Praise for *The Organ Broker*

"A real eye-opener."

—*Publishers Weekly*

"A fascinating, troubling glimpse into the heart and soul of a black market organ dealer, which turns out to be even more complicated than we suspected. He's a man who gazes at the stars while engaging in some of the most nefarious negotiations possible on this planet, a man capable of greed, regret, and love in equal measures. A gripping portrait of a man in conflict with himself. "

—Daniel Asa Rose, author of *Larry's Kidney: Being the True Story of How I Found Myself in China With my Black Sheep Cousin and His Mail-Order Bride, Skirting the Law to Get Him a Transplant . . . and Save His Life*, which was named "one of the top books of the year" by *Publishers Weekly*

"*The Organ Broker* is so richly imagined and executed I felt I was reading a memoir, not a work of fiction. Stu Strumwasser is a hugely talented writer. Read the first page and you won't want to stop."
—Don (D.J. Donaldson), author of the Andy Broussard/Kit Franklyn forensic mystery series and numerous medical thrillers.

"Powerful, original, and gut-wrenching. Stu Strumwasser takes us into the foreboding world of black market organ brokers, where each line crossed proves more dangerous than the last."
—Barry Lancet, author of *Japantown* and *Tokyo Kill*

"A thrilling narrative about the very real world of organ trafficking where human bodies in the third world are spare parts for patients in the first world. When the organ broker has a crisis of conscience, Strumwasser asks if it's possible for him to make amends. The answer is both shocking and provocative."
—Scott Carney, author of *The Red Market: On the Trail of the World's Organ Brokers, Bone Thieves, Blood Farmers and Child Traffickers*

THE ORGAN BROKER

THE ORGAN BROKER

A Thriller

Stu Strumwasser

Arcade Publishing
New York

Arcade Publishing books may be purchased in bulk at special discounts for sales promotion, corporate gifts, fund-raising, or educational purposes. Special editions can also be created to specifications. For details, contact the Special Sales Department, Arcade Publishing, 307 West 36th Street, 11th Floor, New York, NY 10018 or arcade@skyhorsepublishing.com.

Arcade Publishing® is a registered trademark of Skyhorse Publishing, Inc.®, a Delaware corporation.

Visit our website at www.arcadepub.com.

10 9 8 7 6 5 4 3 2 1

Library of Congress Cataloging-in-Publication Data

Strumwasser, Stu.
 The organ broker : a novel / Stu Strumwasser.
    pages cm
 ISBN 978-1-62872-523-0 (hardback) -- ISBN 978-1-62872-551-3 (ebook) 1. Sale of organs, tissues, etc.--Fiction. 2. Black market--Fiction. I. Title.
 PS3619.T788O85 2015
 813'.6--dc23
                        2015004256

Cover design by Georgia Morrissey
Cover photo credit Thinkstock

Print ISBN: 978-1-62872-705-0
Ebook ISBN: 978-1-62872-551-3

Printed in the United States of America

To Owen and River, for giving me purpose and frequent reminders
that there is still plenty of good in this world. And to Jen,
for making me see that they were possible.

CONTENTS

ACKNOWLEDGMENTS

It took me several years to write this book, but several decades to truly become a writer. I'll begin in the beginning: thanks to my sister, born Robin Strumwasser, for taking me—and my songs—seriously, when no one else did. Immeasurable thanks to my friend Mike Hanna for listening to me and my ideas throughout our entire lives and for not letting go of the rope. My gratitude also goes to: Mr. Davenport, my tenth grade English teacher (whose first name escapes me), for encouraging me to take my writing seriously; course Emerson, Thoreau, Kerouac, and Ginsberg; Professors Phil McConkey (who told me stories about his colleague Nabokov), Phyllis Janowitz, and Dan McCall (who taught me about "little blue vases" and was a prick when perhaps I needed it) for teaching me how to write and for being true and weird artists in the otherwise uninspiring ranks of educators at Cornell; my first agent, Chris Byrne, wherever he is these days, who told me in a letter that 1995 was going to be my year—he was twenty years early, but I cannot thank him enough; Jenny Bent, who, as a young reader for another agent, read my first book and took the time to call me and tell me that she thought my book was special and not to give up;

Matt Tonken, Dean Beaver, and Mika Larson for being the most talented and supportive band a songwriter could have ever asked for; Sandy Ross, for coming out of retirement to give our band a real shot and for always entertaining and loving us; Kevin French, one of the best musicians I know who does not play an instrument; Jeff Baum for being a brother; Woody, always an amazing and loyal friend, who found it interesting enough to film; Sven Jacobson, for sharing insights on his home city of Johannesburg as well as the township called Alexandria; Frank Dombrowski, for telling me that my songs mattered; Frank Sica, for being the most supportive investor and unintended mentor; Nick Baily for being awesome; Frank Sposato for being super cool; Sioux Nesi, a gifted and generous photographer; Dave O'Conner, Marina "Hot Doc" Kurian, and Dan O'Conner; Scott Kelly for hosting my first reading at his restaurant; Chris Pavone, for being a gifted editor— before he became a great novelist; Howard Mittlemark for being a brilliant freelance editor; Tom LeClaire for being great at ping pong; Blake Zeff, Peter Finocchiaro, and the people at Salon.com for running my article; my business partner, Ted Werth, for putting up with me and suggesting that I change the title; my agent and new good luck charm, Jim Fitzgerald, and his entire incredible staff at the James Fitzgerald Agency (forgive me for not remembering all of your names); and finally, and most enthusiastically, thank you to my wonderful editor Julie Ganz, my fellow-drummer publicist Sam Caggiula, and everyone else at Arcade and Skyhorse Publishing for taking a chance on a strange, dark story and making me feel a bit better. I can never thank you enough, but please accept the attempt.

The idea of a novel about a black market organ broker had been in the back of my mind for many years before I ever attempted to write it. It wasn't the black market that attracted my fascination but rather the man himself, the broker. Why in the world would an American become an international broker of illegal organs, and what circumstances could possibly put a man in such a position? In March of 2008, I had just gotten divorced, and I traveled with Woody to attend the small, private wedding of another of our closest friends, Bob Pearl, on the beach in Costa Rica. I was drunk, exhausted, and alone when I went back to my hut at 3 a.m. and had an idea about the format within which to write this book. So, thanks Bob, and thanks to the bridesmaid who blew me off at 2 a.m., or I might not have bothered to start writing this story on the back of the motel menu. Thank you, also, to Bob's brother Steve, a filmmaker who took a great interest in my manuscript a few years later and provided me with further motivation to make it better and not give up. Also, thanks to Bob's dad, Mel: it is a terrible burden for a parent to be cooler than his children, but he has shouldered it well.

Finally, great thanks are due to the many people who helped educate me about the black market, organ transplantation in general, or the plight of transplant recipients. Out of respect for their privacy, I will omit some of their names, but I want to extend my great appreciation and respect for: the first organ transplant recipient whom I interviewed in the days when I was just beginning to write the first draft of this book. She is a double-lung and heart recipient, incredibly inspiring—as well as sweet—living a life her parents were told she could never have; the organ broker who is boldly public about being a transplant tourism travel agent, for sharing great detail about his experiences over a bad Mexican lunch; Dr. Jeff Kahn, a bioethicist and professor at the Berman Institute of Bioethics at John Hopkins; Scott Carney, author of *The Red Market,* a shocking and beautifully written tome about the international market for body parts of all kinds; Debbie, John, Moe, Ted, and several others for sharing their intimate, painful and inspiring stories of overcoming broken parts after receiving transplants; and to

Karen Headley and everyone at Donate Life America, as well as Organize.org, who may indeed affect real change and help bring about an end to the crisis of the organ shortage.

To the now more than 120,000 patients in America on waiting lists for life-saving organs, and the hundreds of thousands of additional patients on dialysis but not on a list, I extend my heartfelt sympathies, and my most ardent encouragement: do not give up. Do something. Find a donor who is not a match and then see if you might be eligible to participate in a domino transplant where you and others in need of kidneys essentially trade donors. Write a letter to your Congressperson and tell him or her to pay some attention to this issue and to stop fundraising long enough to do some work for a change. This country needs some modern legislation regarding the disposition of organs, and getting it could save tens of thousands of lives immediately and millions in the years to come. The organ shortage—and the resulting twenty Americans who die every day while waiting for a kidney—is a governmental failure, not a medical one, and it is entirely fixable. Please visit www.theorganbroker.com to learn more.

PART I: LAST YEAR

CHAPTER ONE:
ACCOUNT MANAGEMENT

I've had many last names over the years, but my first name has always been Jack. That makes it easier to remember who I'm supposed to be. I've been selling organs—mostly kidneys—on the black market for about eighteen years. Most of the business takes place overseas so the industry has come to be known as "Transplant Tourism"—and I'm the cruise director.

Last December I was making follow-up calls to some of my former clients like I've done every holiday season for the last six or seven years. It was comforting to check in with some of them around the holidays and learn that many were flourishing. Making those calls was the one accommodation I allowed myself despite my relentless efforts at security. I called them to convince myself that it was justified, that I was somehow absolved. I wasn't just doing it for the money . . . I was saving lives.

I called Marlene Brown's house last year anticipating a routine update. A woman picked up and said, "Hello?" It was quiet in the background.

"Hi," I said cheerfully. "Is Marlene in?" Marlene was a pretty typical kidney case. She had been on dialysis a long time and had a slew of other health problems by the time her family got desperate enough to find Wallace on the Internet. Wallace is a buyer's agent and we sometimes work together. Marlene was a standard transplant tourism trip to Royston, one of my best facilities, in South Africa. She was probably gone for no more than ten days and should have done fine. It had been less than a year since then.

"Uhh, who's calling?"

"Jack. It's Jack Martinelli. Is she around?"

"Jack, Marlene's my mom. Are you a friend of hers?"

Yellow alert. "Yes." Nothing more.

"Jack, I'm really sorry to tell you this," she said quietly.

Shit, I thought. *Marlene's dead.*

"My mom died on Thursday."

"This . . . this Thursday? Just now?"

"Yes," Marlene's daughter replied. "I'm Kim, her daughter. The funeral for Mom is the day after tomorrow. Near their place in New Hope. Do you know where that is?"

"New Hope, Pennsylvania?"

"Yes. If you grab a pen I'll give you directions."

"Oh. Okay. About two hours from New York, right?"

"Yes. Do you have a pen?"

I took down the directions, but I had no intention of going. She wasn't my friend. I had no personal connection to Marlene Brown. She wasn't the first client of mine to end up dead soon after a procedure, but somehow it felt different. She'd hung on for years on dialysis, outlasted renal failure, and managed to get a replacement part. A year later she went and gave up just in time to complicate Christmas.

I felt rattled when I hung up the phone. Maybe it was the coincidental timing of my call. There was a clump of sadness hanging in my throat that I couldn't seem to swallow.

✦

Only a half hour after I had gotten off the phone with Kim Brown I called Wallace and had what constituted, for me, a minor fit. When you're playing with amateurs, you can miss a putt or two, but not with a pro like Wallace. Calling him was foolish.

"Hello?"

"Wallace, Jack," I said.

"Hey, New York," or something like that, from him. Not too excited or glad but always friendly enough. Wallace claimed to live in Connecticut.

"How are you?"

"Good. Happy holidays," he said cheerfully.

"You too."

"Glad you called," Wallace said.

"Oh, yeah?" *Maybe I wouldn't mention it,* I thought. *Maybe it's not a thing to mention.*

"I wanted to touch base and check your availability over the next month or two. Things always seem to get busier after the New Year and I have a few things I'm probably going to want your help with," Wallace said.

"Sure. I'm good," I told him. "The more lead time you give me, the easier—"

"I know that," he replied.

"I'm just saying, sometimes sourcing things can be difficult. If it's something hard to find."

"I'll give you as much time as I can. That's all I can do," he said matter-of-factly.

"Thanks," I replied. "Hey, Wallace, Marlene Brown. That was one of yours, right?"

"Why would you ask me that?"

"It's just me," I said. "It's just that she's gone and I thought you might want to know that."

"Why would you say that to me?" Wallace asked abruptly. "That's not a thing to say."

"It's Jack," I said and forced a small chuckle. "I'm just saying, I thought you might want to know. They were a nice old couple, she and her husband. That's all I meant."

"I don't care if they were nice or who is gone or not gone. Neither should you."

"Fine. Forget it. All I really meant to say is that I happen to know that a woman named Marlene Brown called it quits and I thought that would be of interest to you. You talk to these people. I don't. I just thought you'd be interested. That's all. Don't overreact, Wallace."

"Well, it concerns me that you would have that information, and I don't know why you'd be telling it to me. I don't even know anyone by that name, Jack."

There was a pregnant silence. "Okay," I said. "Have a good holiday."

He didn't say anything right away and there was another pause, and I could almost feel him thinking through how to handle the uncomfortable tension I'd created.

"Jack," he began quietly, "I need to know that we're okay."

"Of course."

"You are my biggest supplier now. I come to you first on a lot of things now. I have to be *certain* that we're okay. That you're steady."

"Steady, Wallace. You're right. It was the wrong thing to say. We're all good. Just call me after the holidays when you know what you need."

"Umm-hmm," he said, and cleared his throat softly. "Okay," he added and then hung up.

I should have never disclosed to him that I had talked to Marlene's daughter. He probably began looking into it right away. That's what I would have done. I've done it in the past. There are things I know about Wallace that he's not aware of. I've kept the information tucked away, available to me if necessary someday in the future. If Wallace uncovered other follow-up calls, he might not necessarily have cared, but it could have cost me business or it could have created even greater risks for me. It was an obvious and uncharacteristic mistake on my part.

I got off the phone that day struck by the thought that maybe it was time to leave the industry, and maybe this time it was really, finally true. After all of those years, despite the way my business had grown and the ease with which we were doing standard kidney deals, perhaps the whole thing had run its course—like an illness. I hadn't thought it through in a long time, hadn't considered what it was I actually did. I hadn't been in a shantytown in years. I hadn't worried much about getting caught either. I laughed a little when I recognized for the first time that I had gotten a little sloppy. I had apparently also forgotten that I was one of the bad guys.

CHAPTER TWO:
THE FUNERAL

Despite that awkward conversation with Wallace about having spoken to Marlene Brown's family, two days later I found myself heading south on I-95. I'm not sure why. Maybe it was morbid curiosity. Maybe voyeurism. Guilt? I had the melancholy sense of making a trip back to my grandfather's village in Ireland.

At the cemetery, I waded through patches of snow in shoes I was ruining. I eventually came upon a small gathering in the middle of an endless parade of headstones all pointing up out of the ground at imperfect angles, resembling long rows of crooked teeth in the mouth of a shark lying dead on a dock. I stayed on the perimeter and a priest was talking and then a line formed and they threw shovelfuls of dirt down on the coffin that contained Marlene Brown. All the men wore black overcoats. Does every man but me own a black overcoat? I hadn't attended a funeral since my father's almost twenty years earlier.

I remembered Marlene being a large woman, obese even. That had probably inflamed her diabetes and made things a lot harder.

I never got close enough to get a look at the coffin. *It's probably big,* I thought. I wondered if they charge more if they need extra wood. The priest made a remark about how she had gotten a kidney transplant and how it had enabled her to spend a few more precious months with Joe and her eight grandchildren. I smiled inwardly, warmed by my own secret beneficence.

Marlene's priest was leading them through the Valley of the Shadow of Death. People huddled around her fresh grave in small groups and held each other's glove-covered hands. There was no wind, but it was cold. We could all see our breath that day in Pennsylvania. White puffs of vapor constantly dissipated in the air in front of our faces as we stood in the graveyard.

She had received a South African kidney. It was standard issue, from a poor black woman who lived in a tin shanty home. The Browns had paid $150K. The South African probably got about fifteen hundred. No one ever made follow-up calls to the sellers. There was a good chance that the South African got no aftercare. She might have gotten an infection or become unable to work.

In his eulogy the priest mentioned that Marlene's husband had gotten a second mortgage to pay for her operation. It didn't fully cover it, but neighbors and fellow parishioners donated enough to make up the difference. I didn't know that. I didn't talk too much to Wallace's buyers. From what Wallace had said, the guy didn't really try to negotiate. He just paid us. It wasn't the new knowledge of how the Browns had funded their purchase that struck me, but rather, the fact that I had been completely unaware of it.

"Traded his home for a few more months with his beloved wife," the priest said, while the cold, wet snow started to seep through the seams where the soles of my shoes met the soft Italian leather. I didn't know a thing about the Browns prior to that funeral. They belonged to Wallace. I had no idea about what they had gone through to buy my extraordinarily overpriced product that had, apparently, only extended her life for another few months. I realized then that I knew so little about any of them. I had stopped asking years ago. It caught me off guard.

Standing there in the snow, I thought about them all, and started to feel sick. I thought about the sellers in South Africa and Asia and South America, poor people living wretched lives all further cut off at the knees by the lies spewed by a network of finders that I had built and managed for years. I thought about all of our American and European clients who we had charged triple the fair price. They all went on to lead Marlene Brown–like lives, in varying degrees—although most did live much longer. Her husband, Joe, was crying, constantly wiping at his nose and his eyes with the fingers of a black leather glove. Then I found that I was crying, silently. It was not for Marlene; it was for me. I was crying for the life I had lost because I realized clearly that day that I had not saved a soul, but instead, I had played a part in destroying all of us. The magnitude of that loss was pushing down on my shoulders, sinking me deeper into the soft snow, pushing me down into the magma in the core of the Earth.

There is one thing that all priests and atheists have in common—they all hope the priests are right. But standing in the remnants of snow on the frozen grass in New Hope I certainly did not believe that priest when he said that Marlene Brown was in a place called heaven.

About twenty people in the US who need a kidney transplant are going to die today. They'll die waiting. A handful of others will die while waiting for a liver, heart, lung, pancreas, or for bone marrow. Twenty more will die tomorrow. The ones with the most money and the most determination are my potential customers. For them, greed for more life is a powerful motivator and that makes for incredible profit margins in my business. The rest spend days, months, and then years waiting, withering away in dialysis centers. The average wait for a kidney on a legit list these days is over seven years. That's no way to put up a fight.

✦

What Wallace had said about things usually picking up in January was true. After the New Year, I was usually required to spend more time attending to some of the mundane and dirty details of my profession. This year was no different. Over the last decade or so, as I built up the business and became more efficient at getting things done, it seems like I've been a little busier each year. Over the last few years, it has also been accompanied by a sickening feeling, an apprehension of a coming closure, of an end—of getting caught, maybe. The more successful I am, the more deals I do, the more I am exposed to risk. It escalates.

✦

In the car on the drive home, I thought about the church I went to, growing up in Queens. We took "Religion" classes on Wednesday afternoons. Sometimes my father picked us up in his big Oldsmobile, collecting us from the nuns and then distributing my friends and me to our respective houses for supper. We always left Religion feeling giddy. We snickered and elbowed each other in the ribs. The rides with my dad were strange, with a pervasive tension filling the quiet interior of his big car, his cigarette burning down gently in the ashtray. "Trayner's dad's such a hard-ass," the others would say at school. My dad drove without speaking. When we piled into his car, he might have managed, "How was it tonight?" sort of rhetorically, to which I guess I said, "Good." That was all. I didn't believe those nuns. He didn't believe them either, not at 5:45 on a Wednesday, the sky overhead already devoid of light.

A few days after Marlene Brown's funeral I was back at home in New York, thinking about her husband, Joe. It was just after New Year's. For a long time I had been aware of what I was doing, but I felt justified. I had endured an abusive father and an uncaring universe—as if that was special. Every kidney transaction I closed felt like another act of debasement that I was somehow forced to suffer, like a martyr. And each life-saving transaction became a small deposit I made in a karma savings account that I thought I could draw upon later. It turns out they were withdrawals, not deposits. When I tally it now, it's impossible to deny the magnitude of the mess I have made.

I pulled out some cash from under the luggage in my closet that I would have otherwise taken to the safe deposit boxes. I placed stacks of hundred-dollar bills into the cutouts I'd made with a box-cutter in the middle of a two-volume set of *The Complete Works of William Shakespeare*. I wrapped the books in tin foil and then wrapped that in bubble wrap and tucked them into a box with a typed note that said: "Joe, Enclosed is $50K. It is for you and you deserve it. You also need it, so don't do something stupid and give it to the Church. Don't try to deposit it in a bank or it will cause big problems for you. Don't tell anyone about your windfall for reasons obvious enough. Just use the money so you can do a little better than you might have done. I am sorry for your loss." That was it. Of course, when he read the last sentence, "I am sorry for your loss," he would know that his anonymous benefactor was referring to Marlene. I hardly felt worthy of making reference to Marlene, but I sent my condolences anyway. In years prior to that, if I had said, "I'm sorry for your loss," I probably would have just been referring to the fucking money. But not anymore.

✦

I thought about that poor guy spending every last penny and then some, and having her go and quit just the same. It was too late to buy her a new kidney. And I found myself shaking my head and fighting off crying while I wrapped those books up in a shroud of bubble wrap. I decided to book a flight to Johannesburg and go see a farm for the first time in many years.

That was the first time that I considered the mechanics of what I am now preparing to do. In addition to quitting, I'm going to have to stop Wallace as well, which is much more complicated. He has been my associate and sometime-partner for over ten years. My plan is to have him meet me in the lobby of the emergency room at Columbia Presbyterian—one of the best transplant centers in the world. Wallace and I have met in person only on infrequent and important occasions. I'm confident that he will come but what I feel, much more than anxiety, is resignation.

I guess the way you're going to feel about all of this depends on whether you place a greater value on kindness or on honesty. It's more important to me now to tell you the truth than to spin the story to try and somehow make you see it my way. The hospital doesn't have a machine to filter out the impurities in one's soul, but in a way that's why I'll meet Wallace there. I think that what I'm looking for, perhaps for the first time, is the same as that which most people are seeking: a little bit of meaning. I only hope it's more than a symbolic gesture.

CHAPTER THREE:
DUE DILIGENCE

About a week after I got back from Marlene Brown's funeral I made the trip to South Africa. I hadn't been there in a while, and felt compelled to check on my supply chain, but something else drew me there as well—that same feeling that had driven me to Pennsylvania.

After our initial conversation about Marlene Brown, the subtle tension that had lingered between me and Wallace remained unremarked upon. Heading into the winter things were getting busier again, as expected, and that was good, but it also made me feel a new kind of urgency about everything.

Dr. Mel Wolff ran the transplant center at Royston Hospital in Sandton, a posh neighborhood about fifteen minutes north of downtown Johannesburg. Johannesburg isn't Joburg anymore. They call it Jozi now. I have no idea why. It's still a pain in the ass of a fourteen-hour flight, even with the new reclining beds in first class. I was staying at the Peermont D'oreale Grande at Emperor's

Palace but asked Wolff's associate, Pierre Kleinhans, to meet me at the bar at the Hyatt Regency downtown.

Dr. Wolff and I had done a little business together prior to his being put in charge of the entire transplant center about six years ago. That's when he called and asked me to come meet him and Pierre in Sandton, and business started really taking off. Kleinhans is a finder from Pretoria who works with Wolff, connecting sellers to Royston. In the years since then, I found Pierre to be reliable and efficient. He was one of those people I figured I could trust as long as he believed that doing right by me was in his own best interest. He wasn't affable like Wolff. Hell, he didn't even play golf—and I didn't like the guy. I didn't like his Germanic Afrikaans accent or the way he talked about sellers as if they were worse than cattle, as if they somehow offended him and his superior sensibility. However, since Wolff took over the clinic, Pierre had probably sourced fifty or sixty kidneys for us. I usually cleared about eighty or ninety grand per kidney, or around half of that if I co-brokered it with a buyer's agent like Wallace. That made for a few million reasons to maintain a good working relationship with Kleinhans, even though he was a slimy prick.

I was having a Balvenie neat and skimming the local paper when Pierre walked in and slid onto a barstool beside me. "Good to see you, Jack," he said, extending his hand. He had an obnoxious "cat-that-ate-the-canary" grin plastered across his face and it immediately annoyed me.

Pierre was wearing a sport coat, rather formal for him, and had a toothpick lodged in the side of his mouth. His hair was thick, dark, and short, and always had a bit of a shine, as if he was using product left over from the eighties. He was furtive and suspicious and cocky, and had the air of a car salesman or mid-level jerkoff in an organized crime family.

"You too, Pierre," I said, smiling warmly.

"I talked to Dr. Wolff. He wasn't even aware that you were in town," he said with his eyebrows raised.

"I came to see you, not Mel."

Something about his posture shifted slightly and I suddenly felt as if the conversation took on a slight air of confrontation. "Oh?" he replied, casually, "Thanks, Jack. It's always good to see you. Why not meet in Sandton like usual?"

"Pierre, I want you to take me to a farm," I said quietly.

He didn't respond at first. He looked away, toward the bar, perhaps considering what to order. He ran his hand over his neat, short hair, patting it into place, forced a bit of a smile, and then quietly said, "Why would you want me to do that?"

"We've been doing this together for years now," I said and then stopped. We looked at each other for a moment. I always thought that Pierre sort of liked me but I would still never turn my back on him.

"You don't want to go there, Jack. New York Jack. Isn't that what your friends call you? New York Jack?" he asked, smiling widely again. "I rarely go myself. It's not safe. Is that why you came all of this way? To ask me about that, Jack?"

"Yes."

"That's a very far way to go, New York Jack," he said. I didn't respond. "We've got an expression," Pierre continued a bit more softly, "'Die doodskleed het geen sakke nie meining.' In English that means, 'He who dies cannot take any property with him to the afterlife.' You know what that means for you, Jack?" he asked rhetorically. "It means, stay the hell away from the shantytowns." He was still smiling, but only to condescend to me.

I took a sip of my drink. Pierre smiled and mumbled something else in Afrikaans and patted me on the shoulder while waving to get the bartender's attention. When the bartender approached us, Pierre pointed at my Scotch and said, "The same." Then he turned back to me and said, "I have a dinner with a young lady in a bit. Going to Michael's. It's a new place. Great steak, Jack. You should go while you're in town. Michael's," he repeated.

"Look, Pierre," I began, more firmly, "I just flew fourteen hours. I need to go there. I need to see it and I have my reasons, but we both know it doesn't really matter why so let's not get into it. The last time I stepped foot inside the gates of a shantytown in Jozi was over ten years ago and some kid threatened to cut my throat. I haven't gone back. I know better. But I am going to see it and I think that it would be better if you came, as it's better for our mutual business if I don't end up as dinner for a bunch of stray dogs."

Pierre knew me well enough from negotiating organ prices to know that I meant what I said. "Ag," he said in a whisper and exhaled. "Okay, Jack. We can't have our partner getting himself sliced in half, can we? I gotta do a thing in Pretoria tomorrow. You still here Thursday?" I nodded. "Okay. Meet me here at noon and I'll take you over. Just for a bit. You don't plan on talking to anyone, right?"

"I don't have to."

"Well it's better if you don't. Don't talk to anyone."

"Fine."

"Did Dr. Wolff tell you the news?" Pierre asked, with the same smug and knowing grin.

"No."

"He was made the head administrator of the entire hospital."

"Congratulations," I said calmly, internally trying to evaluate what that might ultimately mean for me and Wallace.

"You don't sound excited, New York Jack."

"No?"

"Do you know what this means for the rest of us?" Pierre asked quietly. I said nothing and then he answered his own question: "No more oversight. Dr. Wolff *is* the oversight. There is a lot of business to be done now, Jack."

"I'll see you Thursday, Pierre," I said, but the weight of his words stayed with me.

"Okay. Go play some golf, Jack. It'll be beautiful tomorrow. Must be cold as hell in New York these days. Is New York nice in the summer, Jack? Maybe I'll come visit you some time. Maybe in your summertime I'll come see New York."

"Sure," I said. *Good luck finding me,* I thought. "It's delightful. Cool breezes. . . . We'll get our nails done."

"Right," Pierre said, chuckling. "Okay then," he said, smiling broadly again and shaking my hand. "I'm off."

◆

That night, tucked into bed at the Peermont D'oreale Grande, the latest of my recurring dreams began, the one I still have now. I was in that slippery state between sleep and wakefulness, aware that I was dreaming. It seemed real, and it seemed to go on for hours. I was at a dinner table with fine china and white linen and lace napkins. The plates were pearl white, with thin, swirling spirals of dark red along the outer edge. I was at the head of the table, dining alone. On my plate was a large piece of meat garnished with a sprig of parsley, and roasted potatoes adorned with rosemary. There were etched crystal glasses in front of me, one filled with water and one with red wine. Beyond the glasses was a floral centerpiece, thick with red and white flowers. The table was very long and I could feel the presence of unseen others in the room, outside of my field of vision.

Recurring dreams begin for most people when they are seven or eight. There are the dreams about showing up at school naked, and the ones where you realize you hadn't done your homework. They evolve into dreams about important meetings missed, or mortgage payments forgotten. I had those too, but in recent years, it was only a dream about a feast.

CHAPTER FOUR:
LESEDI

Pierre picked me up on Thursday and we drove north toward Sandton, in the direction of Pretoria.

"You just want to look at the natives, Jack? Howzit?" Pierre asked me while he drove.

I didn't answer him. It was December, so it was getting hot as hell in Jozi.

"We'll stop by Alexandra. It's just a few kilometers east of Sandton, not too far from the middle of Jozi. Do you know of Alex? Would they know of it in the States?"

"No."

"Mandela lived there as a kid. A lot of artists and such come out of that slum. They call it the Dark City because it had no electricity for so many years. It's smaller than a lot of the townships but there are half a million natives packed in there. You don't mind the 'natives' stuff, Jack? Right?"

Again, I just watched the road.

"We sometimes call them 'Floppies'" Pierre said, grinning. "That's an old expression. It refers to the posture they assume when shot with an AK-47."

"How diplomatic," I said.

Pierre didn't respond. He kept driving. And grinning. I didn't know what I expected to find in Alex but I wanted to see it. For eighteen years I had bought replacement parts from corrupt doctors in countries with unregulated networks of back-alley brokers who preyed on the villagers. I had created an antiseptic way of touching them through fax machines and meetings held in code-language in four-star hotel bars. I decided it was time to get a better look at the supply chain and stop lying to myself.

"There are no tin shacks you know, Jack. Alex looks like a poor little city. There're buildings and even schools."

I continued to watch the road.

"What is it you're looking for, Jack? Dr. Wolff was worried about me bringing you here."

"It's not his concern. I just want to see where they come from."

"The natives, Jack?" he asked, again grinning.

"The organs, Pierre."

That shut him up for a bit. I had always felt a subtle competitiveness from Pierre, but he usually yielded when the conversation required one party to give way. After a long minute or two of silence, Pierre again said, "Really, what is it you're looking for, Jack?"

"I don't know."

"It's not a zoo, you know," he said more quietly.

"Yes. Thank you."

Again, Pierre side-stepped my sarcasm. "We'll meet one of my people. Two white men can't prance into Alex alone. Dr. Wolff told me to keep you safe."

"Okay."

"Jack," he said, a little more strongly, "you can't ever come here without me. You wander into Alexandra on your own and you're dead in an hour. It's all real here, Jack."

✦

It was only about a ten- or fifteen-minute drive until Pierre pulled over and parked on a nondescript stretch of road. If I looked only to the right the road looked no different from any other in a wealthy, northern part of Jozi near Sandton. To the left, however, was a dangerous slum. I'm no longer surprised by the proximity of the shantytowns and townships to the rest of the city. It's as if they dropped a poverty-stricken internment camp right into the middle of Manhattan and there was nothing more separating it from Chelsea or Soho than the simple knowledge among locals that you don't go past certain streets. Sometimes there is no gate or fence or any structure whatsoever to separate the two worlds. There is merely a stark line of mental demarcation. On one side of the road, there are middle-class white people going about their business and on the other side, in the shadow of their homes and office buildings, are the vivid results of hundreds of years of slavery and apartheid. Government-reported unemployment among such people is about 35 percent, but in reality it is closer to 50 percent. Electricity and running water are spotty. If the homes aren't literally tin shacks made out of scrap metal and duct tape, they are cheap concrete constructions, funded by occasional initiatives, motivated by the desire to keep them out of the rest of the province more than any concern for their quality of life. The land had been purchased a hundred years ago prior to it becoming illegal for blacks in South Africa to own real estate. Crime cannot be measured. In such a place, murder is a daily occurrence and there are essentially no women who haven't suffered rape or sexual abuse at some time or another. These were, of course, the perfect conditions for a man like Pierre Kleinhans to seed a "farm."

Pierre probably spent years making contacts inside of that place, the way I had spent years making contacts at transplant centers. Did he meet them on the periphery, like we would apparently do today? Did he buy them Scotches in the comfort of hotel bars in Sandton?

There were several transplant centers around the world that were on the take and who dealt directly with their own Pierre Kleinhanses, so I didn't have to. I could merely pay off surgeons or hospital administrators and when someone needed a kidney, I faxed them my client's medical details, and they would provide the part, paying careful attention to blood type, MHC, and HLA matching criteria—like an auto dealership that had ordered up a part for your car from a distributor in Ohio who bought it from a factory in Mexico. I never cared much about where the parts came from; I just dealt with the dealerships. I sent them email and faxes from across the ocean. But suddenly I felt touched by it. I needed to see the raw and fertile fields of the farm.

Pierre reached in front of me and opened the glove compartment, revealing a handgun that he tucked inside his belt. "Here he is," he said, motioning to a middle-aged black man approaching the car. "Dr. Wolff said let you get a look and let's not get anyone hurt today so let's make it like that, Jack. Let's get you a look but no problems please."

"I don't want any problems," I said quietly, assessing the man approaching us. His clothes were entirely western. His demeanor was entirely blank. Tough to read. He did not wave or smile but he nodded very slightly to Pierre. That told me a little about him.

Pierre popped open the door handle on his side to exit the car so I followed suit. He walked to the front of the car to greet the man and they shook hands. They exchanged a few words but it wasn't in

English or Afrikaans. It might have been Zulu. "This is New York Jack," Pierre said then and the man extended his hand and met my gaze. I shook his hand and Pierre added, "Thaba," indicating his name.

"Hello," I said, assuming he spoke English.

"You want to see inside Alex?"

"Yes."

"Why?"

"For business," I replied. I felt as if I couldn't just say, "I don't know."

Pierre said something to him in the other language again. Thaba shrugged. Pierre spoke again and then he nodded. "Okay," Thaba said. "Come," and he started walking in the direction of Alexandria, only about a block from our car.

"You give a lot of walking tours?" I dead-panned.

"What?" from Thaba, over his shoulder.

"Jack . . ." from Pierre.

"I'm just a bit excited, Pierre," I said. "Even though it's not a zoo."

✦

The Dark City was different from some other black townships in that the buildings were more substantial, looked more permanent. It was just as dangerous as any other place if you made a mistake, but the people there were apparently a little more acclimated to white people sniffing around. Being white in Alex might indicate that you were from the government—assessing a project to build a school or clinic—or perhaps from a local hospital or some other aid organization. If you were white and standing within the confines of Alexandria, you were probably there to somehow help the local population, so you were more likely to be left alone—unless you carried the scent of money. Wolff probably told Pierre, "If he has to go, take him to Alex." He probably added, "But bring a local, and for God's sake bring a weapon just in case."

✦

We crossed a street and entered what looked like an alley, but it was their equivalent of an avenue. It was lined on both sides by squat concrete structures, pinkish, one-story huts. The population in these places is usually young because those who can get out, do, and for the rest, life expectancy is low. There were young black men standing in doorways, sitting on boxes in the dirt street, some walking past us, on their way to nowhere, I supposed. We only saw a few women, and not many children. Thaba spoke to one or two people in that native language. I didn't know what they said, but it was never with a smile.

✦

We had walked a couple of blocks when Thaba stopped and said something to Pierre. Kleinhans turned to me and said, "He doesn't want to go too deep into the township with you. He asked if there is anything in particular you want to see?"

"This is fine," I said, directing my speech to Thaba. "Just a few more minutes please."

"Okay." Thaba shrugged. "Come."

We walked for another few blocks and made a few turns, mostly rights. He was circling us back toward the car and staying on the periphery of the township. We came upon a sort of large, open courtyard. In the back was a dirt area that appeared to serve as a soccer field. There were some kids kicking a ball around. When they noticed us, one young man broke away from the group and immediately began walking toward us. He picked something up—it was round and might have been another ball—and continued approaching us. He looked about fifteen years old, but he was tall, nearly my height, six feet, and very thin. He had no shoes on and his T-shirt was ripped. As he got close to us, a wide and genuine smile broke out on his face and he said, "Kidney Thaba!" in English. Thaba responded to him in the other language and the boy said, "Oh, Kidney Thaba. I am always friendly!" Then, he turned to me, or perhaps to both me and Pierre, and asked, "Who are you?"

"My name's Jack."

"Kidney Jack!" he said with a big smile.

"No."

"You're with Thaba," he said, "you don't come to buy a kidney?"

Pierre said something to him in the other language and his smile dipped in radiance but was not erased.

Thaba said, "This is Lesedi. He live here. I know him. He want to sell a kidney. He is too young," Thaba said.

"Not anymore," Lesedi replied. He was still smiling. I noticed then that the "soccer ball" he was holding was made of tape, layer after layer of it. It was dirty and frayed all over, not much bigger than a softball.

"I am Lesedi," he said, and extended his hand, smiling this big shit-eating grin like he thought our meeting was rather hysterical.

I couldn't help but laugh a little as I took his hand and said, "I am Jack."

"All right Jack! Kidney Jack!" he said.

"Just Jack."

"Jack! Okay. Jack. When you need a good kidney, you come here to the football pitch. I am always here. Right, Thaba? Come anytime, Jack." Then he lowered his voice, "But bring American money," he added more quietly, still smiling broadly.

I nodded. He gave a short laugh. He was performing, but he seemed sort of smart and also genuinely likable. "So you want a nice drink of water, Jack?" he asked.

"What?"

"He makes a joke," Thaba said.

"It's time to go, Jack," Pierre said, and we turned and headed back the way we had come.

Lesedi yelled, "Jack!" and the three of us all turned back toward him. He flashed that huge half-fake/half-real smile and then did a standing back flip—just jumped up in the air and flipped completely over, backwards, landing on his feet. It was quite impressive. "Two very good kidneys!" he said. Then he waved like a little kid, added, "Merry Christmas, New York Jack!" and ran back to join the others. I liked him.

◆

This is the thing that our government and the uninformed still don't understand: There is no shortage of organs; there is only a shortage of organs in America. And not since the early years have my associates and I had a difficult time locating customers for our imported products. I always had more leads than I could handle. Besides, every time a patient suffering through late-stage renal failure said, "I would never buy a kidney," for some ill-conceived ethical, moral, or religious reason, he laid one more brick in the foundation of the booming black market for organs. Those were the people that sustained the system; the system sustained the black market; and the black market sustained the guys like me.

◆

When Wallace called I had already been back in New York for a few days.

"I need a couple of Eighties," he said. We sometimes referred to kidneys as Eighties since they comprised eighty percent of the waiting list. We called livers Fifteens. Then Wallace added, "It's pretty routine. You want to get those for me? After the new year?"

"Not a problem," I replied.

"Everything's okay?" he asked.

"I just got back from Jozi. It's all buttoned down. Supply is great right now." "But everything's okay?" he asked, clearly referring to the Marlene Brown thing.

"Wallace," I said slowly, for emphasis, "yes, everything is okay. Everything is."

"It's just that you worried me last month," he said quietly.

"Asked and answered."

"What?" he asked.

"Asked and answered. It's lawyer talk for, 'We already discussed this so please don't ask me again just to bust my balls.'"

He laughed a bit. "Okay." Then he added, "So everything's okay in Jozi?"

"Perfect. My guy is running the entire show now. Things will get even easier."

"When you say the whole show . . . ?"

"Yes, all of it. Chief Administrator."

"Wow. Okay," Wallace said. "Good times."

✦

Wallace thinks ahead; I think of leaving. Could I finally just fade away to Tucson? Could I leave New York and let my lease expire and send them a check for a few grand to dispose of the furniture I'd leave behind? I could burn my phones and email addresses—for the last time—and start fresh, with a last name I would keep. I have the money I need. I could get a new phone and email account, accrue contacts. Personal contacts. I'd have the pool, and the golf courses, and dogs barking in the windows of condos, piercing the stillness, to remind me that it is real. I could get that by stepping on the throat of one last seller. Couldn't I forget them? Mark. He's like the fingerprint I left behind at what would have otherwise been a perfect crime scene. He's beautiful, but he ties me to it. I could go to Tucson, but he'd still be in New York. Michelle would be in New York too. How did things get this way? On the driving range, at the supermarket, on the highway driving to Phoenix. . . . Is it too late? I'm forty-five years old. Can't people change sometimes? But Tucson is too close to the border, and to reminders of immigrants, and climbing over fences and dying on the trains at night and selling parts of themselves off for food to feed their families, and soon enough you just find yourself caught up in it all and planning trips to Thailand for old, white men from LA who have drank and eaten their way into renal failure. There are no gold watches for kidney brokers.

PART II: THE EIGHTIES

CHAPTER FIVE:
JACKIE TRAYNER

Growing up in my house was like being a declawed housecat in a home dominated by a large, old dog. My father usually took little interest in me, and I kept to myself, but when we occasionally bumped heads it was bad for the housecat. I was fifteen when I had the worst run-in with my father. One day, I got home around six and he was sitting in the kitchen, smoking a cigarette and reading the paper. That house was small and boxy and as soon as you entered through the front door you could see straight into the kitchen to the right, and straight into the small living room to the left. From their bedroom, my mother said, "Jackie?" and my father yelled, "Stay in there!"

I took a couple of steps toward the kitchen and noticed about half a dozen plastic baggies full of weed spread out on the table. My father took a drag of his cigarette but said nothing. He'd obviously found them in my room. I was terrified. My breathing quickened and I felt a little nauseous. He stood up as I approached, and I stopped a few feet from him, on the other side of the kitchen table.

I expected him to yell and threaten me, perhaps lunge forward with an open-hand slap, but he didn't. After a moment he quietly said, "Go down to my office. I want to talk to you there."

I said something like, "I'm sorry, Dad. I know it's a big mistake. I'm really sorry." I was probably trembling. But he just took another deep drag of smoke and said, "Go." We stared at each other for another moment and then he jerked forward a little so I turned and quickly started walking toward the basement door. I got the door open and made my way down a few stairs, when I heard his heavy foot hit the top step. Immediately, I felt something crash down onto the right side of my head and the top of my shoulder. I lost my footing and sort of crumpled forward and down six or seven steps until I landed on the tiled floor of the basement. I pulled up my knees, curled up on the floor with my eyes closed against the beating I thought I was about to get.

"You think you're going to embarrass me?!"

"No!" I screamed.

"This crap is split up in bags like you're some kind of fucking drug dealer, you little piece of shit!"

He stepped down the last few stairs until he was standing just above me. "This. Is. My. House," he said quietly, with venom in his voice.

I was crying, but silently. I knew that making a sound would set him off and bring down punches. So I tried to speak without stammering, but what came out was something like, "It w-w-was, a . . . big mis-mistake. I know."

I heard the sound of a zipper. My eyes were still closed. There was a splash of light from the hallway above streaming down on one wall of the stairwell but it was otherwise dark down there. He pulled out his big adult cock and pissed on me. On my face, in my hair . . . Warm piss soaked my shirt and hair.

When he was done he moved slowly and that was the meanest part of all. He took his time re-zippering his pants. It was silent for a long moment after that. He must have simply been standing there looking down at me. Finally, he said, "You think you're smarter than me?" His shoe stepped on the tiles very close to my face, making a tap sound, and then the other shoe hit the first step. He climbed the stairs slowly, the steps creaking under the weight of his large frame. It took me a minute or two to calm myself down enough to stand. I pushed my fingers back through my hair, pushing away the piss he had left all over me.

After a minute or two I started to feel that same numbness that always swept through me in those days. Then I walked up the stairs and through the hall and out the front door as if nothing had happened. No one spoke. I don't think I even closed the door behind me. I left the house and started walking with no particular destination in mind. I started to feel something down inside of me. It started out as a gurgling sort of ache but grew into a visceral feeling of pain. There was a feeling in my gut that was becoming animated. I felt it straining against my innards, but it wasn't coming from my stomach. It was lower, nearer to my dick, and it was like a match being lit and I have no idea why it had taken so long. . . . I could have at least put my hands up. I could have fought back once. I didn't have to take it so calmly every time. This time, I thought about killing him.

When I left that house I was wet from urine and shaking a little with outrage. It was starting to get dark out by the time I turned around and doubled back toward home. The intersection of our block and the block it terminated into had recently been repaved and I remember that some of the blacktop was twinkling slightly in the light from the sinking sun. The broken bits of glass that were mixed in with the pavement material were catching the last shards of angled sunlight and for a moment I couldn't help but notice that it looked a little like stars on a black floor of space that had been laid out in front of our house like a supernatural carpet. The front door to the house was still open when I got there—screen door closed but unlocked, wooden door behind it open, saying, "Nice fall day, neighbor! C'mon in!" I no longer felt sorry for myself by then. I assumed the quiet and purposeful gait of a killer. I walked in, and passed quickly through the small dining room and into the kitchen. He was still sitting in there, now in front of a plate of spaghetti and meatballs, newspaper open on the table. His button-down shirt was open, revealing a white T-shirt and gold cross dangling in the gray and black chest hair tufting out above it, his head angled down to read about yesterday's games. I stood in front of him and exhaled like a horse and he finally bothered to look up. Our eyes met and then he had the gall to glance down again, casually flip a page, and then look back up at me. We stared at each other for another moment and then I yelled, "FUCK . . . YOOOUUUUU . . ." and leaned hard into it. I would've puked my stomach up into his face, sacrificing my own guts, if I thought the stomach acids might have burned his rosy cheeks. My father put down his fork but that's all he did. I could hear the sound of my mother's footsteps immediately thudding along on the shag carpeting from the direction of their bedroom. I slowly started to walk away, back toward the front door, and behind me I heard him say, "What?!" and I was sensible enough to break into a run.

I pulled the heavy front door closed, hard, behind me, and one of the three small glass panes cracked—the sound of glass falling to the cement porch behind me somehow made it more real. I was dizzy and felt sick but I ran. I eventually slowed to a fast walk and went all the way to the high school. I sat down on a bench in a dugout next to the baseball diamond and eventually fell asleep. The next day, when I wandered home, I was thinking he'd kill me.

Instead, he never hit me again. He redirected a little more attention toward my mother, but I didn't receive it. I think that if he had hit me again, I really would have killed him. I had it all planned out—thought it through in a logical and practical way.

If my father had hit me that day I truly would have cut his throat while he slept that night. That is my truth for today. We never discussed it and I guess we both knew there was no point in revisiting it. Doesn't everyone have to take their shots?

Instead, he handled me differently. He stopped talking to me. It was almost like the bastard was acting out, like he was the one who was hurt. And for how long did this go on? For how long did young Jackie's father refuse to acknowledge him or talk to him because Jackie finally stood up and said, "Stop"? I guess it was about two years or so.

CHAPTER SIX:
INTRO TO SALES

After high school I attended NYU and lived in the dorms in Manhattan for a while. I was affable, and articulate and funny and I could talk a girl back to my apartment, but I didn't do a lot of the follow-up work required to turn acquaintances into friends. A psychologist I dated once told me that I have Aspergers. I don't really know. We didn't have psychological ailments when I was growing up in Flushing. No one went to therapists. No one we knew did. You kept it to yourself. In the city it was easy to become anonymous without seeming weird about it, and that felt comfortable to me. Being spotted on a crowded city street, or sitting by one's self in the sun on a towel in Washington Square Park . . . I don't think it looked strange to anyone.

In 1987 I was a junior at NYU. That was the year of the big stock market crash and a lot of people got hurt. My dad was one of them. That year the question of whether or not he would pay my tuition took on a new seriousness so I decided to take financial matters into my own hands. I took the initiative and got a "job" of my choosing in order to preempt being forced into a more traditional one later.

Rock was in hibernation, style was, too, but New York was humming. Everyone did some blow in those days. People put mousse in their hair and wore bright colors, trying to be noticed, like putting out "Vacant" signs at a motel. Only a year after the crash, the stock market started to reascend and New York was once again all about money and moving quickly and doing bullet hits of blow in the bathrooms of clubs where you had to know someone just to get inside. The decision to start dealing was so obvious, so easy. First I was just hooking up a few friends from class with a gram here or there. Before I knew it, I was driving to make pickups out on Long Island or in Jersey. My ability to quickly move meaningful amounts of coke on campus, one gram at a time, impressed my main suppliers from Jersey (who I believed to be low-end mafia guys) and even earned me a nickname—"NYU Jack."

I was making buys of a quarter ounce, and then full ounces. That's a lot of cocaine. There are twenty-eight grams in an ounce. By cutting it with baby aspirin, you could get a solid sixty grams out of one ounce. At a hundred bucks a gram (the standard price for many years), you were talking about six grand just to move that one ounce, when I had only paid a grand or two. A four or five thousand dollar profit was a lot of money to a kid only twenty years old. After I built up my list, I could move an ounce in a week. "Screw you, Dad. I'll work it out."

And yes, Jack was the man. I had what they wanted. I was the guy they needed to talk to. By the bathroom. In the car. When I met a group of students, someone always knew who I was, mentioned a mutual friend. The girls looked up at me, furtive, sexy. They were mildly disgusted—in front of their friends . . . but they respected the fact that I was bold and I did things Jack's way. I brought the party and the second wind. At times, it all felt like love.

By the time I was graduating from college, I made more money in a week than most people I knew earned in a semester. I was meticulous about not getting caught. Every time I exchanged a small plastic baggie full of powder and rocks for a handful of twenties, I got a little rush. Every time. For me, the rush wasn't in the doing it—it was in the selling it. In the moments of closing each little deal, I was the one in control of the world around me. It was empowering to feel like I controlled the thing that people wanted, to feel like I was wanted. Outwardly, I pretended to suffer the burden of it; in my heart, I have to admit, I loved it. I romanticized selling drugs, my underground work, my secret identity. Those were golden days.

I wasn't a big enough dealer for the DEA or FBI to come looking for me—and didn't allow myself to become that big—but getting popped with five or ten grams in your pocket could still bring some serious disruption into one's life, even on a first offense. I had all sorts of fail-safes, methods I employed to stay clear about who was okay to do business with, when it was okay to do business, and when to just casually walk away from little deals that simply weren't worth the risk, worth any risk. If a guy in a suit and a black shirt in the bathroom at the China Club acted like we were pals and asked me a question about where I got supplied from—I excused myself and he never got an audience with me again. When some girl I didn't know approached me on the floor at the Ritz without a proper introduction and said that her friend told her I might be able to help her get something—I took the rest of the night off, went straight home, laid low for a few weeks. I mean, I was vigilant. Staying away from people, not letting them get close or get a bead on me—that was something I was already good at.

When I was twenty-one I applied to only two law schools, NYU and Columbia. There were a few simple reasons I decided to go to law school:

1. I liked to argue and was good at it.
2. I enjoyed being able to tell my father that I didn't need his help, that I would pay my own way, that I got a student loan . . . (when in fact I paid with cash and without all that much effort, laundering some of it by pretending to be an independent party promoter and opening a business account).
3. It made no sense for me to leave the comfort and facility of Manhattan college life when business was booming and everything was going my way.

I decided to ride the coke wave for another three years, right through law school. I figured that I could save some money, get my law degree, and then parlay it into some regular straight-up real-world job, get rich and just pretend that the entire experience was in the past somewhere, tucked safely away like the remembrance of a bloody knee or a dream about showing up at elementary school naked. The accomplishments would be locked up in the trophy-case of my memory, but they would always be there for me to privately call upon whenever I might need a boost.

CHAPTER SEVEN:
CARRIE

Near the end of my first year in law school I met Carrie Franco. She was so entirely noticeable. She was a second-year law student. Carrie was so incredible, to me, that she pretty much knocked me right out of orbit and whatever force was holding me in line with the remnants and rituals of my life and routines before her.

We met in a bar, of course. It started with a friendly argument. She was an NYU law student, I was an NYU law student; she was from Boston, I hated the Red Sox; she thought the entire legal system was bloated, inefficient, easily abused, and badly in need of major reform . . . I truly didn't give a shit. It wasn't that long before I started waking up in her apartment.

Carrie had a tattoo of the Chinese symbol for "justice" on the small of her back before any other girl I knew had ink on that spot. I suppose that she still does. Carrie wore sneakers with pretty sundresses. She rocked Vans before they were cool to anyone but skate kids. She wore Hush Puppies for about six months, ten years after

they were out of style and a year before they came back. She didn't
wear much makeup but she sometimes painted her fingernails and
toenails black. You just knew that when she ascended to corporate America she'd be the coolest one in the room, but succeed
without needing to compromise very much. I was sure she'd have
no problem balancing her unwavering irreverence with an ability
to swim in the popular channels and have all the little fish fall in
behind her. She looked amazing even when she looked like shit.
She was sarcastic with everyone, but never annoyed with them the
way I was. She loved every one of the nameless bastards we walked
by on the street every day. I never got that. I still don't, but I no
longer think it's strange. During the time we were together we had
a group of friends, but they were always more Carrie's friends than
mine. I'd say she thought people were silly, but liked them anyway,
whereas I really was disgusted by them—myself at the top of the
list. I loved her and the closer we became, the less alone I felt in the
world. Carrie had plans. She had specific plans about things she
wanted to do. It drove her crazy that I did not.

Meeting Carrie is also what caused me to get into golf, which is
funny because she hated the game, and in the beginning I was only
pretending to play. Once Carrie and I got close we fell into the habit of
telling each other what we'd been up to whenever we'd been apart. I
know this is very common among couples, but it was completely foreign to me, and I could see where it was going. Days I couldn't account
for were going to be problematic. I remembered that Carrie had once
made a comment about hating golf, because it was too slow, and
because it was for the privileged. So I claimed to be a golfer because she
wouldn't want to come along. I could buy a solitary half a day for myself
every now and then, and use the time to buy drugs. I even claimed to be
going to night-time driving ranges whenever I had to meet someone
after dark, but it probably didn't matter. Carrie wasn't fooled for very
long.

By the time Carrie found out the truth, I actually was play-ing a little golf and had even started to take lessons on Saturdays from the pro at the club in Westchester. That original old pro, he's dead now, but I'd pay anything to get a look at his face if he could see my swing now. He was such a sweet old guy. Arthur. He couldn't really play for shit, but he was great at teaching mechan-ics. I haven't really thought about him in years, but writing this down now, thinking about him . . . I miss him. I still belong to that club—I use the name Tuckman. At my club in Jersey I use Caswell. In Arizona it's Campbell. At Pebble Beach I use Induri. I rotate my appearances and avoid playing anywhere too regularly. Once I found out how much Carrie liked coke, secrecy no longer mat-tered. She never liked that I sold it, but for a while there in 1989 she chewed up a fair amount of my product.

Carrie kept a small collection of snow globes on a shelf above her bed. Sometimes when we made love I would try to bang the bed into the wall and make the snow stir up from beneath the hem of Snow White's dress, or from the foot of the Empire State Build-ing, or from beneath a group of tiny running horses. I wonder if she has snow globes now. That's something I do think about some-times. She might have lost some, or left them in Boston. Maybe they meant nothing to her at all. In the years immediately follow-ing our breakup, I thought about things like that a lot. I would fantasize about tracking her down, calling her parents in Boston, securing her new number, then calling her and saying, "Remem-ber those snow globes you had on that shelf above your bed? Why did you have those? Why horses? Why Snow White, Carrie?" Of course I never did.

She wanted me to stop dealing but I couldn't. Not until school was done. I told her that I didn't have rich parents to pay my bills. She bitched about it anyway. I was putting her at risk. I could hurt her, she said. She finally left me—"Pathetic, coke-dealing, lying piece of shit. Pathetic, whining, depressed victim. Unfriendly, arrogant asshole, Jack." And instead of thinking I could love some-one else, I wanted no one. I resented them all. I was alone again and more comfortable with my old surroundings.

When Carrie was graduating, we were still screwing and hang-ing out a little, but I think she was already seeing someone else by then. We were living in the temporary aftermath of the mess I'd made of us. I knew she'd bounce back; I was sure that I would not. I hated her, but I didn't want it to end, and knowing that it would eventually end completely made me hate everyone, at least to some degree.

Usually, when I called her, I got the answering machine. When she was unlucky enough to actually answer the phone, I would try to seduce her through the blur of too many shots of vodka, offering her coke she didn't need or want. Occasionally, she'd let me come over and anxiously undress her and push myself inside of her, too quickly, too awkwardly. Sometimes I thought she was laughing a little. "What?" I would say, going along, trying to exhibit a tiny bit of strength or self-respect.

"Nothing. Go ahead. Just do it."

"What, Carrie?" I'd ask with a wry smile.

"Jack, come here," and she would pull my mouth to hers, pull my hips down to hers and wrap her legs and sculpted feet behind the backs of my knees. "I know you love me, Jack," she would say while I fucked her, calmly looking me right in the eyes. "I'm sorry," she would say.

"You're wrong," I would reply, "Stop talking." I would do it harder, flurries kicking up in the snow globes above our heads.

"I'm sorry, sweetie."

The last month or two really was a mess. She missed her period. We thought she was pregnant. I did too much coke—I had never done that before I got involved with her. She failed a class, couldn't graduate on time, and she blamed me. We thought she might need an abortion. She said that if she did she'd go with Beth and didn't want a drug dealer paying for it. It was too sick and clichéd, she said. She loved me, but wasn't "in love" with me; I wasn't the person she thought I was. She hadn't realized it until lately, but I was less. I was less beautiful. When she told me all of those things, in bed after sex, or on the phone while declining to see me, she didn't even sound mean. Somehow I thought she was being generous. She was right, and she was making the effort to tell me the truth despite how uncomfortable it was for her. It was pity but it was beautiful. She was dumping me with a sense of consideration that only someone as great as Carrie could have mustered. I believed that she deserved someone better than me but I still couldn't bear the thought of letting her go and crashing back to the solitary life I had lived before.

When school ended in May of 1990 she was still in New York for another month or two, living in an East Village sublet, making up that course so she could graduate. I didn't see her. She had quit doing blow before we stopped seeing each other, but once or twice she called me to get something for her friends, probably only when she couldn't call someone else. They had all stopped talking to me. I'd see them around, but rarely. It all just faded.

The clubs sucked, rap was alive, Pearl Jam was rehearsing somewhere in a garage in California, Bush's Dad was making deals with the Nicaraguans, and my father died—he had a heart attack in the car while idling in our driveway. We had barely spoken for years. The resentment had hardened before he died and I was forced to finally look at it. *No*, I thought. *I won't care now.* I felt better, released from something that had been tangled around my ankle until then—his recriminating disapproval.

I felt more firmly planted, more even-keeled—with regard to Carrie too. With Carrie, I had always felt out of control and unsure. There was anxiety that came with wanting things, and it was amplified when I sometimes got them. This was better. The things you want but don't have can cause an aching in your heart, but the things you have and then lose can break you. The trick, I learned, is to not care.

✦

My father's wake was held at a small funeral home in Flushing. Carrie didn't come. She said it might have made it harder for me. My mother was drunk by the time they got started and although I doubt that's unusual at a funeral where half the mourners are Irish, it still caused a few whispers. Now that's drunk. The walls were covered with dark wooden paneling, and you could see a lot of knots in the wood—too many for them to be natural. It was a cafeteria-newspaper-stand kind of funeral. My father's boss, Brad McCloskey, spoke and told a few stories about what a good producer and colleague my dad had been over the years. McCloskey used modest compliments like "good man" and "solid salesman" and described him as funny and persuasive. He made it seem as if he knew my father, which would mean that I did not. I had grown up with somebody else, his stand-in, a drunken, angry and introverted version of the solid, average man Brad McCloskey knew.

There were some guys there from his Elks Lodge. Our neighbors were there. People checked the time on their watches and contemplated their own demises. I sat on a folding chair and listened to people talk about my father, for the last time, and I felt a great resentment toward him because I never got to tell him to go to hell again once I was big enough to look him squarely in the eye. I felt cheated. I have no memories of my paternal grandfather. He died when I was two or three. His name was John Trayner. They called him "Jack." I sometimes wonder what kind of bastard he was in his day.

✦

By the time school started again in September Carrie was gone. She was going to take the bar in Massachusetts, she told me. "No, it wouldn't have mattered," she said. "I would have left New York anyway," she said. "It doesn't matter, Jack. It doesn't matter now," she said, "because that is the past and things are different now. I'm sorry. It's stupid to even talk about." It was better when she was gone. I was cool and focused. *One more year of this shit*, I thought. I took the dealing down a notch. Demand was drying up anyway, and I got by. I paid the bills, and tuition, and I had some cash. A year or so later, the day I graduated, I dumped several grams ceremoniously down the toilet, and made a hard, clean break.

CHAPTER EIGHT:
BILLY KIMBALL

Not long after finishing law school I charmed my way in the door at Blake & Holcomb, a top-tier corporate law firm. And only a few months after I started I could no longer ignore the fact that I had no interest in being a lawyer. Be careful what you wish for, I suppose.

The beautiful thing about an illegal enterprise like selling drugs is that you don't have to pay any dues. The more illegal an activity, the more it becomes a meritocracy. The cream rises, and it takes little time, but only in a fully legal oligarchy like "the law" was one required to kiss the ass of one's inferiors for years. Once I achieved my goals but then quickly realized I didn't want them. . . . Well, I wasn't a lot of fun to be around at obligatory office cocktail parties. All of those Hermes ties hanging down and swinging loose made me cringe the way that one does when accidentally catching an unwanted glimpse of an old man's penis in a gym locker room.

I had been there about a year, and that was the frame of mind I was sporting when a guy I knew from college called and made an appointment to come see me. The timing was perfect, or maybe it just seems that way now. I was not going back to selling drugs; I knew where that eventually landed everyone. Yet I could not resign myself to being a lawyer, to become a regular Joe.

At Blake & Holcomb I had a very small office adjacent to the office of the partner I worked for. When Billy Kimball called and asked if he could come see me I joked, "You know, I'm not a criminal lawyer, Billy." Kimball didn't laugh. He just made an appointment and got off the phone rather abruptly. I agreed to meet him largely out of curiosity. I didn't really have any friends left from college or law school, and Kimball had never really been more than an acquaintance.

What is he doing here? I thought, when he showed up. We shook hands and said, "Yeah, a long while . . ." and, "I heard about Sue, yes. No. I mean, I didn't really know her all that well. Probably not as well as you guys . . ." I walked him into my office. I settled in behind my desk, made a hole between stacks of files piled on my Bob Cratchet apprentice station so we could see each other, and lifted my eyebrows as if to say, "So?"

"You're not easy to find, Jack," Kimball said quietly. He peeled his coat off, moving slowly, as if he was stiff or sore from working out, and laid it gently on the chair next to the one he eased into. His expression was severe. My guard was up, spider-sense tingling.

"Oh yeah?" I replied with a casual smile.

"Yeah. I asked around a little. Michael Baring, all those guys he hung around with in the summers, Hillary, Janie Swanson—she still talks to Carrie, but I guess you two aren't in touch anymore . . ."

"Well," I said, more seriously, "you know how that is."

"I do, Jack. But still. You changed your name?" "Oh, yeah. Yes, I did," I said, smiling again. Def-con 3 now. This is not a drill. "My, uh, stepdad, he died. I don't know if you knew that, that my father died during law school."

"No. I'm sorry." "Yeah. Thanks. But he was actually my stepfather and I had taken his name, Trayner, when I was a little kid and somehow, when he was gone, I don't know, kind of making a new start . . . I went back to my name at birth. Tuckman." Yes, it was all complete bullshit. My father had died, but he was my biological father, not my stepfather. I just twisted all of that into a convenient story.

"Well, just that it was very hard to find you."

"Yeah, you said that."

"I was searching in that lawyer directory, Martindale-Hubbell, for 'Jack Trayner.' I made a bunch of calls, no one from school seems to know what you're up to and then you went and changed your name—"

"Well, here I am."

"The Bar Association had a record of the name change—"

"Billy, what is it you want to talk to me about?"

I was nervous so I leaned back in my chair and yawned a little.

"I've got a problem, Jack."

"Billy, I told you, I don't do criminal law. Do you need me to refer you to someone?" "I don't need a lawyer, Jack," he said gravely. His eyes were sullen and the skin underneath them looked dark, as if from lack of sleep. He was wearing an obviously expensive suit, but it was crumpled, and didn't fit him well. Something about his coloring was off too. He was pale and looked somehow bloated– not exactly as if he'd gained weight, more like he had maintained his weight but had somehow become a bit inflated. His face looked puffy. It's a look that has become much more familiar to me in the years since then. He seemed exhausted but determined. *Oh shit*, I suddenly thought, *he might be trying to cop drugs. Right in my freaking law office, the moron. He could definitely turn out to be a junkie*, I thought.

"Well if you don't need a lawyer, I mean . . . well then . . ."

He cleared his throat a little, sat up a little straighter. "Look," he said. "What I need . . . I need a kidney."

"I'm sorry?"

He stared at me between those stacks of files for a long moment. I'm not easily rattled, but I hadn't expected that.

"Yeah. I'm serious," he said despondently, answering the question I had not even asked. "Unfortunately." His voice was breathy and quiet. I could barely hear him.

"What's that have to do with me?" I asked him. "Aren't there hospitals . . . ?"

"It takes too long, and I could die soon, Jack. I'm not playing around. You knew I was diabetic? In college?"

"What does that mean Billy?" I truly didn't understand the connection, but somehow I assumed it was all bad for young Jack. I didn't like the odds of sitting across the table from a guy with little to lose who had made a major effort to find a guy he was never all that close to in the first place. "It means that everyone knows what you did back in college. No one cares, Jack. Hell, I appreciated it. But a guy who sold blow in college is the closest thing I could find."

"Closest to what? And keep your voice down!"

"Like drug dealers. Or I don't know what," he said quietly. "Someone who might know where to get something like this."

"You mean . . . ?"

He nodded affirmatively.

"Put an ad in the paper. What makes you think I can help?"

"It's illegal."

"Keep your voice down please."

"I'm going through renal failure, Jack. Stage five now."

"Five?"

"Out of five," he said with a weak smirk. "It was brought on by the diabetes and there are some other complications . . ." His voice trailed off. "Look at this, Jack." He moved his right hand across his chest, as if he was about to say the pledge of allegiance, and then pointed to two bumps pushing up under his shirt, on his arm just below his left shoulder. "It's called a fistular."

"Fistular?"

"It's the connection where they hook me up to the dialysis machine."

"You go for that?

He nodded and he then extended his palm toward the two bumps as if motioning to ask whether I needed confirmation, or might want him to otherwise reveal whatever was lying beneath his tailored blue shirt.

"I trust you," I said quietly.

"Do you know what dialysis is, Trayner? Exactly, I mean?"

I said nothing.

"They hook me up to a machine three times a week and I sit there for hours while it filters my blood, doing the job my kidneys can't do anymore. Thing about dialysis is that it will keep you alive, but the longer you're on it, the more it tears up all sorts of other things in your other organs. The only thing that will really set me right is a real, live, functioning kidney. And the wait is over three years."

I wasn't quick to speak. I was taking it in. I was measuring him and the situation. I was considering what he was asking of me. . . . "So, can you wait?"

"Theoretically," he said, quietly, looking down, "I can't. And I've got a bad blood type. We tried everyone we know. We've made a lot of calls. I'm on lists but the lists are simply too long. My dad said to see if maybe there's another way to find something," he said with a little more volume, a bit more animated. "Maybe I know someone who has connections that are, you know—"

"Yes. Softly, Billy."

"Well I really don't know anyone like that—"

"It's illegal?" I cut in. I didn't even know that.

"I don't want to end up being operated on in Thailand or India. You're the only person I could think of. I just don't know anyone else."

"Billy, what does one thing have to do with the other? This is like going to buy luggage at a car dealership. They're both sales-man, but c'mon. What do I know about this? What could I possibly know? And I don't do those other things anymore anyway. I'm a lawyer now."

I could see what looked like some specks of dandruff in his hair. He occasionally scratched at the back of his head with his middle finger while the index finger next to it lingered in the air, curled. He did it then while saying, "You might know one guy who knows a person who could maybe make a difference."

He looked me in the eye then and I saw the look of a young man confronting his mortality. When we're young we claim we know that we're going to die, but we don't really believe it. Billy was a believer. That guy had religion and he was wearing it on his face and on his sleeve. I could also see that he wasn't pissed at me; he wasn't blaming me or anyone else. He was simply trying to solve a problem. His logic required a bit of a leap but it wasn't entirely unreasonable. I mean, he was even right. I knew some people who knew people who might be able to help arrange something like that, or like anything else for that matter, as long as there was enough cash to pay for it.

Still, I replied, "Billy, I'm sorry, and I feel bad, but I just don't think I could help. What I did in college to make a few extra dol-lars, that was casual and it was a while ago. I'm an officer of the court now."

"Jack, we could pay you a lot of money. My dad would. All we need is someone to make the introduction. Nothing else. Maybe you know someone. You might not even realize it. Couldn't you just make some calls, check around?"

"I'm sorry, Billy—"

"We've tried everything. It takes too long. I'm really sick, Jack. My dad would pay a lot of money for this help."

"Hmm. Just out of curiosity, what would the fee be for something like that anyway?"

"My dad would give you twenty-five K. Cash." Cue the house lights and soundtrack. Looking back now I realize that was the watershed moment.

"Not me," I finally replied. "Just someone. Someone else. And we're just talking hypothetically."

"Right. Fine. Twenty-five. Cash. Hypothetical cash. A lot of it."

That's how things start sometimes. By accident. That was about eighteen years ago and I was only one year removed from law school. It was a lot of money to me. "Really," I replied, more to myself than to him. I was considering what I could ultimately extract from a rich man whose first offer was twenty-five grand. I could probably get a lot more than that from a guy whose son would otherwise die. I was thinking about a golf trip to Scotland....

"There are about twenty or thirty thousand people on the waiting list for a kidney right now in this country, and a few thousand die every year while waiting." He said this while looking down at the carpet. He had probably said it a thousand times by then. It sounded like his mantra, and also like his epitaph. "I'm sicker than most."

I didn't speak for a moment. Then I said, "That seems like a pretty big market." That was 1993. The list has tripled since then.

"I don't know about that. But I'm not doing well, Jack. And my family has money. What do you think? Could you help? Do you think you might know anyone?"

"Well I don't really want to discuss it any further right now, but you should give me a phone number where I can reach you."

"Okay, Jack," Billy said softly. I slid him a pad and pen.

"I'll come back to you," I said.

"Okay."

When he said "Okay," he sounded utterly hopeless and I guess it was contagious because I felt infected by his mood. I think it was empathy—thinking how I might feel to be young but dying. I cared about the guy. I wish I could say that it was my primary motivation, but it was not, and I want to tell the truth now. The money is what really captured my attention, and my imagination, but of course I also wanted to help him. Kimball was the same age as me—twenty-seven at the time—but he looked like he was pushing forty. He was always more successful with women, a bigger personality. Now, he looked helpless.

"I will," I said, and stood up. "I will come back to you on this. For sure, Billy." His dull and yellowed eyes lifted slightly to meet mine. "Oh," he said, with a slight smile. "Then I'm O positive. You'll need to know that. Here, I'll write it down."

"Your blood type?"

"O positive. Yeah."

"Weird. Me too."

"Really? A lot of people don't even know." We locked eyes for a moment and in a split second, without saying a word, he asked the question we both knew with certainty that I would say "no" to and I did, with my eyes, and he didn't seem surprised.

He cleared his throat a little. "You'll need this other information, too. It's antigens. HLAs. But they don't have to be a perfect match. Three or four out of six would be great, but it doesn't necessarily have to be any at all as long as the blood type is O positive. These days, as long as you have money you can take this new drug, Cyclosporine. We can get that without help. It's legal."

"Cyclo..?"

"Stops organ rejection. It doesn't matter. Just remember O positive."

"O positive. Same as me. How could I forget?"

"Right. From a healthy, living donor under fifty years old. I'm writing it all down for you. Call me, Jack," he said, smiling again as he got up to leave. "Twenty-five grand," he added in a whisper.

CHAPTER NINE:
JACK TUCKMAN

After I passed the bar exam and before I got my position at Blake & Holcomb, I changed my name for the first time and laid to rest the coke dealer that was Jack Trayner. It was liberating. I did it legally—driver's license, social security—and put a bow around my past and stuck it in the attic. Morphing from one Jack into another paved the way for several more Jacks to come. I read something once about an actor who always tried to have his characters renamed so they shared his actual first name. He said it was easier to remember his cues if the other actors referred to him by his real name. It's true. It's a lot easier to respond quickly and naturally to "Hey, Jack. You see the Mets last night?" or "Jack, hand me that file please" when you happen to be Jack. And Jack doesn't stand out. Jack keeps a low profile.

◆

It wasn't long after I started at Blake & Holcomb that the disappointment set in. And the boredom. "Jack, clean up this draft for me," my boss would say, and drop a stack of papers on my desk so thick that it sounded like a baseball bat cracking into a hardball when it landed. "Here's a list of case law to research, Tuckman. Need it in the morning," he'd say, dropping it on my desk without ever making eye contact. "Gotta pay your dues, Buddy," he would sometimes say as he walked past my station on his way out at six or seven, knowing full well that I'd be there until midnight. *I already paid my dues*, I would think. This is what I spent five years hanging out in the bathroom at the Palladium for? This Formica cubicle is the life I am rewarded with for years of hard work, neverending caution, and the actual "sacrifice" of Jack Trayner?

The stage had been set, and then that meeting with Kimball changed everything. From the moment he left my office I too had one foot out the door. Once I found that first kidney it was all I could think about. I decided to let a few days go by before calling Kimball. I needed to consider whether I really wanted to do this, but I also wanted to make him jones for it for a while—get him nice and anxious before letting him know that I might have something. Many of the skills developed in my previous profession translated to this new endeavor—the sales skills, the caution, the precision, the patience, the egocentricity. Yet, now, when I look back, it's funny to realize how sloppy and clueless I was. The way I worked that deal for Kimball, I should have been picked up by the FBI and transformed back into a half-assed coke dealer by virtue of losing my law license. But I wasn't.

It was 1993 and I didn't even have a cell phone yet. I made outgoing calls from payphones, very cloak and dagger. Back in those days, people drove for an hour just to talk to a guy for five minutes—and I did that too. I started off by calling my Jersey guys. These guys were all pro dealers. First I had to explain where I'd been for the last few months and insist that I really didn't need any blow for the club kids. Then I would have to convince each of them that I hadn't gotten arrested and wasn't trying to cop a plea by flipping on someone else. That was my preamble. Once we got past that, I could explain what it was that I was actually looking for as if it was a punch-line to an old joke. "Actually, I got a sick, rich guy who needs a kidney." There was no real risk in it. I knew who I was calling and none of them gave much of a shit about anything. Sometimes they laughed, or busted my balls a little, or said, "Get the fuck..." and just hung right up on me. But so what? Sometimes they'd say, "dis shit dey teach at college?" I didn't care.

Three or four or six calls into it, the routine went something like this: "Jack. NYU, Jack. Yeah, I know.... No, I don't need anything. It's about something else. No. Thanks. I don't need that either. Shit, that's the last thing I need, Lou," (or Tommy or Ralph or Miguel or who the hell knew their real names anyway). "I've been doing other things. I graduated. Got a regular job now..." I'd say. "Yeah, no. I'm looking for something else right now. I've got a sick, rich guy and I'm looking for a kidney." Pause. No immediate response. "The guy's O Positive, needs a kidney transplant—Yes. Yes. Kidney. That IS what I said actually... Well, that's fucking hilarious. Yes. I said kidney... You want to screw around or you want to make a lot of money? Fine. Yes. You're a real comedian. Fine ... O Positive can only get one from another O Positive, so that's only around thirty percent of the population ... I just know. Don't worry about how I know. Because I do. What are you, a doctor now? I know. I found this all out ... There's also this thing called HLA matching, but it's less important. He'll pay $10K for a healthy one ... No, I shit you not. ... No, I never liked that shit much anyway. I just sold it. Yeah. It is funny. Laugh it up, but I've got a guy with $10K cash if you happen to know anyone who could help ..." It doesn't take long to get a drug dealer's attention with a pile of cash. "Hey, and it's ten, not twenty. I gotta make a living too ... Well, because it's not that good of a job, that's why."

It turned out one of my Newark guys had a guy in Atlantic City whose friend was some kind of multi-tasker who had actually done a couple of deals like this before. A trailblazer. The kidney was coming from some Italian maintenance worker. He was an immigrant from Sicily and lived in a poor neighborhood in southern Jersey, not far from AC. The Atlantic City guy put the word out and the next thing you know he's got some poor schlub who wants to trade a kidney for a better lifestyle. The guy was a janitor at a middle school, friend of a cousin or something. I think about it now and it's amazing. Most everything in those days was happening in India. There was business getting done in South Africa, but not a lot was happening here. This was a fluke. It was just because of who I happened to know in New York and Jersey. I would have liked to think that the guy was raising the money to put his oldest son through college, or to pay for his little girl's asthma medicine or something like that, but I'd bet dollars to doughnuts that at least half the cash went for strippers and tequila and better wine than he normally drank, and that his body couldn't process as well anymore.

I had the merchandise lined up in a little over a week. Much to my amazement, it was easy. I felt a sense of control over things. I had to have that deal, and I started feeling the old charge again. I felt eyes on me as I walked through New York; I felt attractive, wanted, cocked and ready to fire.

During that time I spent hours each night out on my narrow balcony with my best telescope, looking at random stars. I have been doing that since I was a kid—charting stars, reading about what systems might have habitable planets, reading Sagan and Hawking . . . Billions of galaxies, Sagan would say, with billions of stars and countless planets and some that simply have to support life. Some might have hosted intelligent and sophisticated societies that went through their life cycle and died out millions of year ago. Were any out there now? Watching us? Would they see us as friends, or a threat, maybe as food, the way we look at cows and chickens? Would they find some use in harvesting something from us?

The guy I worked for at Blake & Holcomb was named Walter Conway. He wore custom-tailored shirts made of Sea Island cotton. The cuffs and collars were white even if the shirt was a different color, and he wore cuff links—for real, actual cuff links. My excitement about the kidney deal grew in inverse proportion to my waning interest in my day-job. I found myself frequently looking Walter straight in the eye during those days, each time saying something like, "Is that a fact, Walter?" Or, "Is that what I should do, should that be my system too, my ultimate goal?" dripping in enough sarcasm so that he wouldn't even touch it for fear of getting his hands sticky. He'd smugly exhale and turn his back to me and mutter, "asshole" as he walked away, but it wasn't generating the desired effect. Instead of making me feel bad or fear for my job, I thought it was hysterical.

A few days after I secured the kidney I finally called Kimball. It was like waiting to call a girl back for a second date. The more I wanted to make the call the more I felt obligated to wait just another day, and frame the whole thing perfectly. I stroked myself with the anticipation of it, with the beautiful way it made me anxious to think about it—that beautiful feeling of, "I've got the thing . . . I matter." I also enjoyed the ultimate ego stroke of playing the hero. I wanted the money, but I also wanted to have the genuine satisfaction of having saved someone. Anyone.

"Hey Billy?" "Who's this?" he asked, sounding fairly spirited.

"Well, you sound chipper," I said. "That's good."

"Trayner? Is that you?" "Billy, you sound good today. Do you still need the part we were talking about? That part for your car? Because you sound damned rested, like a guy ready for a 10K run."

"Funny, Jack." The verve was gone from his voice. It went off like a switch.

"Do you still need it?" I asked again. "Because I may be able to hook you up, Billy. You may be in luck. But I need to discuss some of the details with your dad." "Why? Just tell me how much they want."

"Your dad, Billy. That's who I need to talk to. Can you arrange a call for us? So your dad and I can get acquainted? Like you said, everyone knew what I did in college and I've been thinking I probably need to be a little more careful about how I conduct myself." I thought negotiating directly with the father of a dying young man would give me the greatest opportunity to get the best price. Kimball didn't believe that I needed to talk to his dad, but what else could the guy do?

I wanted to help Kimball, I really did. No one wants to watch a young man die for no good reason. But I was focused on the money. Of course I was. The Newark guys moved me to twelve grand and never insulted me by claiming to pay the janitor any particular amount. We all knew it couldn't be much more than a few thousand dollars, maybe five grand. They even got me to go twelve-five because at the last minute they claimed the guy was demanding a couple of eight balls and for some reason the Newark guys thought it was only fair that I finance it. I threw them a bone. After all, I got Kimball's father for eighty K. If only they knew! I felt high for days. It was my first taste of the Organ Rush.

✦

I told Kimball's father that the donor and his "agent" were going to need fifty grand, that there was no negotiating with these people. I still wanted my twenty-five all clear or I would waste no less than the count of three to get off the phone and never take Billy's calls again. The guy was agreeable. He even thanked me profusely. I knew they'd eventually find out that I had lied and kept most of the money, and I didn't care about that either. It was so much easier than I expected. I felt a tinge of guilt but after all, I was saving his son's life and what's a fair price on that? Time was working against him—it was limiting.

My first closed sale in the business. I often think back on it with a feeling of nostalgia, on the events and details, and I always get a real kick out of that part about the janitor wanting coke. "Okay, sir, here's your receipt, here are your antibiotics—make sure to take them every day and not risk any life-threatening infections. You're short one kidney now, but you should be fine. Oh, and here are your two eight balls. Party on, goombatz."

The craziest part about that first transaction, my initiation, is that I was so jazzed about it, so proud of my role as hero, that I actually drove Kimball and Michael the janitor to a meeting at the clinic in Jersey City. Executing on a nephrectomy and kidney transplant can take months here in the US—lots of tests and a few meetings before the surgery gets ordered. Looking back, it's hard to stomach how clueless I was then. I was even in the room while the doctor asked some of the qualifying questions. Michael was presented as an altruistic donor. They can direct their organ "donation" to anyone of their choosing with no regard for lists or matching criteria, but the doctor still has a professional obligation to make sure that the match can work, and an obligation to ensure that no money has changed hands.

"Yes, doctor," Billy Kimball said, "my second cousin. Once removed, I think. My mother's side. Well, her maiden name is Barrett but her mother's mother, my maternal grandmother. . . . That's how I'm Italian. On that side." Kimball was well-rehearsed and smooth. He was a smart guy and he never had to try too hard. "Cousin Michael is a saint. We were closer as kids, but people get busy. But he tells me he'll come and save the life of a cousin he hasn't even seen more than twice since we were ten . . ." Michael's hair was neatly combed and somehow I just knew that had been a special effort. He wore a WalMart-issue suit with a shiny sort of faux shark-skin finish. He looked like an older version of a poorly dressed recent college grad on his first round of interviews.

For the most part, the doctor didn't seem to really care. Kimball's preparation was unnecessary. The doctor had a clipboard and made notes on a form as they spoke. It seemed like he was going down a checklist and barely noting the answers. He often glanced at his nails while Michael or Kimball responded to one of his rote questions. You see, it's like this: if they turn down the procedure, they lose a lot of money and that money will just go elsewhere, and who is really helped by that? One way or another, legal or not, somewhere else or some other country—it's going to get done. Once it's done, a life has been saved. Why not be on the side of saving lives—and getting paid? The doctors were very easily convinced by thin cover-stories. They still are. After that, I even insisted on being there for the procedure when it was done.

I waited at the hospital for hours until it was over, but I did not remain glib. That kidney moved from Michael in one adjoining room to William Kimball (of the Greenwich Kimballs) in the other, and I got sick to my core. Kimball's family was scattered around waiting, pacing, talking, not talking. I don't mean to imply that I got nauseous. It's bigger than that. There was a subtle but penetrating sickness that spread to everyone in that waiting room. It spread through me like fog in a science fiction movie, washed over me like the slow, black swell of an ocean wave. I was disgusted at what I was part of, the baseness of it, the way I had relieved Kimball's family of so much more than a fair price, and of taking that poor moron's kidney so he could do some blow and patronize the local hookers for a few weeks—or whatever it was he intended to do.

At one point a nurse asked me, "Are you his brother?" I laughed inwardly at how incredibly stupid and careless I had been, standing right there in the waiting room. Since the passage of NOTA (the National Organ Transplant Act) in 1986 it's illegal to exchange "anything of value" for an organ. I never sold someone a gram in college and then stuck around to watch him do bumps in the bathroom. I had even made some of the arrangements in my own name at the time—Tuckman—and then debated for weeks if perhaps I should change it again. I was concerned that if I did, it could raise a red flag for the bar association. I decided to leave it alone and just start using new names going forward. All the time. And rotate phones. A lot of this stuff is probably obvious. The Internet changed everything.

As for Billy Kimball, he's living in Connecticut, working for a hedge fund, and he's fine. It's actually amazing, considering all of the circumstances. Billy Kimball has three kids—at least three kids. It could be more by now. I'll bet they're glad I found him that kidney. I occasionally check up on him by casually touching base with one or another person from our NYU days who knows someone who thinks that perhaps he and I were friends. It's enough to get me a rough update. "Yeah, his firm this, and such and such deal that" or "Yeah, Billy's wife's brother was the guy on that show about everyone trapped on an island," without it ever evolving into, "Hey, I'll tell Alex to tell him Jack Trayner says hi. What's your cell number?"

In the beginning, he was the only one I checked up on. Maybe I should have kept it that way. Those damn follow-up calls; that's how the infection started. I kept a distant eye on Kimball's progress for years. You see, he's alive. And at least three more people—his kids—are alive, and it is because of me. I did that, and no one can ever take that away from me. That has to count for something.

When it was over and settled, I put about thirty grand in a safe deposit box in a bank here in New York. Then, I actually took the time to fly to Tucson to open an account and put the other thirty into a safe deposit box out there. (No, there was no real significance to the choice of Tucson. Carrie and I had been there one Thanksgiving to visit her relatives. I just needed any place far away and random. Not LA or Chicago. Not too small a town either. Meticulous Jack.) I spent a lot of time at the driving ranges for a day or two before I came back. I was starting to hit the ball well then. The following week Walter dropped a bomb on my desk, making a loud clap with the papers—which I thought was intentional—and said, "Sorry, pal, but I need it all in the morning," as he walked by without bothering to make eye contact. He was pulling on his waistband to move his pants a little higher on his hips as he walked away.

"Yeah. Well, fuck you very much!" I said with a bright smile and without hesitation, as if I were joking. Of course we both knew that I was not.

He didn't say anything, but he stopped. He turned to face me and looked me squarely in the eyes. I expected him to make some condescending false-bravado threat about teaching me a lesson, but neither of us spoke. A smile crept over his face. He didn't even have to say anything. From that moment on, I didn't work there anymore, and we never exchanged any words about it. I was of no consequence. He turned and walked away and I yelled out one last comment: "Starting my own firm, Walter. See you at the club, my good man!"

✦

Now, I will end my years as an organ broker. It will finally end. It began accidentally, in 1993 with Billy Kimball, and then I worked toward the goal of growing the business, but there was never a plan. Now I have a plan. And I know two things about plans: the fewer plans you have the less likely you are to be disappointed, and the more complex a plan is the more likely it is to fail. So mine is a bad plan; but it's mine.

I am going to arrange to kill my partner and by doing so, help save a lot of innocent people. I'll be like a rat on the stand at the Gotti trial, but I will also be Robin Hood again, finally on the side of doing what's right. I am also going to take down the murder-ring-organ-farm I helped to create at Royston, burn it down like an old email address, and with it my entire career. I have no choice. If I have learned anything through this whole miserable affair it's this: to do any good in the world requires an element of self-sacrifice.

The client will be incredibly wealthy. He will need to travel but we'll be on a private jet, provided by his father, with a ton of medical equipment and an attending nurse sitting beside him. This is not a kidney. Wallace will be on the plane. He will have to travel with me on this one and will gladly do so to serve his own agenda of wanting to someday cut me out of the loop. The money will be on the plane. The client, and the broker, and the supplier. Wallace will be told that the plane is headed for South Africa, but it will go to Rio instead. I have few friends in this world, and fewer still who I can trust, but my friend in Brazil is one of them and he won't let me down. Most situations are controlled best by money, but some require more.

Wallace may note at some point that we are heading south and not east, but he may not, and either way, it will not matter. There will be nothing he can do. There will be no guns on the plane, no parachutes. When we land in Rio we'll all be transferred to a limo to take us to the hospital, but the limo will be followed. This time the conspiracy will be mine; the plan, mine.

Leaving the airport the limo will be followed by two motorcycles, each with two men on them. A few miles away from the airport, on an open stretch of highway, the motorcycles will pull up beside the car. The men on the backs of the bikes will point guns at the driver and order him to pull over, and he will comply. They will order us out of the car. There will be confusion. They will ask our names, in English. I will say, "Jack," and offer to fist-pump the man talking—not shake hands, not high-five . . . "fist-pump" and "Jack" will be the sig-nal. Then, I will say, "This is Wallace," and point at him. Wallace will turn and look at me, a knowing look of shock mixed with fear and outrage and he'll loudly say, "Jack?" and the man will quickly put two or three bullets in my partner's head. The nurse and client's father may scream. They will be told to shut up. The men will carry Wallace's lifeless, bloody body and place it into the trunk which the driver will have already opened. I will say, "Get back in the car," to the others, while thinking, "don't think, don't think, don't think, don't think." One of the armed men will get into the limo with us. The motorcycles will speed away and the limo will speed away and the cli-ent will probably say, "Jack, what the hell happened?" He might say, "Jack, why did you do this?!" and the only answer he will get will be, "Shut up. We're going to save your son." He might say, "Take us back to the plane," and all he'll hear in response will be, "Shut up. We're going to save your son."

The driver will know the route to the hospital nearby. He'll drive quickly. He will make the call to alert them that we're just ten min-utes away. We will enter through the delivery entrance near the large kitchen. There will be a gurney there for the client, and another for what was once Wallace Kendrickson. My friend in Brazil will have arranged it all. They will rush the client and Wallace toward the ORs. They will have four hours. There will be another patient, form-ing a domino chain wherein a donor and recipient who don't match become part of a multi-party exchange. Wallace wasn't a match for Philip, but he was for someone else waiting in that hospital. The heart that other recipient might have otherwise received could then later be gifted to Philip. Throw in plenty of forged paperwork and a few well-placed bribes . . . and no one goes to prison. This was the only way. It will work.

After the ER personnel retreat back down the hall from which they came, with Wallace and the client, the client's father and nurse *trailing awkwardly behind, I will return to the limo. We won't speak. He will drive me to Leblon, to my friend's rarely used summer home. On the way there I will make the call that will soon burn down Royston, and Wolf and Kleinhans and all the finders they may know in the shanty towns. I am Robin Hood. I'm Batman. I'll live in Leblon for some time, for months, maybe longer. I don't know what I'll do after that. I really do not know. I have no plan for that at all— perhaps that's the only thing that might get me out of this alive. Having no plan for what happens after this also means that I won't be disappointed. Maybe there's a chance.*

PART III: NEW YORK JACK

CHAPTER TEN:
THE ADDRESSABLE MARKET
OPPORTUNITY

After the pre-surgery interview I went to with Kimball and the janitor eighteen years ago, I chatted up the doctor in the hall. He told me that, "Nearly 80 percent of the people waiting on those lists need kidneys. People have two of them so altruistic donors like your friend here are possible."

"And Billy's cousin, Michael, he'll be fine afterward?" I asked.

"Should be."

"So why don't more people do it?" I asked.

"Would you?"

I answered the question with another. "How long do people usually have to wait?" I asked Kimball's doctor.

"Usually over three years," he replied. "A guy like your friend, in stage four or five, that's a real problem. They can get bumped up the list, but it's dicey."

✦

"Doc," I asked, "what happens to people who don't get one in time? What else can they do?"

He shook his head slightly. "There's *nothing* they can do."

That was eighteen years ago. The lists have gotten much longer since then. The average wait for a kidney now is around seven years. It could be ten years by 2020. Since NOTA was passed it's against US law to receive "anything of value" for donating an organ. Like it always does, making any form of goods or services illegal instantly creates a black market for it. Such is the case with my industry. Whereas immunosuppressants made organ transplantation broadly possible after 1983, it was the passage of NOTA, three years later, that signaled the coming of the organ rush.

✦

After that first kidney sale, I was struck by how I was able to find the merchandise with relative ease. About a month later, I put the word out to my Jersey guys that I might need one more thing like we'd gotten from Michael the janitor. Two days later one guy called and said, "Hey, Jack. You want to maybe stop by the place sometime tomorrow? Grab a sandwich? I might have something you're looking for."

"Maybe sometime next week," I said. "Would it be the same price?"

"A little more probably," he replied.

"Oh. I was thinking a little less probably."

"Well, stop by. We'll talk."

I was caught off guard. I didn't think they could find something like that so quickly. It actually still surprises us sometimes ("us" being me and my colleagues) that organized crime hasn't taken a greater interest in our little business. I figured that the

Kimball transaction must have opened their eyes a little. But the word-of-mouth-disseminated-through-Jersey-based-coke-dealers methodology was obviously inefficient and unsafe, so I turned them down. I was optimistic that I could build a network of suppliers, but the tricky part was finding buyers in a safe and efficient manner. That was the rub. Kimball was an accident. He had come to me. That thought lingered in the back of my mind for years: if I someday figured out an efficient method of finding buyers, the business could explode.

I changed my name to Jack Campbell. And I got started, right after leaving Blake & Holcomb. I got myself a shitty little office in The Garment District and set myself up offering "general services." It was on 37th Street, a block where every storefront sold knock-off versions of designer clothing. I connected with a few local banks and mortgage brokers and got some spot work here and there doing residential real estate closings, but I was jazzed and gearing up for something bigger. I had cleared sixty grand in cash from the Kimballs and my mind was in business-plan mode.

✦

When I returned from Tuscon I placed a call to the United Network of Organ Sharing, the quasi-governmental agency that oversees organ transplantation in the United States—and all of the lists.

"UNOS. Paul Sheridan."

"Hey. Hi. My name's Jack Campbell. My, uh, wife, she . . . I have some questions about, you know, to apply for an organ transplant—"

"To get on a list, you have to coordinate it through your local hospital's transplant center."

"Oh, right. Okay," I said. "It's just . . . well, our doctor, he told me there are like thirty thousand people on the lists. Is that true? Are there that many people waiting?"

"Yeah. That's about right."

"And most of those need kidneys?"

"Yes. Is your wife in need of a kidney?" he asked.

"Yeah."

"Well, a lot of people are getting them now. Your local hospital can help you through the paperwork and application process."

"And the rest, they're mostly livers?"

"That's true," he said, "but that won't affect your wife."

"So most of the people on your lists need a kidney or a liver?" I asked.

"Almost 95 percent."

"So, if 95 percent of the people on waiting lists need a kidney or a liver, and kidneys are redundant and livers regenerate, that seems like a lot of people looking for organs who could get them from someone alive. Right?"

"I'm sorry. What did you say your name was?"

"Jack. Anyway, Paul, is there any way to legally pay and somehow get an organ faster? To move up higher on the list? Like paying a rush fee?"

"No. Of course not."

"But that's a pretty big market then . . ." I said.

"Market?"

"I mean, it's just a lot of people that need help."

"Yes. It is. Sir, what was your last name again?"

✦

That conversation took place in the early nineties. Paul Sheridan. I loved that name. I used it for years when I used to reach out to potential clients posing as a guy from UNOS. Surely it got back to him a few times over the years—must have driven him crazy. Now, in 2011, the list is over 107,000. That makes for a little over 100,000 kidneys and livers. Do the math. What if the rate to save one's life was $50,000? $100,000? It's actually even higher. Then consider that the average commission for most goods and services ranges between 5 and 15 percent . . . And there you have the seduction . . . I earned far more than the surgeon on Kimball's kidney transplant. I was the rainmaker. I had found my niche.

✦

I started traveling to India, South Africa, and Brazil. I found doctors I could pay off, whole hospitals and transplant centers that were already on the take, administrators who could be gently greased to look the other way . . . I made trips to Thailand and the Philippines, Indonesia, Eastern Europe, and later to China as well. In those parts of the world everyone knows what's going on, and everyone accepts it as part of the way things are. It may not be discussed openly, but it is understood—like having a mistress in France, or not paying taxes on cash income.

CHAPTER ELEVEN:
RISK/REWARD

Sometime late in '93 I went to see a doctor at a hospital in Recife, Brazil. Recife is in the northeast part of the country. There are no direct flights, so you fly to Sao Paulo and then double back. Sao Paulo is as far south of Recife as Florida is south of New York, but it was either that or make three stops. The doctor I was meeting with, let's call him Genaro de Mendoza. We had spoken on the phone several times and as I often did back then, I said I was looking to source a kidney for my sick wife. Once I got to the local market and met the local docs—and felt them out in person—only then would I decide whether to make a pitch, cold and off the cuff, or just politely excuse myself and glide out of their memories.

Dr. Genaro de Mendoza wore a white lab coat and was seated behind his desk when I was led into his office. He wore glasses with large square frames, and his eyes were unsmiling behind them. His skin was dark and blotchy, his hair thin and swept sideways across his balding scalp, and he sat with his hands clasped in front of him on the desk.

"So, Mr. ah. . . ." he began in English.

"Just call me Jack."

"All right. So your wife, she needs a kidney transplant? That's what you said?"

"Yes."

"And your friend, your friend a nephrologist told you that you might have better luck finding a donor more quickly outside of the States?"

"That's right."

"Why here, Mr . . . Hmmm? Jack? What brings you to Recife? You have very fine hospitals in New York, don't you?"

"Of course, Doctor, but as I explained to you, this UNOS they have in the United States, it's a terrible system."

"Yes, you did say that."

"It's prejudicial, and my wife is not high on their list and I have tried to talk to them. I am willing to pay anything for the proper care but they say—"

"Well, it's not about money, Mr. Jack."

"Jack."

"Hmm?"

"Just Jack."

"Yes. It's not about money." "Isn't this a very expensive procedure?"

"Well, yes, of course, but that has no bearing on who is chosen as the recipient."

"I understand that Doctor, but I'm just saying that I want to get my wife the very best of care."

"Well, Jack, we have done many kidneys transplants in recent years. We run an excellent facility here, so that much is true.

"And you see, Doctor," I said calmly, "if I were to bring Susan here—Susan's my wife of course—if that went well, and your people were able to help us, I think that I might be able to refer you other similar patients from the United States. Perhaps that way everyone could benefit. Maybe many people."

"I'm sorry, Jack. I don't understand. How might you refer patients? What exactly do you mean?"

"I mean that we've met many people who are dealing with the same challenges we are. At home, back in NY, we've met others who need a transplant and are frustrated by the bureaucracy. Many are wealthy. Like me, they'd probably be very comfortable paying for the best care if they could get it expediently. They would probably pay a premium even. Do you think they could get that here? Expediency?"

"Jack," de Mendoza said without a smile, his voice soft and gravelly, "are you offering to pay me to get kidneys for people?"

"Of course not, Doctor. That's not legal in your country or mine. But my friends would surely pay you an appropriate fee for a costly operation. And to get better care sooner than they would in the States, from a system that is arbitrary and inefficient."

"I see," he said, still speaking softly and in perfect English. "Could you excuse me for a moment? I have to consult with a colleague regarding a patient. I won't be long."

"Of course."

He got up and walked out of the room, through the exterior office and into the industrial-looking hallway. Twice I noticed his secretary glancing up at me. I thought about bolting but only moments later de Mendoza returned with another doctor, also wearing a white lab coat, over a button down shirt and slacks. He was stout and broad-shouldered, with a friendly air, and he was trailed by a security guard. My pulse may have barely moved but intellectually I immediately grasped that I had fucked up and overreached. "Mr. Jack," the other doctor began in a rich, almost melodic voice, smiling genuinely, "may I speak with you for a moment?"

"May I ask who you are, Doctor?" I said casually, also smiling.

"I am Doctor Juan Guillermo. I am the hospital administrator," he said. The security guard stepped forward and took up a position beside him. De Mendoza had returned to his desk and was seated again. I looked back at the security guard. He was shaky, and his shirt was creased and stained. He rested one hand on the gun in the holster on his hip, but he wouldn't shoot a man for this. I could rush past him—there might be no other way.

"Please Mr. Jack, may I speak to you in the hallway?" Guillermo asked again, still smiling broadly.

"Sure," I said and exhaled. "You can speak to me in the hallway. What's the security guard for?"

"Him?" Guillermo chuckled, "he's for de Mendoza. This debil mental," he said in Porteguese, motioning at de Mendoza, "he doesn't understand capitalism. Idiota. Do you like rum, Jack?"

"Well, I prefer scotch. Scotch whiskey," I said, standing.

"Okay, this way," he said and clapped me on the shoulder.

That's how I met my friend Juan Guillermo. I've bought about a hundred kidneys from him since then. Still, it wasn't long before I learned that it was safer to talk on the golf course.

✦

Sellers are everywhere, all over the globe, easy to find, easy to line up, and easy to pay off with chump change. You simply bait them with money. From the time I started in 1993 until '97 or '98, the challenge was always finding buyers. Once I did, negotiating the price was not that difficult. "No" is illogical. It means death. I have never, in my eighteen years, met a single buyer who could fund the purchase but who decided, in the end, that he would rather pass the wealth down to his kids than stay alive. Never.

In the mid-nineties I still had to be very creative to find clients, and take some risks. I sometimes paid off mid-level administrators at transplant centers here in the States for names on their lists. A few times when business was slow I even placed ads in newspapers. What cop doesn't know that every, "exotic massage studio" advertising on the inside-back page of the newspaper classifieds is actually granting rub-and-tug happy endings to anyone with the nerve to ask? Who believes that there is a single "Escort Service" that actually sends young, beautiful women to "escort" older, rich gentlemen to functions? No one cares. And no one seemed to care about my vocation either.

Transplant Consultant for Hire

If you are waiting for an organ transplant we can help expedite getting the lifesaving help that you need. We work with a global network of high-quality healthcare providers to secure you a good match and provide the very best care. If you are currently on dialysis that poses no restriction. Any stage of renal or liver disease can be considered. Call Jack Thompson, at 1,2,3,whatever-the-hell-my-number-was-that-month . . .

◆

By 1996 or so I completely stopped practicing any kind of law and I was obsessed with solving the international marketing challenge for organs. In 1997, I did. Not too many years ago there were personal ads in the classified sections of newspapers. Eventually, most classified ads migrated to the Web. The Internet launched the organ rush into high gear the way the railroad did for the gold rush in the middle of the eighteen hundreds.

Suddenly, finding customers was easy from behind hidden IP addresses in cyberspace. UNOS launched its first website for people interested in organ transplantation in '95. Two years later I began hunting there too. Here's my analogy: UNOS is the Mexican government and guys like me are the drug cartels. The cartels usually win. In fact, it's usually a blowout. Once, back in 1999, I got a memorable invitation to an Instant Message chat:

W: *I saw your ad online.*

Jack: *Which ad?*

W: *Is this the transplant consultant? The listing on the Internet?*

Jack: *Yes. How can I help you?*

W: *I need a kidney. Can you help me with that?*

Jack: *I can advise you, yes. I can help direct you on where to obtain the organ you need.*

W: *How can you do that?*

        I hesitated. I was rotating cell phones. IP addresses were essentially impossible to pinpoint then, but still . . .

Jack: *I work with hospitals and transplant centers around the world. I represent them and sometimes I can arrange travel for patients from the States.*

W: *You represent them?*

Jack: *Yes. Why?*

W: *Hmm. It's just that I actually represent this buyer. It's not for me. I represent them.*

Jack: *In what capacity?*

W: *Representative.*

        Pause.

Jack: *I'm Jack.*

        Pause.

W: *I'm Wallace.*

Jack: *Do you represent more than one person looking for a kidney?*

W: *From time to time.*

Jack: *Maybe we can help each other.*

W: *Maybe we can, Jack.*

◆

That's how things start sometimes.

CHAPTER TWELVE:
THE MAN FROM DALLAS

Hermann Coburn is an eccentric older guy from Texas. In recent years, he's become known in my industry as The Man from Dallas. Unlike the rest of us, he does not keep a low profile. In fact, he's a bit of a publicity hound. He's often quoted in articles about the black market for organs. The Man from Dallas is a true "travel agent." He arranges trips for desperate, wealthy Americans in renal failure to one of two foreign facilities known to be far more concerned with the bottom line than the Hippocratic Oath. He has skirted the law by claiming that he is merely arranging travel accommodations; the fact that these trips all happen to be to foreign transplant centers is not against any US law, and not his problem. Most of his clients live for many years, whereas twenty other people suffering with renal failure in the US will die today.

✦

For the most part, Coburn's a buyer's agent like Wallace. However, where Wallace takes too many chances, The Man from Dallas takes *all* chances. Wallace finds buyers. He sources them; he gets referrals; he trolls organmatchmaker.com looking for leads. He follows subtle tips from doctors and hedge fund managers and lawyers. And when he finds them, he usually brings them to me—his supplier. But he does so without using his real name. He hides behind his rotating Florida cell phone numbers (a technique he copied from me) and the security of ever-changing email addresses. The Man from Dallas does not. Hermann Coburn is a crusader, and men with a cause don't hide—they seek out trouble. They wear arm bands and badges. It's remarkable that The Man from Dallas hasn't spent more than a short stint in prison. It's even a little surprising that he's still alive.

✦

The Internet made the business infinitely easier, and meeting Wallace made me realize that the marketing challenge of finding enough buyers might no longer be a problem if I outsourced the buy side of the transactions to professional partners. I had already built a network of suppliers around the world, and realized I could simply provide the parts, representing only the sellers. After Wallace and I got acquainted, we did a couple of kidney deals together in 2000. I cautiously sought out more brokers to whose clients I could provide merchandise. A few quick Yahoo and Alta Vista searches on "transplant tourism," and "buying a kidney," led to the public contact information for Coburn. I decided to go and meet him late in the summer of 2000. It was over a hundred degrees in the shade for ten days running when I landed at DFW.

✦

I arrived at his house in the early afternoon. The street was fairly empty but I parked about a half a block past it, on the opposite side.

He lived in a modest suburban home on a small lot. It couldn't have been more than fifteen hundred square feet, and there were similar houses crowding in on both sides, only a few feet away. Somehow I had expected something more rural and more grandiose—a structure tucked back away from the road on a sprawling Texas-sized piece of wooded land.

In the front yard was a garden of sorts, which looked at first like it might have been growing wild, but upon closer examination, it simply looked messy due to overcrowding. There were countless seedlings and guide-sticks jutting out of the ground, with no formal rows or sections, all mashed together in a small space surrounded by a short concrete border. What looked like wild tomato plants—or possibly ivy—extended over the concrete in spots like the tentacles of a mutated octopus climbing onto a dock in a scene from a bad science fiction movie.

Behind a screen door, the foyer looked black from where I stood in the bright sunlight outside. I walked up the path that split the front garden, and before I reached the door I heard a man's soft and pleasant voice say, "Jack? Welcome to Dallas."

◆

The Man from Dallas made iced tea, and we sipped it while sitting at a small, wooden kitchen table. The chairs were rickety on the hardwood floor and made soft creaking noises, like a playground swing, as we spoke. "Tell me about your wife," he said. I maintained a pained expression, but inwardly I was probably laughing a bit—flippant prick that I was back then. The Man from Dallas. I had anticipated a man far less likeable, perhaps more like Wallace.

I told him all about Susan, my imaginary wife. I related the details of her condition, her deterioration, the fistular in her upper arm, the losses, the pain, the hopelessness, and how I had stumbled upon him on the Internet. I told him my name was Campbell, but that he should call me Jack. I called him Herm, at his request. He smiled and nodded reassuringly. He understood. He knew. He would help us. He was sincere and it made me feel regretful.

✦

When he talked about the business, the pace of his speech quickened. "They'll pay fifty grand a year for dialysis but they won't pay for Susan to get a kidney transplant. And why? Because of the insurance companies, the HMOs. Who do you think owns Congress anyway?" he said quietly, but emphatically. I nodded, and I got a little sermon in Hermann Coburn's kitchen: "It's the military industrial complex. Don't you see, that's the chokepoint. That's where the government is able to control it. . . . Why do we need the government to regulate our own bodies? . . . This brave new world . . . Life, liberty and the pursuit of happiness. Life, Jack! That's the very thing." He was nearly whispering. When he finally went silent and the nodding motion of his head had slowed, I said, "So . . . how much would it cost?"

"About seventy thousand dollars," he said without hesitation and then did not add another word. He was also a better salesman than I had expected.

"Why so much?" I asked, pretending to be naïve.

"Pays for all the travel, accommodations, the expense of surgery, aftercare, all incidentals, and my fee, which is ten thousand dollars."

That was eleven years ago, but eighty grand was still well below market. Ten thousand dollars, I thought. That explains the shitty house and the octopus display where the front lawn should be. He had not even mentioned the part—the kidney.

"How much is it for the kidney?"

He peered at me intently and suddenly had a more focused and intelligent look in his eyes. After a moment he said, "Nothing." I waited. "Are you a cop, Jack?" he asked, still smiling.

"No. Oh . . . no," I replied, also smiling, and calmly added, "I am not a cop. Sorry if that came out wrong . . ."

"Are you affiliated with any law enforcement agency?" he asked, still smiling casually.

"No."

"The organ is donated, Jack. I don't deal in organs. I just make arrangements for your wife to go to an excellent transplant center in a foreign country where the government doesn't have its hands around the throats of sick people. Think of me like a travel agent. What you do while you're on this particular trip, at that particular facility—once you get there—is your business. But I can tell you this: she'll get what she needs, and two weeks after that surgery, she'll feel better than she has in years."

The hospitals must be paying local finders, I surmised. The price of the organ must come out of the overall fee for the surgery. "And you get ten thousand?" I asked him.

"Jack, I need to make a living too. And to pay for my research, and—"

"Herm," I interrupted him, "I wasn't complaining. It seems too low."

✦

He was taking ten grand per kidney. Back then, I was probably getting at least triple that, and that was only the sell-side commission on the transaction. "So if you don't get involved with getting the actual kidney, who does? How do we know it's the right, you know, match, and that she'll be healthy?" I asked.

"Good questions, Jack. The hospital handles all of that. Before you and Susan make the trip—I assume you'd be going with her? . . ." I nodded. "Before you go, I'll be in contact with the medical team at the hospital, send them her chart. They'll secure a kidney from a living donor that's a good match. You're paying me for my contacts and experience. I have worked with these people for years. I know where your wife will get the right care. And I know where she would not get the right care."

"And these people just donate kidneys? They don't get paid? Why would they do that?" I asked him, feigning the genuine concern of any intelligent, but uninitiated, man.

"Does it matter?"

I paused for what I thought was an appropriate amount of time, then said, "I suppose not." Then I added, "Herm, it doesn't sound like you make all that much. Your house, you're not living extravagantly . . . do you mind my asking . . ."

"Why I do this?" he asked with a fatherly smile.

"Yes."

"I didn't go to medical school, Jack. I'm not a doctor. But I get to save people's lives. These people who come to me, many of them would die. With my help, they will live, maybe just as long as you or me. And without me, they'd wait through four years of dialysis treatments while the US government played God with their lives." He paused. "I do this," he said sincerely, "for love."

✦

There was no air-conditioning, but he had ceiling fans spinning in all of the rooms. They pushed the hot air around but did little to cool the house. It was cooler than it was outside in the sun, but probably still well into the mid-eighties. Insects from the garden buzzed about outside of the screened windows. My shirt was sticking to my chest.

"So no one bothers you because technically you're not selling organs or anything..." In my head, the word "love" was reverberating in his voice, like an itch or a headache.

"Now you got it, Jack. I'm just a travel agent."

"Herm, what's the deal with those stories about guys losing kidneys in Vegas? Waking up in bathtubs full of ice with a note that says to get to the hospital or they'll die? . . . Is any of that real?"

"Kidney thieves?" he said with a bit of a smile. "Forget that. That stuff doesn't really happen. At least not here in the states. You need an operating room. Two. A sterile environment, and anesthesia and nurses and . . . it's mostly just urban myths."

"All that stuff about hookers luring drunk businessmen to hotel rooms . . . I read something about some guy, 'The Siren' they call him. 'The Siren?' Runs a ring of kidney thieves. That's not real?"

He snorted a short laugh. "The Siren is not real," he said, shaking his head. "But I won't say this business isn't without danger for guys like me."

He calmly got up from the table, turned, reached toward a kitchen drawer behind him, and removed a handgun. Maybe a .38. He looked into my eyes as he placed it on the table between us and sat back down. The gun made a solid "tap" sound as it came to rest on the wooden surface of the table, muzzle pointed straight toward me. Coburn reached over and turned it slightly, so it was pointing toward the wall. "I gotta be careful," he said.

I smiled, yawned a bit, and said, "Why? Why do you have to be careful? Who cares?"

"I told you. The government. The healthcare industry. FBI. The FBI is always watching me. They're tapping my phones right now. They drive by the house now and then. Like I don't know why a white Buick is coming by. Or a green Oldsmobile. Like I don't know which cars they use. . . ."

"But if the FBI wanted to catch you, you'd be caught already," I said. "You're not hard to find. It took me five minutes on the Internet."

"Not catch me, Jack. Just keeping tabs on me. And my work. I am close to some big discoveries in cryogenics. I could show you. Downstairs. I have been working with spider venom, and human growth hormone. Injecting myself. I'm close now. I may have it solved soon . . ."

"Solved? What?" "Eternal life. When a part wears out, you replace it. Like a kidney. But there's more . . ."

"I see."

"They can't have that."

"Who?"

"The government. I told you. The FBI. The pharmaceutical companies need *sick people* for customers. . . . But they don't bother me because they need me. That's how I stay a step ahead. Smarter than them," he added with a grin, pointing at his temple.

"They need you?" I asked.

"Every time those Keystone cops get a lead on a black-market organ ring, who do you think they call for advice?"

This was eleven years ago. I knew little then about the way things are balanced in the business and the legal system, but his words quickly sunk in. "And do you advise them?" I asked casually.

"Of course."

◆

When I left his house I went to the car and opened the trunk. I got my bag and changed my shirt right there on the street, removing my sweat-soaked button down and replacing it with a clean, dry t-shirt. I got in the car, cranked the air conditioner, and drove away. I never spoke to Hermann Coburn again. When I got to the hotel, I burned every single one of my email addresses and cellphone numbers. I knew I would have to contact all of my associates and provide them with new ones once I got back to New York. It was worth it. I wanted no connection whatsoever to The Man from Dallas. Now, when his name comes up, I pretend to have never spoken with him, but I can tell you this: I secretly root for him. I wish him well, and I'm glad he helps people. I pray that he's right, and that what I do helps people too. I hope he gets it right and finishes his "research" in time—before his heart gets too old or the FBI changes their minds about him. But I don't want to be in his Rolodex on the day that either one of those things happens.

CHAPTER THIRTEEN: WILL YOU CALL ME AFTERWARD?

In the late nineties and into the beginning of the twenty-first century, the organ rush was on and blossoming. I built a network of foreign transplant centers and local finders through which I could find sellers and source parts. I co-brokered more and more deals with buyer's agents like Wallace, making the risks associated with tracking down rich, sick, desperate, and open-minded Americans and Europeans less and less of my concern. I met fewer buyers and spoke to none of them after their wires hit my Bermuda or Cayman accounts. Until I called Connie Laughlin.

In December of 2004 I was on my balcony in New York late one night focusing my telescope into the cold, clear black of the winter sky without purpose and for some reason I thought of Connie Laughlin. She was one of mine. I had sourced her myself off a website and negotiated the details with her and her husband, growing unintentionally fond of them. I remembered her more clearly than most because she wasn't just a kidney. Actually, I remember them all, but Connie a bit more. Connie needed a kidney and a liver and the Laughlins exhausted their savings and also took a second mortgage to come up with the fee. Only a month or two after her procedure she called one of my cellphones and invited me to dinner. She really did. I declined of course, but I was touched, and felt guilty. Perhaps that's why I thought of her around holiday time a few years later and why I made that very first follow-up call.

Connie and her husband were always on the phone together each time we spoke, one always yelling to the other saying, "It's Jack! Pick up downstairs!" The Laughlins had been very focused on getting Connie better in time for their daughter's wedding. They were Irish and made a point of their heritage and I couldn't help but disclose that I too was partly Irish. Connie started referring to me, for some reason, as Jack St. Peter, which I suppose is better than many of the things I've been called.

"Kentucky Fried Chicken!" she answered the phone cheerfully in 2004. It had been a couple of years since we had spoken but I knew it was Connie right away.

"Connie, it's Jack."

"Oh, I'm sorry. I'm making chicken tonight and the kids are all here. Who's this?"

"Jack. Jack St. Peter."

"Jack! Oh my god, Jackie St. Peter! Jack. Hello. Hello there. How are you, Jack? Is everything all right now?"

"Oh yes. Connie, I was just calling to make sure everything's all right with you. We haven't talked in a long time. I don't want to intrude but I do like to check in sometimes and make sure my clients are doing well."

"Oh, Jack! Jack St. Peter, my hero, Jack. How sweet of you, Jack."

"Do you want me to hold on while Michael picks up too?"

"Hold on a minute," she said, and there was some silence. After a moment she returned and said, "He can't, Jack. He's working with the boys. Making drawings with Annie's little ones. The twins are here. It's a madhouse."

"I understand. How are you?"

"Thank God," she said more calmly, "thank God, Jack. Thanks to you, too. Jack, hey, Jack, do you live in New York?"

"Why do you ask?" I replied casually, guard going up.

"Just that I'm making a load of chicken, Jack. You practically saved my life, you know. And I have a ton of chicken here. We're in Brooklyn, in Red Hook, the part with all the Italians. West of where the blacks mostly live. Come right now and have some dinner with us, Jack. We always—hold on a minute, please . . ."

Even with her hand held over the phone, I could tell she was speaking very loudly, yelling maybe. She came back on and said, "That was just Michael. He says not to bother you and you're probably with your own family. But surely we'd love you to come."

"Connie, how are you? How are you feeling?" I asked.

"Good days and bad days, Jack. Good and bad. Are you sure about dinner?" She paused. "It's practically Christmas Eve."

"I'd love to," I said, "but I'm in Chicago. I just wanted to say hello and make sure you're okay." I was in Manhattan, of course.

"What's that?" she asked. She had her hand over the phone again and this time she was certainly yelling at her husband who I could hear in the background garbling something or other about "no goods" which I assumed might have referred to me.

"I just said I'm in Chicago but that I called, I called to say hello, Connie. To make sure you are okay, and you are, and I'm glad for that. That's all really."

"Well, good days and bad, Jack," she said cheerfully although a little less energetically.

"Have a great Christmas with your family."

"You as well, Jack St. Peter. Merry Christmas to your family."

Why did she do that? Why did she invite me to have dinner with them, as if we were friends somehow? That was the very first follow-up call I made and it got me a Christmas dinner invitation. After that they rarely went all that well. They were usually short and awkward conversations with former clients who mostly seemed to resent me for having saved their lives. I didn't care. They were saved. I had saved them despite their resentment. Sometimes there were brief, disjointed talks with relatives who explained that I was calling a dead man, but even the dead ones had at least been given a chance. Connie Laughlin had no chance without Jack St. Peter. She'd be a statistic. Did her husband get that? Did he think an aging Irish woman from Red Hook who was a secretary at a restaurant supply wholesaler was getting a kidney and a liver from the God Committee at a local hospital? I should have gone there and eaten all of his fucking fried chicken.

If I hadn't started that shit in 2004, maybe I wouldn't have turned it into an annual tradition, maybe I never would have called Marlene Brown, never started on this path. It was that damned funeral. Why had the priest spoken about her operation? About the money? Why did it make me think about my own father? Why the hell did I ever drive to New Hope, Pennsylvania? If I'd just gone to Tucson maybe I wouldn't have ended up on the phone that day and life would have just gone on uninterrupted.

✦

In the early days of my business, when I traveled the world, before every trip I surveyed the books and maps and travel guides and located the few decent golf courses in those mostly destitute lands. I played at River Club, Glendower, and Durban in South Africa. For a brief time I was practically a member at Leopard Creek, far from the city and close to Kruger Park, but also one of the best courses in the world. I've enjoyed Bangpoo and Best Ocean in Bangkok, and Caxanga in Recife, Brazil, with its flat landscape and beautiful ponds, an oasis of security within the chaos that sometimes surrounds it in that economically splintered city. I've played all of those courses with doctors and businesspeople who ran hospitals. I played with local leeches and they all smiled eagerly at my explanations of the clients I could bring them.

It was the winter of 2005. In New York we were still suffering through the midwinter gray and chill of February. I had been working for years with some people at the Royston Clinic in Johannesburg, South Africa and I had a meeting there with my main contact, Dr. Mel Wolff. Wolff had recently been named the head of the Royston Transplant Center, an important division of the hospital. Mel had always seemed particularly entrepreneurial and since he had taken over we had been talking about getting together. There were ways we could expand our business relationship, he explained.

Despite the fact that I knew him for a few years, I vetted him all over again. I checked him up and down. He had been a doctor and in the hospital business all his life. He was twice divorced—also a good sign. That made a man more likely to be easily influenced by money. I waited nearly a year before taking him up on the invitation. By the time I went to see him, I was certain he was just trying to make money, not being secretly righteous.

In Joburg it was summer and felt hot the minute I stepped off the plane. After about ninety minutes getting through baggage claim and customs, I entered the terminal and saw a young black man in a black suit holding up a sign that said, "Jack Campbell."

"I'm Jack," I said as I approached him.

He smiled broadly. "Okay, let's go, Mr. Campbell. Royston Clinic sends me to get you and take you," he explained, reaching out to relieve me of my bags.

"I'll hold on to this," I said referring to my shoulder bag; in it were a couple of hollowed-out books holding neatly arranged stacks of American dollars, fifty grand or so. The X-ray on the baggage check read it as interior pages of the books. I was stockpiling a little American cash at a safe-deposit box in Joburg.

We walked to the car without speaking much. He said, "Dr. Wolff said to take good care of you."

"Thank you."

He opened the door for me, let me in, closed the door behind me and got into the driver's seat. It was a white Mercedes. I sat in the back, wishing I had just taken a cab.

"The Michelangelo, yes, Mr. Campbell?"

"Yes."

"Thank you," he replied, still smiling in the rearview mirror.

I had booked a room at the Michelangelo in Sandton because Wolff and I were to play River Club in the morning, right nearby. He had someone he wanted me to meet. It sounded like a local finder or some sort of go-between with the local population. My plan was to talk with Wolff, try not to play too exceedingly well, and then charter a plane to Leopard Creek and stay there for a few days and play by myself, leaving another day or two for game rides. Leopard Creek sits right at the foot of Kruger National Park, one of the better places in the world to see lions in the wild and not get eaten. On the third hole at Leopard Creek I have actually scored a hole-in-one.

When I arrived at the bar at the clubhouse, Dr. Wolff was already seated next to a younger white man. Wolff was wearing beige slacks and socks and white shoes and a crisp and tailored-looking white dress shirt. More appropriate, I thought, for Capetown, or a rerun of "Miami Vice," but I guessed that it was the guy's day off.

"Hier kom hy," Wolff said to the man, then added, "New York Jack," He motioned toward the other man. "Pierre Kleinhans."

"Hello," Pierre said, standing slightly by placing his feet to the floor but never really lifting his ass from the barstool. He shook my hand firmly. That was the first time we met.

"Afrikaans?" I asked, referring to the language.

"I'm from Pretoria," Pierre said. "Dr. Wolff explains that you are from New York?"

"That's right."

Pierre looked fine but not trustworthy. His hair seemed matted down a bit by sweat. I didn't find him appealing on a personal level but that didn't preclude him being a good finder. In fact, it might have been a positive characteristic as far as that specific job description might go.

"Gee hom 'n streep," Wolff said to Pierre. I didn't understand him, but it sounded like an instruction, and when Pierre left to fetch my drink, the dynamic of their relationship was rather clear.

"I don't speak any Afrikaans," I said to Wolff bluntly, but politely.

"I apologize, Jack. Just habit. I ordered you a Scotch."

"Thank you."

Pierre returned with my drink and pulled a barstool around so the three of us could sit in a triangle, facing each other. The clubhouse was nearly empty, not that it mattered much.

"Jack, I have explained to Pierre how you help people in the States. How you and I have worked together over the years. Now that I am running the transplant center at Royston I would like to help a lot more people in need of that type of care, and I think you know that we run a world-class facility."

"I do, Mel. I have always thought that of Royston."

He smiled sincerely. "Thank you, Jack. I appreciate that."

He extended his glass to mine and we clinked them. Pierre pushed his own glass forward and we both clinked his as well. I had a rocks glass nearly full of Scotch, one solitary cube floating in the amber pool. I took a big swallow. It was a very fine single malt. All the South African white guys shared my affinity for good Scotch.

"So Pierre works with the hospital. He coordinates with the local population of donors, as a liaison, and helps to facilitate matching and proper tissue typing," Wolff said, spewing euphamisms. A finder—I was right. He turned to Pierre and said, "Jy het gekry dinge vir kliënte van Jack se reeds."

"Please, Doctor," I said politely to Wolff, "English."

"I apologize again, my friend. I only told Pierre that he has already found things for clients of yours. I will try to maintain my speech in English. Bad form. Please forgive my rudeness."

"It's nothing," I said.

"And now, gentlemen, with me running the entire transplant facility, couldn't we work together and help a far greater number of patients coming to us from the States and Europe looking for the very best care?"

"Jack," Pierre began, his thick Germanic accent obtrusive against the South African version of English I was more used to. "Dr. Wolff says that you represent sick people who need organs. People who need lifesaving help and can afford to travel to a facility like Royston to get the best care, without fighting the bureaucracy in the States for years."

I didn't reply. I watched his facial muscles. I listened to the tone of his voice.

"With Dr. Wolff in charge now, it greatly expands the nature of what I can provide to those patients."

"Pierre," I said quietly, trying to suggest with my own volume that he should lower his even more, "that's already been the case, effectively, at Royston for years."

Wolff let go of a small chuckle, and then said, "But not like this. If we did a couple of transactions a month, that was good business.

Now, I could do ten times that amount. And all the other things people need beyond kidneys. Pierre can get anything, almost any match, full MHC with multiple HLAs, all sorts of matching criteria for various other organs, not just kidneys, on a few days notice. Don't underestimate the value of that, Jack."

His statement was weighty. Most people, if confronted with an opportunity to triple their business, would get very excited. Jack usually excuses himself to the bathroom and leaves town. But this was the business I knew. I knew this facility. I would be warm and safe and halfway around the globe when the transactions took place.

"What about things that are hard to find?" I asked, looking directly at Pierre.

"Nothing will be hard to find now," he said offering up a smarmy smile that made me think of my old coke dealer friends. "There are so, so many of them here."

"Sellers?" I asked.

"The poor," he replied and laughed.

That's how things start sometimes.

✦

Before I even got back to the States, I placed one call from Leopard Creek. I called Wallace.

"Hello?"

"Wallace, Jack."

"New York," he said brightly. "I see you're out of the country. Visiting friends?"

"I am."

"Is that good for our team?" he asked jovially.

"As a matter of fact, it is. Wallace, I just cut a deal that can make us a lot of money."

"What kind of deal, New York?" he said more quietly.

"To source anything we need, on just a few days notice, for anyone able to travel and pay. Hard to find goods. I have no idea how long this might last, but my guy here was just put in charge of the transplant center and seems anxious to make money. We should leverage the opportunity while we can."

"I like the way that sounds, Jack," Wallace replied. "Let me know when you get home. Safe travels."

◆

That was early in 2005, over six years ago. The wait on the legit lists for kidneys was about four or five years by then. How about that for a growing industry? It is so many kidneys ago, so many trips to Jozi and Tucson ago, and more than one Jack ago. It always is. Back in 2005, when Pierre said they could get anything, he meant "any kidney from a living donor and any harder match from a cadaver donor." Now, in 2011, when Pierre smiles and quietly says that he can get us anything, he means it literally.

CHAPTER FOURTEEN:
CHRISTMASES

After talking with Connie Laughlin in 2004 I made follow-up calls every December. Those calls became my holiday ritual; those former clients became my cousins and aunts and uncles. In December of 2009 Maria Thomsallei was my girlfriend and one Saturday afternoon she said, "You have to come to my parents' house for Christmas dinner, Jack."

"Not a chance," from subtle Jack.

"My father personally said to invite you. He'd be offended if you didn't come."

"What's your father's first name?"

"Tony."

"No fucking way."

"It's Anthony."

"No."

I eventually felt guilty and agreed to go to Long Island with her. As I had done several times in years past, I prepared myself to tell stories full of lies before tables of glassy-eyed younger brothers and cousins and parents who all desperately wanted to believe that I was something I am not. You sit at a man's dinner table, holding his adult daughter's hand, in front of a huge roasted turkey on a china serving platter, and you know that the poor guy can't focus on anything other than, "Please dear Lord, thank you for this bounty we're about to eat, but much more importantly, please don't let this Jack guy turn out to be an abusive, lying prick. You know, like me, Lord. Please don't let him turn out to be like me." God apparently never did right by those guys. Every year I drove up to some family's house in a new Jag or Lexus and told them tales about cases won, about courtroom drama and huge settlements wrestled from unethical insurance companies. They sat there and ate it up with their rice pudding while they daydreamed about their precious daughter ending up as my sidekick on a TV legal drama created about our lives. I rarely thought twice about it back then.

Maria's parents lived in Levittown—a middle-class enclave in Nassau County built one small, cookie-cutter structure after the other, right after World War II, to house returning soldiers. I was dreading dealing with her family and my back-story more than I normally did. That was still a full year before I went to Marlene Brown's funeral but the sense of ennui, of being sick of it all, had already started to creep in on me.

✦

I made more follow-up calls than usual that year and one of them was to a guy named Tom Walsh. Walsh was a kidney, and a pretty typical case. However, despite a strong profile and proper post-surgical treatment, he had some complications afterward. At one point it looked like sepsis; it briefly appeared that he might not even make it. That's unusual for a buyer who's in renal failure but otherwise reasonably healthy. I had worried about Walsh, but I was also always reluctant to follow up too soon for fear of giving the impression that I wanted to maintain an ongoing relationship.

A woman's voice answered the phone: "Hello?"

"Hey, is Tom around?" I asked, trying to be as casual as possible, as familiar as possible, so as to suggest a sense of existing friendship.

"Can I ask who's calling?"

"It's Jack. Thanks."

"Okay." Then it was quiet. In older households there is more silence settled in around things—not as much background noise or people talking, music, activity . . . Holding on the telephone was sometimes like a little vigil when I called the older ones. I would stand with my feet planted firmly and hold the receiver firmly, bracing myself. I occasionally reminded myself not to submit to the temptation to pace. You see, I had taken their money, but I also wanted them to be okay. And I didn't want to feel responsible.

A man cleared his throat. "Y'ello?"

"Tom?"

"Yes."

"Tom Walsh?"

"Can I help you?"

"Hey there. Jack. Jack Campbell. Do you remember me?"

Silence.

"Tom?"

"Yes. What? What, Jack?"

"You know who I am?"

"Of course I do."

"It's been a couple of years. Merry Christmas. I just—"

"Yes."

"It's been over three years now. I wanted to just say hi and see how you're doing."

"During the holidays," he said. "I'm fine. But you shouldn't call me, Jack. I got a house full of people here. My grandkids are here."

"Yeah. Sorry. So everything's okay?"

"I'm a lucky man," he said very quietly.

"Well, that's what we like to hear, Tom."

"Okay."

"Well, just wanted to check in—"

"You said that," he interjected flatly. "Jack, please don't call here."

"Okay. Well, thanks." The line clicked and went dead. "Have a great year," I added.

◆

Maria had four brothers. The oldest was named Anthony Jr. There was also a Peter and two much younger guys, one of whom was named Louie and one whose name I never got. She also had a sister named Rose. She had grandparents and nieces and nephews and a few cousins. It would be chaos, I imagined. Eventually the spotlight would fall on Jack and then the crowd would fall silent and I would be forced to recount some of the spectacular details of my imaginary law career. That year I just didn't have the stomach for it. With each comment or question directed toward me by members of her family, Maria squeezed my hand tighter under the table and snuggled up closer to me until she was finally halfway off her chair and onto mine.

At one point Tony Sr. said, "Shut up for a minute, shut up everyone, because we got a lawyer here and I want to ask his opinion." They all more or less complied and shut up and he then directed his attention at me and asked, "Jack, what do you think? You think Giuliani could be President? Could he ever win?"

"Oh, I really don't know," I said.

"But couldn't he do for the rest of the country what he did for New York? I mean, didn't he clean up Times Square and straighten out the moulignons and kick Osama's ass a little?"

"The moulignons?" I responded.

That cracked up a couple of Maria's brothers, one of whom said, "The eggplants. The troublemaker blacks." Maria threw a fake slap at him as if to suggest that he was being inappropriate and embarrassing her in front of me, but she did it for comedic effect.

◆

In the car on the way back to the city Maria said, "I'm sorry, Jack. My brothers are a bunch of morons."

"It's fine. Don't sweat it."

"That's why I had to move last year."

"Last year?" I asked.

"Yeah."

"Where'd you live before then?"

"With them."

"But you're thirty."

"Yeah. That's why I had to get the hell out of there."

I knew I couldn't break up with her before New Year's because doing so would have mandated twice as many late-night phone conversations in order to talk her down. I'd have to wait a couple of weeks. I was driving back on the LIE and trying as hard as I could not to say anything that would initiate more conversation. I was thinking about Tom Walsh. He wanted no part of me, no reminders of what he'd done to stay alive. It made me feel something that I could only describe as "hurt." I was on my third Maria. Jack Tuckman had no family, no friends from college. . . . How could he? He hadn't even existed then.

✦

After the holidays things picked up a bit, as they usually do. It was January of last year, 2010. After I ended things with Maria it seemed that often my phones didn't ring at all, but when they did, it was usually Wallace. He told me about his fishing trip in the Florida Keys. We were working on a couple of trips to Moldova for kidneys and getting a liver from Royston for a guy named Max from Miami. Max was sick as hell and would die soon no matter what we did but he was intent on taking his game into overtime and Wallace was intent on charging him for it.

✦

"I want to get your input on something," Wallace said.

"What's up?"

"Is that gmail address good?"

"It's fine."

"Well, around Christmas I emailed a guy who was offering out an altruistic donation on organmatchmaker.com."

"Now why would you be on there? Should I be offended?" I asked.

"Because some things in life *are* free. It was slow, I was bored, I don't know . . . I don't usually bother with it," he replied. "But never mind that. We traded an email or two over the last few weeks and today I had an IM chat with him. You won't believe what this guy just said to me."

"Tell me."

"I cut and pasted it into an email I just sent you. Take a look."

"Hold on," I said, and reached over to my laptop to open a browser window.

◆

Wallace: Hi. I saw your listing and wanted to get more information. It says you are willing to donate a healthy kidney to the right recipient. And you're O positive, so you could donate your kidney to almost anyone?"

TS: *Not me. My friend that I am helping . . . But yes, O positive.*

Wallace: *What do you mean, "friend"?*

TS: *I have a friend who wants to donate a kidney. I am helping. If you are O positive and a good match—and deserving—we could talk offline about the possibility and the other details.*

Wallace: *Well, it's not about whether I am a match. It's for a friend. I am also helping a friend.*

TS: *I see.*

Wallace: *Yes. We seem to both be helping friends. Mine is very anxious to get the kidney he needs. He would be very appreciative.*

TS: *That would be apropos. I'm sure my friend would expect gratitude. May I ask your name?*

Wallace: *It's Wallace.*

TS: *So then you're Wallace from Connecticut?*

Wallace: *Who are you?*

TS: *I am The Siren.*
   LONG PAUSE.

Wallace: *Seriously?*

TS: *The Siren.*

Wallace: *Ha!*
   END SESSION.

✦

"This is not good," I said to him quietly. I was shaking my head a little but he didn't know that of course.

"Do you think it's really him?" Wallace asked.

"Maybe it's the Loch Ness Monster."

"Jack, seriously. You think that guy could be real?"

"It's an urban myth, Wallace."

"Are you sure?"

"Does it matter? You can't do anything about it either way. Even if he were real, then that guy would make the Man from Dallas look cautious. Just burn all the contact info he has of yours and forget it."

"But he was offering up a part for free. No offense, Jack, but that's a bit better than your pricing."

"Wallace, he was *advertising* a part for free. The real offer is still coming. When he gets the buyer on the phone, whoever that guy is, The Siren, or Bigfoot, or Spiderman, he's going to suddenly need fifty K for 'expenses' at some point. I'm not pitching you or trying to make a buck here. We don't have an exclusive and you're free to do business with other seller's agents, but don't go and bite off a big piece of trouble like this."

"You never know . . ."

"Wallace, those stories about kidney thieves in Vegas having hookers lure drunk businessmen into hotel rooms, slipping drugs in their drinks and then harvesting kidneys, that's all nonsense. You know better than that. You need two legit operating theaters to do a nephrectomy and a transplant or it's murder. That never happens. Never. Why commit murder when you can just pay some poor schlub a grand or two? It's a fairy tale. 'The Siren' is just a nickname for fifty different morons who've spouted off in strip bars over the years while making up stories to impress other morons. Burn the fucking contact info and forget it. Really."

"Relax, Jack. I already did," he said with a slight chuckle.

"Then what's the point?" I asked, not amused.

"Just kidding around. Relax, New York."

"You testing me?" I asked, half-pissed.

"Fucking with you."

"Well, someone is fucking with you, pal. You are way too loose with who you talk to and who you think might be your friends."

◆

In 2009 I still resented the risks Wallace took. Soon it will be Christmas 2011. Now I will take the risks. I will be The Siren. That's how I can fix some of the mess I've made. The world's not watching our business yet but change starts with an event. I will be Columbine. The Rosa Parks of organs. There's a fiscal cliff approaching in the balance between UNOS and the black market for organs. It might as well be me.

And soon, I'll have to meet with Wallace. That's coming too and it will be my last opportunity to try and change his mind. Can a junkie get clean, can a hungry man skip a meal?—because you ask him to, because it is right and you merely ask him to?—it's possible, but very unlikely. Those will be my odds with Wallace. Even if I had three million dollars to ask him to walk away from this deal, this bad and different deal we've gotten into, it would only be temporary. He'd just lie. Wallace is a man who needs the meter on his bank account always clicking, the balance always growing larger. It isn't just about the money; he needs the rush. I understand because I've been like that for a long time too.

◆

When that last meeting comes—in a hospital lobby—there will be no "New York!" greeting, or "Strange place for a meeting. I hear the food's not so great." His hair will be gray at the temples. He'll look common, a little thicker in the middle these days, no different than any other guy walking down West 168th today thinking about his prostate medicine or whether he'll make his year-end bonus.

I imagine our conversation will go something like this:

"So what's the problem, Jack?"

"Don't you know?" I'll say.

"I think I do, but I was hoping I'd be wrong."

"This isn't what we signed up for." There will be animosity in our eyes, but also affection and regret.

"I didn't sign up for anything, New York. I'm just running a business." Then, he'll add, "Why would you want to ruin things now, Jack? Now, when there is so much money to be made. We help people, Jack."

"Not really. We help some, but only at the expense of others. And this is different. I told you from the beginning this is a different thing."

"It's getting done, Jack. No matter what you say now it's still getting done."

"What if I asked you not to? Wallace, what if I asked you to leave here, and go get a drink, and tell the client that in the end you just couldn't get the part? Could you do that? Could you consider that maybe we've taken enough and just go get that drink with me instead?"

He'll look at me, concerned and also sorry, but mostly he'll be unflappable. I know that's what will happen. There's a chance that I am wrong, but it is very unlikely. So I'll have my answer and it will not be a surprise. Not yet. But soon. I feel it coming and it carries with it the same kind of rush. I am going to stop him. I am going to burn Royston and Wolff and Pierre and maybe in the end it won't change much, maybe they'll be typing out thousands of people in advance in *the streets of some poor province in India soon. Maybe they'll be taking blood samples from all new prisoners in Russia soon—especially the ones who wrote disparaging articles about Putin—but not in Sandton. We can only imagine what they're already doing behind closed doors in North Korea where the only national export we know of is missiles. Shit—I could probably consult for those guys . . . So perhaps things won't change. But I can. I will change, and for that I do feel lucky.*

PART IV: HOW THINGS START SOMETIMES

CHAPTER FIFTEEN:
MARK

In January of this year I met Mark. It was about a month after the shit with Marlene Brown and only a couple of weeks after I got back from Jozi and my trip to the farm at Alexandra. We were busy, but things between Wallace and I were still awkward and tense. It was raining that day; warm for winter but still cold. The rain was being blown horizontally, drifting into the sides of buildings and under everyone's cheap, disposable, New York-deli umbrellas, soaking the legs of their pants. I was on my cell phone, opening the interior door of a diner where I had just eaten, and he was standing between the interior and exterior doors where he later explained he had been waiting for me to finish eating for twenty minutes.

"Jack?" he said, casually. Alarms went off but I didn't flinch and just kept walking past him, pushing outward on the exterior glass door and stepping out onto the wet and dirty sidewalk. Mark walked up right beside me and said, "Jack?" and then, "Jack," again. So I stopped, turned toward him—nervous about pretending to not hear him since he had been clear and forceful—and motioned with an index finger for him to wait a minute.

I said, "Yes. Fine," into my phone. "I'll call you then. When I'm back in the office. I'm on the street now," or some other random thing to whomever I'd been talking to. We looked at each other for a few seconds and I wasn't just nervous; I was flat-out scared. I thought I was getting arrested and I became afraid, for a moment, that maybe I was even about to get killed.

He was dressed in a worn black leather jacket, some sort of stylish jeans, and black shoes, but he had no hat or umbrella. He was ruffled from the rain. He looked far too young to be an FBI agent, too young even to be a regular cop—and that worried me. I thought he might be the relative of some unhappy customer who wanted a rebate, maybe a few organs of my own. So I smiled confidently, shook my head just slightly, and said, "Do I? . . . I'm sorry, but . . ."

Mark looked frozen. He was a beautiful young man, fully grown but still appearing genuine enough to be a kid. He stood on the sidewalk in front of a wondrous New York backdrop. There were trucks and taxis and shoes stamping through puddles and expletives being shouted off down the block and the wind-whipped raindrops. Mark said nothing at all. I thought for a second that perhaps I should run but instead I extended my hand and asked, "Do I know you?"

"Look, Jack. Please . . ." He was shaking his head up and down then.

"What?" I asked with another broad smile, feeling comforted somehow and yet a little panicked too. He seemed to be alone. There didn't seem to be anyone else on the sidewalk or in a parked car watching us. I noticed some paint on the fingers of his hand. Some blue and specks of yellow. I didn't think he was a cop.

"You know me," he said, maybe starting to tear up a little. I was trying to survey the sidewalk across from us.

"No. I don't think so." There were sirens exploding in my head then.

"Well, you know my mom, Carrie Franco. You know her, right?

The smile lingered on my moronic face. I know it did. I might have tilted my head, just a little, like a puzzled dog, but that was all. If I could have done it, perhaps I would have cocked one ear. It bought me a second or two. Mark looked a little over twenty. A little over twenty years since Carrie. Could it really have been twenty years? Could this be? Carrie had said that she didn't want me to come with her to the doctor if it turned out that she was pregnant. She had stopped doing coke—I thought it had been about us. She moved back to Boston to be with her parents. . . .

It only took a moment for me to understand that I had a son, that I had miscalculated, that I had missed it all and fucked up everything more than I even knew. And I smiled and shook my head up and down and that kid must have felt sick from the sight of me. Maybe he knew I actually considered running. Mark. Just like his mother, twenty-two years before him. I kept my grip on his hand. I was afraid to let go and let him slip back to Boston or wherever he might go to. I have never been so surprised or caught off guard. I felt a little dizzy. It made sense that I found him so appealing in the first instant I had seen him. I had thought, what a nice-looking kid who's come to arrest me.

✦

"So how is she?" I asked once we were back inside the diner, working as hard as I could not to sound hopeful. I was trying to remain settled, but it was hard. I was not surprised to discover that I still cared, over twenty years later, but I was surprised by the force and speed with which it swelled up inside of me.

"She's good," he said, with a very slight smile that displayed some grace beyond his years. And pride. Shouldn't he be freaking out too? But he was not. After just a moment he seemed calm, composed, and relieved. He sat with his hands clasped on the table in front of him, sitting still and appearing comfortable. I was stirring my coffee, taking small sips, adding sugar several times. "I mean, generally she's good," he added, like an afterthought. "I haven't spoken to them in a few weeks."

I nodded, and I guess Mark somehow surmised that it was a question and then added, "My parents. 'Them' being my parents. Mom got married when I was three and my stepdad raised me. I call him 'Dad' and all." It sounded almost rehearsed and I wondered if he had thought about what he might say to me for a while, maybe even for years . . . Then he added, "But I haven't talked to them in a while. Been kinda pissed. Because of this. Because of you and wanting to meet you."

"They're angry?"

"More that I am," he replied. Then he added, "Jack," as if to amuse himself, or perhaps to somehow insult me. We were on a first-name basis. We were meeting for the first time. I was his father. The guy who had wiped his ass and gone to all the Little League games and paid the bills . . . not him. No, I was actually his father. Jack. Some guy across the table at this diner.

"You're angry because Carrie didn't want you to meet me?" I asked. "Because she didn't tell you who I am sooner?"

Mark has eyelashes as long as a woman's. I remember looking at him then and thinking about that rule: "The more a man looks like a woman the more attractive he is, but the more a woman looks like a man the less attractive she is." I remember noticing how simply attractive his face is. I was thinking, "He's probably normal and well-liked and invested in life," and hoping it was true. I was thinking that I couldn't deny him the chance to talk to me and get some answers, but also that I had an obligation to get away without upsetting the creation that Carrie had set in motion. I didn't want to poison the fact that he was Carrie's son, and not mine.

"I'm pissed off . . ." he finally began. "I guess I'm pissed at my mom because, well, you knew her. I doubt she's really all that different now from when you knew her. I mean, people don't really change, right? My mom's pretty cool. You probably understand that. And we have this honest sort of relationship." He paused and looked up at me, conducting a further evaluation, perhaps beginning to see the disappointing truth. "When this stuff about Ken not being my biological father first came up I was around ten or eleven. It was hard for a while. After that, my mother's story was always that she literally didn't know who my father was. She had been seeing a few men, she wasn't proud, she was doing some drugs at the time. . . . She admitted all this shit. But she loved me more than everything else and she moved back in with my grandparents in Boston and got it together—for me—and not long after she met Ken Carson. And we're okay. You know?" he said with a bit of a self-conscious grin. Actually, Mark always seems a bit self-conscious. "But she always told me she didn't know who my father is. A couple of months ago I turned twenty-one. She gave me a letter she had written to me just a few months after I was born. A big part of that letter explained her mindset at the time and why she wouldn't tell me who my real father is until I was an adult. When I turned twenty-one."

"She was trying to protect you."

"Yeah . . . that's kinda bullshit," he said quietly. "She wrote this letter. She said that she wanted to put it all down and tell the truth and let me judge it all for myself, when I turned twenty-one. I think it's sort of self-righteous—the way she claims that she didn't want to influence my opinion, my judgment of her—it's just as much about her."

"Everyone lies," I said.

"Exactly." When he said that, he really did look like a kid, young and beautiful and wreckable. "Look, I go to Columbia, Jack. I'm a senior. I've been living in New York for almost four years and I never even knew you were here. And she tried to preempt me with some bullshit letter she wrote twenty years ago, when I was a baby, because she's a good lawyer and she planned her defense out in advance. And she lied to me."

"What's with the paint?" I said, pointing to his hand.

"That? Nothing. I was in the studio before . . ."

"You're an artist?"

"No," he said, looking down, shaking his head a bit.

"Mark, the person I was," I began in a low, gruff rumble of coffee-voice, "your mom was right to tell you the way she did. The way I have . . . structured things, lived my life. . . ." I felt exhausted. The mere fact of meeting him, of knowing that I had created a son with Carrie Franco, that alone was enough to send me to Tucson for a month of recovery.

"Yeah?" he said, asking me to finish.

"I'm just glad that she kept you from me," I said rather quietly and without a sense of melodrama. I wanted to leave.

"That's shitty."

"I don't mean it that way," I said, "I mean that I am glad for your sake."

"Yeah, I knew what you meant," he responded. "But it's shitty *to you*."

"You don't know me," I said, a bit sadly.

His hair was starting to dry. It was ending up a little curly, not much like mine, I thought. His eyes were blue. They were just like mine—not pure blue, but bluish-green swirled, a bit like marbles.

They were the same knowing, calm, cynical, observant pair of eyes I'd been seeing in a mirror for forty-four years.

"That's true. I don't know much about you, dude," he said, and for the first time in twenty minutes took a big draw on his coffee. "I know some things about who you were twenty-two years ago, but all I know about you now is that you live in New York, you're a lawyer, and you are really, really hard to track down."

"Harder than you know." I smiled a little.

"My mom did love you, you know."

"Oh?' I said, casually, Def-Con Two ringing somewhere in the back of my head.

"Yeah. But a lot changes at this time, my mom says. You leave school and things start to have consequences. Mom keeps telling me that this is an important time for a person. Decisions made for you guys then, for me now, she thinks it matters a lot. She keeps telling me that lately."

"Does she know you came to meet me?"

"Jack," he began, in a stronger tone, "I want you to know that I'm all good. I am pretty happy. I like school—"

"Does she know that you came to meet me?"

"Yeah. She knows. I said that. We fought about the whole thing. Anyway, sometimes I think I should have majored in something with a career path—I mean, I'm a philosophy major, a *philosopher* of all things—but I may go to law school. You wanna know this shit, right?" I nodded affirmatively. "I have a great boyfriend, and we're genuinely in love. I came out to my mom when I was sixteen and she didn't flinch." He paused. "By the way, you look like you're flinching a bit yourself right now there, Jack."

"No. I'm not. That's fine."

"Okay. Well, I love him. For real love. My parents do too. That took a while—he's twelve years older than me—but they do now.

And I have great friends and I don't need anything from you. My parents are pretty wealthy. I'm good. I just thought that we should know each other. But I don't have any kinda agenda. Just to meet. Cool?"

"I don't know what to say."

"Say we can grab a cup of coffee again some time. That's all, and we're cool."

"Mark, do you . . . don't you have anything you want to ask me, to know about me?"

"Of course," he said. "But I thought maybe I could get to know you a little rather than interview you. Whenever you want to tell me is fine. Is there something you wanna tell me *now*, Jack?" he asked with a grin.

He was likable.

CHAPTER SIXTEEN:
MARK AND PHILIP

Mark and I did meet again, but it wasn't for a few more weeks. In late February he suddenly called the cell number I had given him. It was two months after the Marlene Brown funeral and I still didn't feel like myself. We agreed to have dinner together. We made a plan to meet at Antonio's on Seventh in the Fifties. I was sitting at the bar drinking the Macallan Eighteen neat and Mark was about ten minutes late. When he finally arrived, I noticed him right away, saw him checking his coat and smiling nervously to another young man who was trailing him. He saw me at the bar and approached.

"I'm sorry," he said.

"It's ten minutes. Don't worry."

"No, about Philip, I mean." Then he motioned toward the other man and said, "Philip." He gestured toward me and said, "Jack."

"Hi," Philip said quietly, and we shook hands. Philip was young too. Mark had mentioned that he was twelve years older than him, putting Philip in his early thirties, but he looked younger. He wore a black pinstriped suit that looked custom-tailored. He unobtrusively waited for someone else to lead the conversation; somehow his demeanor seemed almost apologetic. I took him for smart and there was something I liked about him immediately.

"Jack, we're late because, well we had a little debate about Philip coming and then we also debated whether we needed to give you a heads-up or maybe just not concern you by making a big deal and I just hope it's okay because I—"

"I insisted," Philip interjected with a slightly conspiratorial smile as he leaned into the middle of our little circle by the bar.

"He insisted," Mark said, sighing a little and smiling.

"I hope it's not impolite," Philip said.

"It's fine. We'll play it where it lies."

"Oh, do you play?" Philip asked, picking up on the golf reference.

"Yes."

"Great," Mark said softly and facetiously, biting at a nail.

"He doesn't?" I asked Philip, pointing toward Mark.

"Jack," Mark began, "about Philip being here, I just wanted to tell you, we've been together over four years now. He's been with me through this. I mean, learning about you and meeting you . . . a father's important—"

"I think it is too. Let's sit down and discuss it with a few drinks in us," I responded.

✦

Philip put his hand on Mark's shoulder. For some reason I felt a surge of forgotten and terrible longing for Carrie and for those months when we were in love. It occurred to me that those events were twenty years behind me. I felt as if some unseen force had yanked open a spigot in my gut and released a wave of emotions that I thought had been obliterated years before. I can't say that I remember feeling hopeful in those days with Carrie, but I do know this: in the moments now when I realize that it may be possible to be happy, what I'm left with is regret.

I wanted to take Mark, right then, and go to Boston, and sit with him and Carrie and just watch them together, simply interact as mother and son. I had nothing to say to them, and it was irrational, but I thought that maybe seeing Carrie and Mark together could somehow unsteel my heart. That thought stayed with me permeating the air in the restaurant like humidity. I finally realized that Mark and Philip were at the table and stood to go join them.

I sat and no one spoke at first. We passed those small and formulaic "lip-press" smiles to each other, packaged with half-nods.

"You're a lawyer?" I finally asked Philip.

"A lot of lawyers around here," he said.

"It looks like I'm going to law school after all," Mark explained.

"Oh," I said and nodded.

"What do you do, Jack?" Philip asked.

"Corporate. International."

"No one I know knows you," he added casually.

"Should they?"

"I don't know. Just attorneys."

"I rarely do much here in the States anymore. I represent companies in India, China, emerging markets mostly. I travel a lot. My own little firm. Less of a lawyer than a businessperson these days really."

"I see," Philip said. Mark smiled slightly, and I think Philip took his hand underneath the table.

"Why'd you change your name?" Mark asked bluntly, and then seemed to almost regret having asked. It was matter-of-fact.

"It's just that it was nearly impossible to find you," Philip chimed in.

"I changed it a long time ago, after my own father died. He was my stepfather. Like Mark," I lied, "I was raised by my stepfather. So I changed it back to my real name, Tuckman, after he died. Your mom must have told you that." I actually had no idea if Carrie knew that I had changed my name.

"She didn't. But she does think that maybe you don't want to be found because you were a drug dealer. Because a lawyer doesn't want to be identified with having been a coke dealer," Philip said.

"No. That's not it."

"You weren't a drug dealer?" Mark asked.

"I didn't say that."

"But you changed it again?"

"Sometimes in business I use a pen name. It's, well, it's international matters and sometimes it's complicated."

Mark nodded, and said, "Sure. Pen name. Nom de plume. That makes sense," he said grinning.

"What about you?" I asked, looking toward Philip and smiling comfortably, condition yellow, but not emergency-mode. Right then the waiter came by and asked for our drink orders. I ordered another Scotch and Philip asked if I might be persuaded to drink some wine as well and I agreed.

"The Gaja Barbaresco?" he said to the waiter.

"Of course," the waiter said with a sincere smile.

"It would be my treat of course," Philip said. He seemed genuinely concerned about not committing any sort of faux pas. I knew that bottle and it costs about four hundred dollars.

"The Gaja is great, Philip. And I appreciate the offer, but I'd like to take care of dinner tonight." I told the waiter to bring the Scotch while the wine was decanting. Then, turning to Philip again, I asked, "So, what's your practice like?"

"I did labor relations and employment matters mostly, occasional civil rights cases which I found to be a lot more engaging, but in the last few years some things have changed and I've been focused more specifically on the civil rights actions and doing a lot of pro bono work for non-profits."

"I'm proud of him," Mark said quietly.

"I do mostly pro Jack work," I said.

"As is your right," Philip returned, smiling slightly. I laughed, just a little. Then Philip said, "I do a lot of stuff for gay rights groups now. I'm trying to help."

"Okay," I said.

"The last bastion of institutional racism," he said matter-of-factly.

I nodded. He seemed passionate and genuine, but not self-righteous.

"Jack," Mark said with a slight clearing of his throat, "Philip . . . what changed is that he's positive. You know? He's *HIV* positive."

I took a moment and studied him. Watched for signs in the muscles of his face that might tip me off to his emotional state, his reaction to Mark's words. Almost none. That in itself was telling. I looked then at Mark.

After a moment he said, "I'm not," very quietly.

"Quite an introduction, huh?" Philip said. "Can we drink the wine now?"

CHAPTER SEVENTEEN: RECRUITING

In March of this year I went back to Johannesburg. The morning after I arrived I left my passport and wallet in my room at the Michelangelo, took some cash and the car keys, and headed out in the rental car. A few minutes later I pulled up on the side of the road near the outskirts of Alexandra, exactly where we had parked a couple of months earlier when Pierre and I went to meet Thaba. I left the cash in the glove compartment and stashed the keys under a large rock nearby when I was certain no one was looking. I had nothing on my person of any value. I thought I might be satisfied after the visit in January but I was not. I wanted to talk with the sellers and I knew it would be risky to ask Pierre to bring me there again so I decided to go by myself. It was unlike me.

I remembered our path from the previous visit. A right and a right and a left and straight for a while before again making two more rights to reach that large clearing. Walking into Alex I felt tired. Tired of my routines, of the travel, of the pretense and the facades. But more than anything, I felt sorry. Perhaps I had gone there to punish myself, but there was no one to apologize to. Over the years I have not spoken to most of our sellers, and I have met only a handful. I walked up the alley and passed men standing in the doorways wearing dirty T-shirts, their vacant stares directed vaguely in my direction. Dark shadows filled up dimly lit rooms behind them. There was a tiny Vodafone office on the first corner. It surprised me that anyone in Alex could afford a cell phone, but also that I had somehow missed it on our first visit. I headed toward that clearing and noticed that one of the men I had passed was following me. He wore a blue and white striped shirt and was hanging back unobtrusively. I decided that he was probably just curious about the white guy and not out to hurt me. And if he was, I would be dead soon and it wouldn't matter.

There was garbage in the alleys. The puddles contained maggots that I could see moving at the edges of the water. The structures all seemed lopsided, slightly shifted on their foundations, as if every little building was created and then sort of screwed into the ground to make it stick, each ending up on a slightly uneven angle. After two more turns I came to the clearing and squinted against some dust that was kicking up in the agitated air. I moved aside a little and sat down on the dirt with my back to one of the concrete buildings that made up the square. The air was hot, but not intolerably so. It was March and already getting cooler in South Africa.

Then I saw Lesedi in the back portion of the square where they played soccer. He was sitting while some kids nearby played a pickup game. His tape ball was on the ground beside him. He noticed me quickly, the only white man in the township, and our eyes met. I didn't even know I was looking for him until I found him. He did not wave and he did not flash that phony-yet-charming smile of his, but after a few long moments he stood and approached me. Around the same time the man in the blue and white striped shirt emerged into the square, leaned against a wall, and lit a cigarette. Lesedi came to a stop only a couple of feet in front of me. He still wasn't smiling. He might have even grown an inch or two, I thought. His tape ball was tucked under his arm.

"You are Jack," he said, standing above me.

I was squinting against the sun and looking up at him. "Hello, Lesedi."

"You remember Lesedi's name." He paused and seemed to be thinking a moment. There was a problem, I knew that, but I didn't yet understand its nature or how severe it might be for Jack, now vulnerably sitting in the few square meters on earth where he least belonged. He seemed dirtier, a little gaunter than he had appeared to be two months earlier. "Kidney Jack is who you are," he said, somewhat loudly.

"I told you, just Jack."

"Well you come last time with Thaba. Thaba tells me ten thousand rand for a kidney. Ten thousand to fix the water and help my sisters. But I only get six thousand Rand and Thaba says not to talk to him now." Ten thousand rand was the equivalent of about fifteen hundred US dollars.

"Did you . . . ?" I scrambled to my feet. The man in the striped shirt was about fifteen feet away, smoking. Lesedi was right in front of me. Everyone else in the area—about eight kids playing soccer and four or five adults sitting on cheap broken chairs or standing and talking—had taken notice of me and then gone on about their own business. "Did you sell him a kidney?"

He smiled a little finally, but this time it was facetious and mean-looking. "My mother died last year, Jack," he said quietly. "I went with Thaba to Royston Hospital." He pulled up the left side of his shirt and twisted his thin frame a little and there cut into his lower left side was a nephrectomy scar, not yet fully healed. I thought, *No*, but I said nothing and just looked at it until he dropped his shirt. He still didn't speak.

"Wait," I said, and then motioned for him to lift his shirt back up. He obliged me. There was still some redness in one or two spots and what looked like dry and hardened pus, but nothing too bad. It looked like some minor infection that he was actually beating without complications. He was up and about. I wasn't that alarmed.

The man in the striped shirt then yelled something that I did not understand.

I didn't even turn my head. "Did Thaba give you any pills?" I asked Lesedi.

"Yes, he gave me the pills for after but he only gives me six thousand rand and not ten thousand. You give me four thousand more."

"I didn't come here carrying any money," I said and he seemed to believe me.

Again the man in the striped shirt yelled. Clearly it was meant for me.

"Lesedi," I said. "Thaba is not my friend. Walk out with me now, and don't let this man bother me, and I will give you your money that you deserve."

He looked at me for a long moment before responding. I imagined that he was considering whether it was worth four thousand rand to see a white devil bastard get cut open in the village square. He nodded in agreement, opting for the cash, and we turned toward the man in the striped shirt. Lesedi barked something at him in their native language and the man laughed. We passed without incident and made our way back toward my car. It was too hot to be chasing some white guy down the alley in the middle of the African day anyway.

We crossed the road and I recovered the car key and opened the door. I removed what was about five thousand rand from the glove box, plus another hundred in US dollars, and handed it to him. He took it from me, but he was not satisfied either.

"I bring shame to my family and my sisters say not to talk to them now. I hid the money in two places and one of the places is found now and the money stolen away from Lesedi."

I tried to show him respect by not apologizing or trying to rationalize anything. I said nothing.

"I do this for my sisters but now they are not my sisters no longer," he said, finally allowing sadness to infect his speech. I had heard of this, of sellers being ostracized from the very communities and families they were trying to help, but I didn't expect it in a place like Alex. It was urban and close to a large city. It was incredibly poor but it had a modern sensibility. So many parts must have already come from inside of there. Didn't Lesedi know what would happen? He was young, but no one is a kid who lives in a place like Alexandra. I wanted to help him, but what could I really do? I couldn't bring him back to New York and set him up with a job at my make-believe law firm and take him on camping trips. I couldn't start sending child support checks to the Alexandra Western Union. Pierre certainly wouldn't help him. All I could do was let the kid have that cash and leave him knowing he'd probably be dead by thirty, assuming he took his meds and lived through the next month.

CHAPTER EIGHTEEN: THE DINNER PARTY

I didn't hear from Mark for a while after that dinner in February. I wasn't sure if his curiosity about his "father" had been satisfied, or if I had somehow offended him or Philip. He called me sometime in March and we chatted briefly and casually and then he disappeared for another couple of months. Perhaps I was supposed to follow up? I never seem to know.

◆

I was still seeing Lizzie, although it was mostly over by then. She was a brand manager at P & G. I woke up at Liz's place on the Upper East Side one morning in May and said, "I might go to California for a few days. Play some golf. Maybe you want to come."

"I don't play, baby," she replied.

"Well, you could hang out, do some shopping. We could go out together for dinner at night."

"No, I'd be bored while you're playing golf."

"Yeah?"

"Why don't we play some tennis?!"

"I don't play. I'm a golfer."

"But we could play together. You need a partner for tennis," she said playfully, stroking my arm.

"Yeah. That's why I play golf."

"That's obnoxious," she said.

"I guess," I replied without offering any kind of apology.

"Plus the world is ending on the twenty-first anyway."

"What?"

"Some guy in California says the world is ending this month. It's the End of Days, like that movie."

"What movie?"

"I don't know," she said dismissively. Then her tone changed, and with some humor she added, "You've got until the twenty-first."

"Do I?" We had already been dating for a few months and it had run its course.

So I ended up flying out to California again to play Pebble Beach by myself, the way I often do. Pebble Beach is the real deal—a beautiful and perfectly designed golf course, and simply a beautiful piece of the world. I belong to several different clubs because it reduces the risk of other members starting to feel too chummy, and the dues aren't much of an issue. The best way to ruin a lovely round of golf at a world-class course is to join a foursome with some radiologist who remembers me from a prior year and who then forces me to apply part of my brain to remembering details of my back story when I really only want to focus on gauging the crosswind cutting into that dog-leg left.

I was on the driving range just hitting a few balls to warm up when one of my cell phones went off, piercing the tranquility.

"Jack? This is Philip. Mark's friend. Your son, Mark Carson, I mean."

"Yes. I know. Is everything okay?"

"Yes, Jack. Absolutely. Mark and I are having a little dinner party this Friday and we got to talking and well . . . we'd just like you to come."

I was a little taken aback. I had met them for dinner, but that was in a restaurant. I meet people for dinner in restaurants. That's the proper place to conduct a meeting. It's a way of doing things. That the invitation related to my son, that I even had a son in the first place, that he was reaching out to me, was unsettling. The fact that it was Philip calling me, not Mark, to make the actual invitation, was touching.

"Well, sure. Okay," I said.

"You'll come then?" he asked. I knew that it was for Mark's benefit. He was probably sitting right next to Philip on a couch somewhere in Hell's Kitchen.

"Yeah. I'd like that."

"That's great, Jack. It's this Friday, at eight. I'll ask Mark to email you our address. Mark, you have Jack's email, right? . . . We'll see you Friday, okay?"

"Yeah." I wasn't booked on a flight back until Sunday, but I changed it and got out the next day. They had clearly made an effort and I didn't want to disappoint them.

"Jack," Philip said, "you understand that our friends, some are straight, and well, several are not, and so, they'll be there too."

"Yeah. I gathered that," I said with a slight smile.

"Okay then," he said cheerfully. "Bye."

◆

The next morning my other cell rang early. It was already past nine on the East Coast but I was still in California. The area code appeared to be one of the new Florida creations.

"Hey, New York," Wallace said.

"Why don't you just get New York area codes on your phones?"

"Ha. Coming from you."

"Fair enough," I said. "How goes it, Wallace?"

"Can we get together? Maybe grab lunch?"

I paused. The sun was coming up from behind the hotel and my window was facing west, toward the ocean. The light pouring down on the beach was growing clearer and less golden-hued. "Is this about that thing before the holidays? That old client of ours I mentioned that time?"

"Jack, I don't hold grudges," he said quietly.

"Then why the meeting?"

"I need a Fifteen," he said. "Fifteen," as in the fifteen percent of people on the list who need livers. We called kidneys Eighties and livers Fifteens but didn't have much need for other code words. When it came to lungs we simply said Lobes. We sometimes joked about Blocks (heart and double lung transplants) and dominoes—three or more transplant patients all forming a chain—because those were parts guys like us could never obtain. Livers, on the other hand, were possible. Most livers come from brain-dead donors on life support. Because the liver regenerates they sometimes find legitimate altruistic donors—the recipient's cousin or something—but it is much more rare than a kidney. In recent years we've even had finders in Johannesburg or China come up with sellers. China had been great for a while—when they were mining the prisoners on death row—but that ended abruptly when the government got more sensitive to "human rights issues for prisoners," which was code for "we're keeping the fucking organs here in China now that we have people who can finally afford them, you has-been westerners."

"Fifteens are tough," I said matter-of-factly.

"And this customer has restrictions."

"Such as?"

"Let's grab lunch, talk about it then."

"Wallace, I'm not in New York right now."

"When do you get back?" he asked, casually.

"Tomorrow."

"So maybe lunch on Monday?"

"Can you tell me what kind of restrictions?" I asked.

"You know that Coney Island Diner, Jack? The place on 46th off Broadway?"

"I think so. Maybe."

"Meet me there on Monday at one. There's a lot of detail with this so it's easier if we get together."

"Wallace, can you just tell me what kind of restrictions?"

"Pain in the ass ones."

"So he's going to have to travel, Captain Steubing?"

"Certainly will, Gopher," he said, chuckling.

◆

In the cab coming back from Kennedy, then getting ready to go see Mark and Philip, I thought about the past a lot and frankly, in the moments when I think about the past, I think about Carrie Franco.

I thought about her in the suburbs of Boston, maybe Quincy or maybe Needham, sitting at that very moment with Mark's father, Ken, watching a movie. I put on black Valentino pants and a gray Hugo Boss shirt, open at the collar. I went to a good wine shop and found an Antinori Tangianello. I remembered Philip ordering the Gaja Barbaresco and thought he'd probably like another big Italian red.

They lived on Fifty-seventh between Seventh and Eighth Avenues, a little north and a little east of Hell's Kitchen and what it turned into—the chic new haven for actors, artists, and the gay community that got tired of Chelsea. It was Philip who opened the door.

He wore a thin black sweater with an aqua Izod-looking collar sticking up from under it. That had been in style when I was in college, but apparently it was now retro and stylish again. He smiled when he saw me and said, "Mister Jack." *He's drunk*, I thought, amused.

"I brought you something," I said, and held out the bottle with the label turned up so he could see it.

"Oh, God, yes!" he said, and laughed a bit, but he seemed subdued. "You will come to all of our parties now, Jack."

Philip pulled me behind him like a kid as he led me through the apartment. His grip was loose. The apartment was elegant and there was almost no clutter. There were odd sculptures sitting on antique end tables and expanses of untouched wall space obviously left bare by design. There was no television visible, although I later uncovered a hidden and sunken flat screen in the bureau next to the living room curio. When I was twenty-one, like Mark, I had my things in plastic supermarket crates. As he threw my coat on the bed Phil said, "I dragged Mark to the driving range last week. His swing isn't too bad actually."

"I thought he didn't play," I replied.

"He's been coming with me sometimes lately. But I think it's because of you," he said with forced nonchalance.

I tried not to think about it. No one should be making decisions about anything because of me. That was around six months ago. Mark and I have gone to the driving range together a few times recently. His mechanics aren't too good but I don't spend much time telling him why or making suggestions. That wasn't Phil's point. We talk about other things.

Philip and I left the bedroom and joined the others in the living room. Mark was wearing linen pants and flip flops. He also looked loose. There was some whitish film on his hands and wrists. It looked like white paint that had been washed off with turpentine, leaving a thin, bleach-like, residue behind. There were only around twenty-five people but it was sort of crowded because the apartment, while beautiful, was not particularly large. Most of the crowd was older than Mark, probably around Philip's age, and far younger than me. "Hey," Mark said. I put my hand out to shake, and he embraced me instead and it was awkward.

◆

"You don't mind the marijuana, right?" Mark said very quietly. There were a few people passing around a joint.

"Marijuana?" I said, teasing him for his use of the formal name. "No."

He laughed. "It's kind of a smorgasbord," he said. "We don't sit down for dinner so just help yourself to whatever. Don't eat the sweetbreads. That's Philip's thing and it's shit, but I humor him."

"Got it."

He looked at me sideways and said, "Thanks for coming, Jack."

"No problem."

"Philip really appreciates it too. He's got this thing now about you and me becoming besties. So, thanks."

I smiled and said, "Okay. Painting today?"

"Oh, yeah," he said, waving his hand. "Let me introduce you to some of our friends."

They were an eclectic group of varied age and race. There were several people who identified themselves as lawyers but most of them couched that introduction with a clarifying statement about the non-profits they worked for, or the fact that they were with the ACLU, or even that they were going back to school for graphic arts. Although not a particularly corporate-looking crowd, several wore suits. Others looked no different than the homeless guys playing the sax or the djembe down on the IRT platform.

"You're Mark's stepdad?" I was asked by a short and thin young man, no bigger than a greyhound standing on its hind legs.

"Sort of. Biological father. His stepfather really raised him but—"

"Oh yeah, yeah, yeah. I'm sorry. I meant biological. Have you had the shrimp? These guys do the best Cajun stuff. Philip's mom is from N'Orleans. Try this," he said extending a toothpick with a huge shrimp skewered on it. I hastily accepted it and chewed while nodding in an effort to express both my thanks and approval.

"Philip?"

"Ha! Yeah. Yes. Do you like Death Cab?" he said, pointing straight up, which I took to indicate the stereo system and therefore the music. "Kurt, by the way," he added, extending his hand.

"This band?"

"Death Cab For Cutie," he said, and then before I had a chance to answer he added, "No? After your time, maybe?"

"Not bad. Sort of like the Eagles a little?"

"Oh, you are a funny one," he said, sort of hunching over a bit with a laugh and elbowing me lightly in the side.

"Thanks."

"You're a lawyer, Mark said. Isn't that right?" Kurt asked.

"I am, yes," I replied while reaching for another shrimp.

"All fucking lawyers," he said with mock disdain.

"Why, are you a lawyer?" I asked him.

"Hysterical," he said without laughing. "I must tell Mark that his biological really is a funny one."

I talked to more people and spent a good amount of time talking to Philip and Mark. I even took a hit of a joint with my "biological." I began to feel so enamored with them after an hour that I felt compelled to make up a story about having another engagement. Even though I had flown back from California to be there,

I started to feel claustrophobic and exposed. They all knew my name before I told them. They all knew about me and Mark and that I was a lawyer and played a lot of golf.

◆

Then I noticed Philip sitting quietly on the couch, somewhat slumped in his posture, fingertips of one hand to his forehead. I turned to Mark and found that he was already looking intently in my direction. When our eyes met, I knew.

"Is he sick now?" I asked softly, so that no one but Mark could hear me.

Mark nodded. "He's pretty sick," he said, also speaking very softly.

"What does that mean?"

"His T-cells started spiking. They changed his meds but it only got worse. He's got full-blown AIDS now."

"But what does that mean?" I asked again, like an idiot.

"It's AIDS, Jack. It means what it means." Mark paused for a second, and turned toward Phil and then back to me. "We haven't really started telling anyone yet, except our parents, but it's getting unavoidable now. Something was wrong with his medication . . . It caused problems." He sighed. "It's . . . he's got heart damage. A problem with his heart now."

"They have the cocktail meds for AIDS," I said. "People live for years now. . . ." I was looking over at Philip, and Mark was doing the same. He looked back at us, from around twelve feet away. He knew Mark was telling me.

"They do have medicine for it," Mark said, sort of absent-mindedly. "Phil held out for a few years but everyone's different," Mark added.

"And now what?"

"Well, for one thing, he thinks I should know you better and I have to play fucking golf now. I told him I would. I just do whatever he tells me to right now."

"He's a good guy, Mark."

"You don't even know, Jack. He could live off his father's money, do nothing, like his brother. But Philip works sixty-hour weeks fighting for people who have no one else. It's all he does these days. The sicker he gets the more he works."

A few minutes later I finally made my exit. Philip hugged me when I went to leave and then Mark wrapped his arms around me as well. That was the second time that Mark hugged me that night. While I liked them both for their ease and genuine affection, I was also too uncomfortable to linger in the doorway. I pulled my chest back, gently patted Mark's upper arms with my hands, and said, "Okay, goodnight," and made my way toward the elevators.

CHAPTER NINETEEN: STARFISH

Wallace got to the diner right on time. So did I. We walked straight toward each other from opposite directions on Forty-sixth Street. He's always right on time.

"How you been?" he asked jovially as we approached each other. He wore sneakers, as always, a light and stylish leather jacket, and had a backpack draped over one shoulder. He looked like an aged college student, maybe fifty, heading off to class.

"Hey, Wallace."

Once inside we ordered coffee and neither of us looked at the menu. I noticed that his hair looked gray.

"Been a while," I said.

"Couple of years."

"Getting a little gray, pal."

He smiled and nodded, touched the side of his head with his free hand. "Well. . . ."

The waitress came and we ordered. Wallace got a tomato and spinach omelet, egg white only. He had not ordered an omelet with me ever before. He had once ordered egg salad. I got the turkey club. "So?" I asked, smiling.

"Yeah," he said. "It's for a woman. Very wealthy husband. Family office wealthy. I've networked into some of those channels the last few years. Very concerned about privacy."

"Tough blood type?"

He shook his head energetically in quick, short motions. "AB positive. A snap," he replied. "Universal receptor."

"Then what's the problem?"

"Husband doesn't like the traditional route," he said. I didn't follow. I cocked my head a bit, and probably looked a bit like a Labrador. "Gotta be a living donor," he added nonchalantly, taking a big bite of eggs and ketchup.

"Shit."

"New York Jack!" he said, more loudly, motioning at me with one hand extended outward, palm up, as if he was introducing me on a nightclub stage.

The place was packed, buzzing with loud conversation, the sound of silverware and glasses clinking, chairs pushed along the tiled floor. There were tourists everywhere, odd variations of out-of-place Americans. It was comforting. The normal lunchtime chaos was easy to blend into. I wondered if we had come to know each other too well.

"You're talking about a big project," I said quietly.

"It's a half million. That's two-fifty each. I'm not negotiating. That's the real deal and we split it."

I didn't say anything. The money worried me. It was too much. For a liver I normally got around $200K total, meaning about a hundred and fifty to me. If I co-brokered it, with Wallace for instance, it might mean only seventy-five grand. A half a million was big, and that meant a commensurate risk, despite the fact that Wallace would surely argue otherwise.

"You can't do that deal here in the States," I said.

"And thus," he said, looking up from his lunch and smiling, "I called you."

✦

Wallace knew greedy doctors in the US and circulated in wealthy circles. Fifteen or twenty years ago, when this all really got started, he was a nurse at the Cleveland Clinic, one of the leading transplant centers in the US. I learned that tidbit years ago through a doctor I stumbled upon who knew him. I've never told Wallace. Hell, his last name is Kendrickson and he lives in South Norwalk, but I never had a reason to tell him I knew that either.

Wallace still took risks to unearth buyers, exposing himself in small ways I had stopped doing years ago. I fully expected to see him destroyed one day, either by a jail sentence or something more gruesome and unexpected. He was one of the main reasons I never let down my guard or relaxed my protocols, always rotating phones, always changing email addresses. He was a pro, and he managed his risk, but he was arrogant, and that brings men down.

"They're gonna have to go to Jozi," I said to Wallace.

"That's what I already told the husband. Johannesburg, I told him."

"Lucky she's AB. At least that's easier."

"That's what I told him."

"So I'm going to have to travel too," I said. "I wouldn't want to arrange this by phone. I'm going to have to go back there now."

"Okay," he said without looking up.

"I'll need fifty up front."

"I brought you a hundred," he said quietly, motioning to the backpack on the seat beside him.

◆

A week later I went back to Jozi to find the Fifteen we needed for Wallace's client. Sitting at the hotel bar of the Michelangelo in Sandton with Dr. Mel Wolff and his slimy sidekick, I was feeling fatigued. I didn't want to be back in South Africa. I was sick of the long flights. It did allow me to move a few hundred grand in cash to Jozi, but it made me feel caught up in the baseness of the business. Even in the wealthiest neighborhoods in Jozi you always run the risk of a good car-jacking. I wanted to be back in Tucson, by the pool at my condo, listening to some old Texas blues and thinking about my putting. I needed some time with a woman whose touch was a balm against my isolation. I was tired of Wolff and Pierre and Wallace and the thought of that kid with a nephrectomy scar etched into his lower back.

"The human body, it is an amazing thing, an amazing network of interrelated systems all perfectly in sync. I take it you don't believe in God, Jack?" Wolff asked me. I returned his gaze, giving him all the answer he needed. He laughed. "Well, if you were a surgeon you might."

"Why's that, Mel? I thought men of science don't get religious," I said, softening a little at the sound of his laugh and the sight of his smile. The man was a crook, and a bit of a fiend, but he was likable as hell. I always gave him the benefit of the doubt.

"Quite the contrary. We see his handiwork firsthand." He smiled, almost paternally, and continued. "What we're talking about here, a liver, it's very interesting. Some things in the human body, some organs, they don't regenerate. But many do. The liver does, and this is why we can get you a living donor. You see the liver has two main blood supplies—"

"I know," I said. "I know it regenerates."

"Like a starfish," Wolff said.

"Okay. So you just explain that they are selling a third of their liver?" I asked very quietly.

"If the donor even needs to know that."

"What do you mean?"

"Jack, Pierre suggested that we just source a kidney donor and while we are in there we could easily remove the portion of the liver needed for your client. It doesn't have to be complicated. Why does the starfish need to know?" He sipped his Sauvignon Blanc and turned and looked at Pierre who remained silent.

"Wait," I said, and a laugh escaped me. It didn't even feel like me laughing. It almost surprised me. "You're just going to clip a third of the guy's liver and not even tell him?" I felt the corners of my eyes contract in a slight grimace, involuntarily. "Really?"

"You know, Jack, I said too much. I apologize." Wolff placed his hand on my shoulder. "My friend, don't get caught up in this. At Royston all of these donors get the best care. We give them real after-care. This isn't India. We don't dump them on the street to get sepsis. You know that. Let Pierre deal with the common aspects of all of that mess. You and I are in the healing business."

"What you're saying isn't right, Mel."

"Jack, together we have done a hundred transplant procedures. Every single one of them saved someone's life. Now that I am in charge of the whole hospital we can expand, help thousands, not just hundreds. Send your client to us in Sandton. We can do this as early as the week after next. It's going to cost more of course, but I have to look that over with Carolyn. I'll email you next week when you're back in New York. Okay, my friend? Not to worry."

Again, I said nothing. I was distracted by the sound of the chatter in the background.

"Okay, my friend?" he repeated.

"That's fine."

"Jack, now that I'm in charge we can source anything. Anything. For the right price, Pierre can get anything we might need to help one of your clients. Like this liver. We have a very good system and we are accomplishing something important here that will help save a lot of lives in the coming years."

For the first time I understood the magnitude of the word "anything" when it was coming from Pierre Kleinhans or Mel Wolff. Perhaps, I mused, I had tapped a pipeline to living donors as significant to the US transplant tourism demands as the Alaskan pipeline was to California's oil needs.

When Wolff was in the restroom I quickly said to Pierre, "I need to go back to Alexandra."

"No, Jack. You saw it already. There's nothing there for you."

"Pierre, I need to go back there tomorrow and I need Thaba to come with me. If you don't want to come that's fine but I want you to tell Thaba to meet me here at noon tomorrow so we can take a ride over to Alexandra. Don't bring Wolff into this, just tell Thaba."

"Jack, that's a very bad idea."

"Pierre, you need to have Thaba go with me or I am going to Alex without him."

We stared at each other for a moment and Kleinhans looked as if he might spit in my face. His lips seemed to pucker slightly with indignation. Perhaps he was clenching his teeth behind his pinkish lips. "All right, Jack. Anything for a friend," he said in a saccharine tone. "I'll call your tour guide and we'll come pick you up here at noon. Will it be just another short visit?"

"Yes."

"All right then, Jack. And this will be the last one?"

"Fine."

✦

Once we were all in the car the next day I told Pierre to take us to the same place we had seen the first time, back in January.

At one point, without turning around from his position in the front passenger seat, Thaba said, "Have you been back to Alex since we went together, Jack?"

"No."

Then, he and Pierre exchanged some words in a local language I could not understand. Did they know? We entered Alex through that same alleyway, and I led them to the clearing, not worrying that I might seem too familiar with the route. The square opened up before me and I immediately saw Lesedi, sitting on the ground in the dirt near the boys playing soccer, his ball made out of tape lying beside him in the sun. He might never leave that spot, I thought. From across the yard, when I saw his attention focused on us, I waved him over. He slowly stood and strode right at us. He saw that I was with Pierre and Thaba, and he said nothing. Neither did my colleagues. Finally I said, "Thaba, give this boy four thousand rand."

"What?" he asked, laughing a little.

"Give it to him."

"What are you talking about, Jack?" Pierre asked.

Thaba said something to Lesedi that I didn't understand and I cut him off and yelled, "Don't talk to him!" I turned toward Thaba. "Don't talk to this child. Talk to me. You told him a price, now give him the rest." All of the kids that had been playing soccer and the handful of other people in the square were looking at us.

"You don't belong here, New York Jack," Thaba said confidently and calmly. "Go back to Sandton."

"You told him ten thousand. Do you know what you took from him? Give him the other four thousand rand."

"You should have told me this before we came, Jack," Pierre said. But we all stood there and stared at each other and had ourselves a bit of a Mexican standoff, right there in the middle of hell in Gauteng Province, South Africa.

"I don't have that money," Thaba said.

"Get it from Pierre," I said, my voice dripping with anger. "He'll give it to you and you can give it back to him later."

Pierre stepped between us and said, "All right, all right..." and removed his wallet and handed the cash to Thaba. They exchanged soft but heated words I didn't understand. Thaba handed the cash to Lesedi without looking at him, and then spit at Lesedi's feet.

I looked at Lesedi. He looked like a kid again, a tall and lanky kid who could have come from the Bronx or Brooklyn, who might have fought his way out of that mess, who still might, but probably wouldn't.

"There is nothing else I can do," I said to him.

"No one can do anything," he said quietly. Those were the first words he had spoken to us that day. Tears were welling up in his eyes.

"Your sisters?"

"I do not have sisters now," he said.

"Good luck," I said quietly. I turned on my heel in that dirt and walked away. I could hear the footsteps of Pierre and Thaba behind me. I thought for a moment that I might feel the sting of Thaba's knife piercing my skin and spine, but I did not. I was still their connection to the customers. I still had leverage, and the ability to walk out of the Dark City unscathed.

CHAPTER TWENTY: RETIREMENT PLANNING

We got that Fifteen off to Royston okay in late May and she was back at home in Washington DC about a week after Memorial Day. A half a million dollars. Two hundred K for each of us after expenses. I felt the rush, but I felt ready to put it aside. Sometimes scoring a big deal made me want to pause, to savor it and be patient, like a serial killer. But for Wallace, I knew that the scale of the opportunity unfolding before us was going to be problematic and too hard to resist. I knew he couldn't leave it alone. It's funny, but if the government ever asked the pharmaceutical companies to add up how much cyclosporine and Prograf and other immunosuppressant drugs they sell to transplant recipients, and then cross-referenced it against the number of legal transplants done domestically off of the UNOS lists, they would find a huge disparity that would equate to a rough representation of the illegal foreign organ trade. But they don't ask. That's the protocol.

It wasn't until after we did that Fifteen in May before everything seemed businesslike and back to normal between me and

Wallace. I was careful not to impose on his confidence again after the mistake I had made by mentioning Marlene Brown. When he contacted me at the beginning of July, a month had slid by since the live liver deal. I would have preferred a little calm followed by a few regular Eighties shipping off to Jozi for Mel Wolff, bolstering my portfolio incrementally, fifty K at a time. Not Wallace.

In early July he proposed something different than anything I had ever before encountered. That was the second thing that changed it all for me.

"This is a very different thing," I said then, thinking about the fact that he had somehow truly become my partner.

"Yeah. More profitable. Like *done* profitable," Wallace replied.

"Wallace," I said, matter-of-factly, "ten deals. That's more profitable than one. Or five is. But this is a different kind of deal. It is a different enterprise. Do you follow what I'm saying? It is not even our *industry*."

"But it *is*," he said. "Jack, this is like winning the lottery and then pretending there's a decision to be made about whether or not to redeem the ticket."

"It's different . . ." I said, more to myself than to him.

"I find buyers; you find sellers. That's how it is. How it's been. This is not different. The only thing different is usually it's extra money, maybe that new car, a condo down-payment—like the Fifteen last month. But this time it's a finish line." He paused, then added, "Really." The "really" somehow sounded like a threat. "You know, you're not the only seller's agent."

"Hmm." It was a remedial negotiating tactic and we both knew it. I wondered if he even felt embarrassed for saying it. We both knew it didn't matter at all. In our business, the more tense a situation, the less negotiating that actually takes place. The more critical a situation, the more weighty the merchandise, the less margin for the push and pull and dance that consumes so much time in more frivolous transactions, like real estate, or the stock market, or love.

In our business, the best players negotiate by simply showing up, committed to the deal.

"With us," Wallace said, "it gets done. I can call the man in Seattle. The people in Rio, they can always be called . . . But why do that when you and I . . . It gets done, and I can't risk this not being done correctly."

"Because," I responded, calmly, "it is different."

"Yes, Jack. Fine. Of course it is." That's how things start sometimes.

"Wallace," I said, "even if I wanted to do this, what makes you think I could?"

"Because no one else can and it has to get done."

"But without the Chinese, how could I even do this now? Even if I wanted to?"

"The way we both know it's going to happen."

"Wallace," I said, hearing myself pleading a bit, "even if my guys were up for this at Royston . . . I mean, let's say they could do it. Even if they could type it out in advance and. . . ."

"Now, New York Jack!" Wallace said, more animated.

"Now wait," I said, "because you only get four hours with a heart once it's outside of the donor's body. A kidney can last two days on ice, but not this. So the guy would have to go live there at the hospital, for months, waiting, and maybe that's still not long enough. It would be very tough."

"That's why you had it right the first time. They have to type it out in advance. Just say it already, Jack. Who fucking cares? You can say it, New York. No one's been listening for years. All of this changing phone numbers . . . No one cares."

"Do you realize what we're ultimately talking about?" I asked in a near whisper.

"Yes."

"Do they understand it? Do these people who hired you understand what they're asking for? What it takes to get a living donor *heart*?"

"I don't care," he said casually.

"Well you sound pretty cavalier in light of what we are talking about."

"I am not."

"It is, a heart," I said gravely.

There was a long pause. I felt like we were both waiting, like two gunfighters about to draw in the high noon sun.

"A contract hit," he said quietly. "In this country you can get something like that done for as little as ten or twenty grand. In some countries it's a few hundred bucks. This is something very specialized. It's for very rich people who know exactly what they need and want top-quality merchandise. The fee is five million, of which you will be paid two."

There was a long uncomfortable silence. "Suddenly we're sixty-forty?" I asked.

"On this we are."

"Five *million*?" I said, almost involuntarily. I might have guessed one, and I was struck by it.

"Yes. Cash. They're good."

"Someone on a god squad could be paid off for a lot less."

"Not on this. Even paying off someone on a hospital's transplant committee wouldn't help. There are other complications," Wallace said.

"And?"

"There is no other way to fill this order," Wallace said. "Not for this particular patient."

"Why? Why can't we just bribe someone on a committee or send him to wait in a hospital in SA and just pay his way to the top of the list? Is he such an impossible match? We shouldn't even be going back to Royston right now. I should do it in the Philippines. Plus, the thing about a heart, he could be kept alive for a while with an L-VAD while he's waiting. People sometimes last for a year on those now. It could buy him the time he needs. . . ."

"L-VAD? One of those artificial heart pumps—"

"Yes. An artificial heart pump."

"It wouldn't matter. It would buy more time but it wouldn't make a difference. Not for this guy. He has AIDS, Jack. All the time in the world can't help this guy. He needs us to get it for him. There's no other way. No list is helping a guy with his profile. So, it's five million, Jack. Two for you."

"Yes. I heard you the first time."

There was a pause, and suddenly I felt a little sick. *Philip?* I thought. *Could it possibly be for Philip? No . . .*

Wallace interrupted. "Then why aren't we working out details instead of debating whether or not to accept a gift?"

◆

Someone HIV positive who needs a transplant does have an outside shot now, but certainly not one that you could bank on. They remain extremely low on the legitimate lists and only get secondary merchandise (someone also infected with AIDS who went brain-dead; someone with Hep C; perhaps an organ from the elderly). It's tough because putting a second-class organ into an already compromised immune system that has to sustain the stress of major surgery, and then tolerate immuno-suppressant anti-rejection drugs. . . . It doesn't make for good statistical outcomes. And that's if the guy only needs a kidney.

What Wallace was alluding to—getting a black market heart without going through the legitimate channels—of course it's not the same as sourcing a kidney, or part of a liver, or a lobe of a lung. A patient with AIDS will simply not get a heart off a UNOS list, and even a facility on the take can't hide that a patient has AIDS. How could anyone explain that the recipient was chosen despite being completely ineligible? We were dancing around whether or not to be complicit in conspiracy to commit murder. For this AIDS patient's family to buy what they wanted, we would have to know in advance who the donor was and where he lived, in what miserable god-forsaken shanty-town he had been seduced by Pierre Fucking Kleinhans, and have the patient ready, because they'd only have four hours. Believe me, I tried to say no. I wanted to be a man who said no to such things without consideration or weighing the fee against the risks, or the harm. But sadly, some part of me was still a man who said, "How much?" even as I made myself sick from it. I know better now, today, as I recount all of this, but only a few months ago I still didn't.

✦

"Two million is a lot," I said to Wallace. I didn't want to ask anything specific about Philip. I didn't want to show Wallace any of my cards yet.

"Twenty kidneys, Jack. Double that if co-brokered. Maybe that's a retirement plan. I assume you've got other money. I've got money, but a few extra million would always help."

"What's his name?"

"Forget it, Jack. Not on this. Just understand that he's young, early thirties, I think. Family is loaded. They started at a million and I moved them to five. From one to five. Think about that."

"Can he travel?"

"Yes, but who knows how long it will be that way."

"Blood type?"

"O. Sorry. It is what it is."

"Any other stuff?" My mind was racing.

"AIDS issues. Give me a new email address and I'll send you the medical records. Send it to your guys at Royston because that's where it's got to happen, right? This will be huge."

"You realize what we'd become a part of?" I asked him, still not sure I could even do it; but still not sure I could resist. I was wondering about the patient, about Philip, and I have to admit that I was also finding myself lusting for the fee, drifting along in a dreamy way like a teenager with a crush. I felt the adrenaline charge that preceded the rush. It's just like that excitement that builds while someone is still cutting up the lines, before a single one has been snorted. It's the rush; the lusty feeling of addiction—and satisfaction. It might not even be Philip, I thought. What if it is? Philip's father, Harold Lauer, was very wealthy. He was probably the kind of man used to getting what he wants, no matter what the cost might be, and he could spare a few million.

"Nothing. I'm not part of anything. I just tell sick people who they should talk to and if they get what they need that's great but it's between them and some hospital in Timbuktu. I have nothing to do with anything else," Wallace said casually.

"You have knowledge of it."

"I don't, you see. And please do not start this shit again Jack because now is not the time to get weepy or unprofessional about who we are. That's what you need to get your brain around, Jack. Don't ask questions you don't want answered and you'll be a lot better off in life."

✦

I thought a lot about what Wallace had said and daydreamed about the fee. "A retirement plan," he had said. There are fewer than a thousand names on the lists who need hearts. Often UNOS actually takes care of them. Black market heart transactions have always been mostly unheard of. This deal on the table with Wallace was unique in that the guy had AIDS and would never pass muster with a god committee at any transplant center at home. This couldn't be done through regular means. It required the intervention of New York Jack.

✦

Why does someone want and want and want even when he already has more than enough? I think it's partly addiction and also that money just happens to be the metric. There has to be some measurement for our lives, a reason to get out of bed. The money somehow became mine. I wondered if the client might possibly be Philip but the odds against it were too big. I thought about all of my justifications and I wanted to let them go but it always felt as if doing that would be like falling off a cliff. Over the years, in my rare moments of introspection I sometimes thought about The Man from Dallas. I tried to convince myself that we were cut from the same cloth, crusaders against some vague injustice.

The biggest realization I had while considering Wallace's heart transaction was something I imagine most people accept when they're still kids: life's just not fair. For years the illusion had somehow fueled my vindictiveness and solitude—but not since I met Mark. Once I met Mark I felt more like a part of things. Ironically, that made me feel more like I had things to answer for.

That night I spent a lot of time peering into my telescopes. The skies were clear and there were unimpeded views. The closest star to us other than our own sun is Alpha Centauri. It's 4.3 light years away. It would take a craft traveling the speed of light 4.3 years to reach us from there. The pinpoints of light we see in the night sky from some stars began traveling toward us hundreds, thousands, or millions of years ago. Looking at them is like reaching into a grave and pulling out ghosts. What has happened there since then? Ever since I got my first telescope when I was a kid I hoped to find something out there, skipping over billions of people right here on earth to do so.

CHAPTER TWENTY-ONE:
GHOSTS

The next morning I got in my car before rush hour and drove up the FDR to the Queensboro Bridge. It's been renamed for Ed Koch, the former Mayor. "How'm I doin'?" he used to say on the news when I was a kid. He had a thick New York accent. "How'm I doin'?"

The bridge was almost empty. It led me to Queens Blvd and then I drove through narrow side streets into Flushing and parked across the street from the boxy little house I had grown up in. It sat tucked between two other boxy little houses, with shared walls, vinyl siding, and dingy gutters. When I lived there the house was a gray; now it was light blue, and it looked cheery. There were wires hanging down from a broken cable connection, and the ivy was thick and overgrown on the right side of the building.

I climbed the three small stairs to the front door and knocked. It wasn't yet eight a.m. After a few moments I knocked again, louder. Then I heard the creaking of the thick, wooden front door being pulled open. It was dim inside, and in the shadows was a small woman in an embroidered housecoat. The screen door was closed and she looked up at me and I could see the features of her face jutting out from the dark, old and wrinkled, but familiar, like a weathered painting of the woman who had raised me many years before.

"How you doin', Mom?"

She squinted behind thick metal-rimmed glasses and said, "Hello?"

"Mom?"

Her mouth opened wider and then her eyes did as well and she mouthed the word, "Jackie?" I nodded. "Jackie, what are you doing here, son?"

"It's been a long time, Mom. Can I come in for a bit?"

She seemed to think about it, looked behind her and then back at me, and said, "Okay, Jackie. For a bit. C'mon in."

She retreated into the room and I stepped into the house. I had never been there before. I had not lived there. It was someone else. It was a dream.

The dining room was a shambles, cluttered with plates and boxes and stacks of old newspapers and magazines on the table. The carpet was stained and littered. She pulled her housecoat tighter around her.

"Come this way, Jackie," and with a wave of her small hand she led me into the living room. Her hair was thin and gray and stiff with hairspray. She sat on one of the two couches, and folded her hands in her lap. I sat on the other.

"How are you?" I asked quietly.

She nodded, as if to say "Okay," then asked "What brings you by here all of a sudden?"

I looked at her. She was dissolving into the shadows and crevices of that house. She was fading into the arguments still bouncing off those walls. "Maybe I shouldn't come here and bother you. I didn't mean to do that. Do you hear from Elena much?"

"Your sister? No. But sometimes. Not like you."

This time I nodded, but it was a nod of dismissal. Then I said, "I came to ask you something about Dad. Can I do that?"

"Why do you want to do that, Jackie?"

"Is it strange?"

"It's strange you coming here now. Eight in the morning on a Wednesday when I have my doctors to go to in the afternoon. I have to get on two buses, you know. Yes, I'd say it's strange. What is it you want?"

There was a lamp on the square wooden table where the ends of the two couches met. It was turned on, and one of the thick curtains was drawn open, but it was still dark in the room. The ceiling fixtures were off. In the beams of light streaming in from the side of the living room window between the curtains and the window's edge there were dust particles gently floating upward against gravity. "Is there anything you could tell me now, Mom, about my father . . . about what was his problem with me all those years? I mean, he was hard on you and Elena too, but why did he treat me the way he did?"

"Treat you what way? Jack was a good man. You kids made things hard for your father. He had to go on the road and sell. He had to make meetings. He had to go to all the meetings in all the places, selling shoes to pay the bills and keep a roof over our heads."

"He sold jewelry."

"Well."

"He hit you, Mom. A lot. We never talked about this. But we knew it. Elena did and I did."

"Well, I'm not going to talk about that. Those stories."

"Are you saying it's not true?"

"Is that what you came here to ask about?"

"Don't you remember that day, the day Dad found that pot in my room? And he made me go to the basement." I turned my head and looked at the entrance that once led down a shag-carpeted hallway to a basement door. "Don't you remember?"

She shook her head. "No," she said firmly.

"And he hit me and pushed me down half a flight of stairs."

"He did not," she said incredulously. "Oh!"

"But he did. And you know he did. And he urinated on me on the floor. My own father did that. You know that. You know all of those things."

"I do not know such things. Watch your mouth. That is a story. Did Elena tell you that?"

"What?"

"Look, your father worked very hard. And sometimes you broke the rules. Sometimes I broke the rules. He didn't even want children. But we were so young and then I got pregnant with Elena and we were Catholic and so things changed and he always told me, 'She's your doing, Joan, so you take care of her,' and he was right to say so."

I was struggling to stay controlled but I knew that if I got upset or angry the conversation would end. She was only partly lying anyway—I believed that she truly did not remember those things. "And it was the same with me?" I asked.

"No," my mother said, "you were Jim Peterson's boy, not his, and he hated that. He allowed it, but he hated that you were Jim's and he had to feed and clothe you."

"Jim Peterson? Jim the old cop who lived down the block?"

"How could you blame your father?"

"What are you saying?"

"Look," she said more sharply, "did you come here to upset me? You don't come by for years and now you want to ask all these questions? Now?"

"No." I felt tired.

"Because you tell Elena she can fight her own goddamned battles!"

"Alright, Mom. Please. What do you mean about I was Jim Peterson's boy?"

"Your father was in Army Reserves in Korea then, and you know how these things happen. Jack was gone for months at a time and I often thought about taking little Elena and moving back in with my mother in New Jersey. Jack had a mean streak, now that's for sure. But when he came back he said we were Catholics and I had to have you and he wouldn't let me go and move back with my mother. And he even named you Jackie. Just like him, and just like his father."

"He wasn't really my father? Is that what you're telling me?"

"That's enough now, Jackie. Now, do you want tea or do I have to ask you to please go? I have two buses I have to go on."

"You're kidding . . ." was all that came out of me. I was back in that room upstairs, waiting to see how he might react. I was falling down the basement steps. I thought he'd kill me in the basement that day. Maybe he did. I stood up. I left the living room and crossed through the tiny dining room that connected it to the kitchen. That was the same way I had walked that day, that day when I yelled back at him. I remembered that walk, that gait of a killer. I remembered how it felt, momentarily, to no longer be afraid.

"I am not kidding!" my mother said. "It's the Q-26 and then I have to switch at Roosevelt Avenue. Why would a person lie about buses? Why?"

She had gotten up and I brushed past her and walked to the basement door. I opened it and looked down into the dark at the empty stairway. She stood behind me in the hallway.

"There!" I yelled. I lunged toward my mother and grabbed her coat by the arm and pushed her to the top of the landing. "There! Those stairs! That's where your Jack threw a boy down a flight of fucking stairs."

"Let go!" I yelled again, seething. "That is where your Jack pissed on his own broken son, his *adopted* son, apparently. The sick bastard! And there is where you let him," I said, pointing past her to their bedroom door. "Every time."

"Get out. Get out!" she yelled. "Don't come back here. And you tell that Elena I'm through with her too! Who needs it?!"

I am not my father's son, I thought, but instead of glee or relief I just felt more anger. And nothing felt changed by the news. Nothing. The news was about genetics, but it didn't change the circumstances of my life in any way at all. I walked out of that house and was tempted for a moment to walk down the block and find Jim Peterson. He'd have to be in his eighties. I wanted to find him and shake him and make him tell me why he never shot that prick Jack Trayner in the face.

CHAPTER TWENTY-TWO:
A HEART TOO BIG

A few days later, late at night, I had been out on my balcony with my telescope for hours when my cell phone rang. It was Mark. I was fixated on a tiny point of light I knew to be a double star. The warbling caused by two massive bodies circling and pulling on each other wasn't detectable with an amateur device like mine, even if it was an expensive amateur device.

"Jack. Is it cool that I'm calling you now?" He sounded anxious.

"Yeah. It's fine." I was distracted. *There might be planets orbiting that double star*, I thought. Imagine what a double-star sunset would look like.

"I called the other number. I guess that phone's disconnected now? So I tried this one, like you said." He sounded hoarse.

"That's fine," I repeated.

"You know, we only know each other a few months now, Jack."

"Yes." I was thinking about his grandmother, sitting alone in that dusty living room, holding on to redacted memories of her version of her life. *How will I tell him the story of our family? One day, I'll have to tell him*, I thought.

"But I wanted to call you. Is that strange?" I didn't answer him.

"Jack, what is it that you're always keeping from me? What don't you want to tell me? Philip says you have some sort of secret and it makes you untrustworthy? What is it?"

"He says that?"

"What is it?"

"I don't know, Mark," I said.

"Sure you do. It's something big I think." He was practically whispering. I thought he might be drunk. "Who goes and changes phone numbers like that?"

I kept my eye on that double-star. *It could be millions of light years away*, I thought. *This could be light from the dinosaur age. What could be happening on that double star now, today? It could be anything. It could even be completely gone.*

"Philip was admitted today," he said. He paused, then added, "Jack, he's so sick. So fast . . . with the, uh . . . the medication problem . . ." He sounded like he might start to sob.

There were lights gleaming up from the street below, and lights behind the window-shades protecting people's privacy in the hundreds of apartments in the buildings I could see from where I stood. There were stars above me, some glimmering and some—it was more like they were glowering, almost sarcastically. They all shined down on me and I could see plenty with my eyes, despite the New York light pollution. I could see thousands with my scope and there were billions beyond them, all going about their business.

"Jack, I know it's late, but could I stop by?"

"Here?"

"Or, we could meet somewhere else. If it's not too late for you. Do you want to come by our place? I'd rather talk about this in person."

"Mark, just tell me what's going on. How bad is it?"

"He's dying, I think." The words came out like a wind between two buildings pushing down a narrow alleyway, scattering stray leaves and candy wrappers.

"I thought he was doing okay."

Then Mark was crying. "I know. I know," he said quietly through tears.

I sat down on the concrete floor of my balcony. It was still warm after soaking in the sunlight all day and I could feel it through my pants. I had no idea what to say.

"He's gained weight lately. You saw him. Kind of a lot in the last few weeks," Mark said. "Water weight mostly. I hope it's okay that I am calling you. I talked to my mom and dad an hour ago. It seemed like I should call you. Mom said to call you—"

"She did?"

"Yeah. They're in Boston. Phil's gained weight and started having difficulty breathing, and he finally went to the doctor and then to a specialist and he didn't even tell me for a day and a half."

"Mark," I said, "it's okay that you called me. It's good." It was well past eleven and it seemed like every apartment in the building across the street was lit up. *I have no idea what any of them are doing in their apartments*, I remember thinking.

"He has cardiomyopathy.

"Hmmm," I said, feeling myself grimacing against the news. It felt like burning my hand on a stove.

"You know? You know what that is, Jack?"

"It's an enlarged heart."

"Yes," he said, crying more audibly then. "It's an enlarged heart. It started last year. From a viral infection. And the HIV cocktail, the medicines had an interaction. Phil always takes his pills, every single morning, every night. People live that way a long time now. And it happened anyway and now he's collecting fluid and they say because of the cardiomyopathy it's very hard to treat. Congestive heart failure."

"What stage is it?"

"Stage?" Mark repeated. "I think four. I think that's the last one." He was more subdued then, and seemed to have stopped crying.

"It is."

"It is, right? How do you know?" Mark asked.

"They won't offer him a transplant because he has AIDS," I said.

"That's right."

I was silent again. I saw a light in an apartment across the way go dark. *Oh God. Wallace's heart must surely be for Philip.* If Harold Lauer went searching for a heart for his sick son he would spread around some cash for information, and there are only a handful of people a search like that would lead to. One of them uses Florida cell numbers and gets most of his parts from me.

"It's so ironic," Mark said. "He's dying because he has a heart that's too big."

"There's nothing poetic about cardiomyopathy," I responded softly.

"Ironic, I said."

"Yes. I see."

"Jack . . . could you help him?"

"Me?" The yellow alert went off in my head. "How could *I* help him?"

I was sweating a little and could feel it beading up on the sides of my forehead.

"My mom thinks that maybe you can help," he said more soberly. It was then that I became instantly aware that Mark knew more about his "biological" than he had previously let on.

"How, Mark? Why would Carrie think that?"

"Because my mom says you did something once for a man named Billy Kimball."

I resisted reacting and went into damage-control mode, wanting to get a handle on what Carrie and Mark did or did not know about good old Jack.

"I see," I replied evenly. "So you haven't been honest with me I guess."

"Not completely. I'm sorry," Mark said in a voice that no longer sounded drunk at all.

"What did Carrie say about it?"

"She said that you both knew a guy in college named Billy Kimball, and after law school you somehow got him a donor for a kidney transplant and it saved his life but that you charged him a lot of money for it. There was a rumor that maybe you were some kind of kidney broker or something, but she wasn't sure. She isn't sure now either." Hearing him voice that made me feel tired, like another round of changing phones, another flight to Johannesburg.

"Well, she's right." I would not have said that to anyone else. "I got Billy Kimball a kidney back in the early nineties."

"You did? Can you help Philip?" he asked, choking up again.

"Is that why you came to see me, Mark? After all these years, is that why?"

"I wanted to meet you, Jack. I wanted to know you anyway."

"But was that why? Was that the reason?"

He paused, and then quietly said, "That's the reason for the *timing*, yes. Why I wanted to meet you *now*, but I swear it's not the only reason I wanted to meet you. And I'm glad."

"Okay," I said. At that moment I wasn't sure if I would ever talk to him again. That's another dirty truth. It wasn't out of anger or a sense of betrayal—the kid just knew too much about me. That's just the way I've become accustomed to doing things.

"You'll help us?"

"I doubt I can do anything, but I'll help you if I can. But you can't discuss this with anyone."

"I won't," he said. "I just want to help Philip." There was some silence again, and then he added, "You know, Jack, in the eighties, Reagan and them, they did nothing about AIDS at first. It was on purpose. They were glad it would kill off the gays."

"That's not exactly true, Mark," I said. *I should go*, I thought. I need a heart for a recipient with AIDS. What are the odds? . . . Royston. Mel Wolff and Kleinhans, I thought.

Any indecisiveness I had felt about helping them was already waning. He is my son. Philip is his love, the way Carrie had once been mine.

"Mark," I finally said, "what are you going to do now?"

"Do? Marry him. Before he dies."

"No, I meant what will you do now? Tonight. To be okay?"

"There's nothing to do," he said. He sounded exhausted too.

✦

I didn't sleep well after that. First I sat down on my balcony and drank more Scotch. For eighteen years I had stolen from the poor and given to the rich. I was the Anti-Robin Hood. Eighteen years— enough time to age the best scotch whiskeys . . . with Wallace, with this proposition about procuring a heart for a dying rich kid with AIDS—it was about the money, but maybe it could be about a dying young man with AIDS and maybe that gave me the opportunity to finally do something right.

I had been alone for so long until Mark found me and I again felt like a part of things. I loved him, I supposed. I still barely knew him but I loved him anyway. I couldn't bear the thought of Mark having to lose him, to feel that pain, when I knew that I happened to be about the only person on earth who could actually prevent it from happening. They were probably using me—Mark and Carrie—but I didn't blame them for it. It made sense. And it evoked a great sense of outrage from me to think that perhaps I could *not* prevent it—that I was required to live in such an unfair world. *I could get Philip a heart,* I thought, *and I could save him. I could get the money and the absolution.* I know that is convoluted logic and in a way just a rationalization so I could get my fee, but that's what I thought. Mark being alive in the world, and beautiful and kind and having actually come from the one love I had ever been a part of, that made me determined to save Philip for him. I lay in bed that night for hours, unable to sleep, feeling like a timer had been started.

✦

It was the fifteenth of July when I went with Mark to Cornell Presbyterian Hospital to visit Philip. Mark and I met at a coffee shop at 68th Street and Second Ave. and walked over together. The walk was mostly silent but for the sounds of traffic and the city. The sky was clear and the air was warm and sticky. When we entered the building, security asked us for identification and we both showed the guard NY State driver's licenses, mine bearing the name Jack Campbell. They didn't record anything or make us sign in. For some reason they just wanted to make sure we could drive. I guess no one intending to blow up the hospital is a licensed driver.

The Lauers lived in the East Seventies, and I suppose that's why they brought Philip to Cornell. Cornell is part of NY Presbyterian and has a good cardiac unit, but they don't do heart transplants. Those procedures are done at Cornell's sister hospital, Columbia, on the Upper West Side. The doctors and administrators had already decided that this one doesn't make the list so it didn't matter.

We found him in an ICU, which was not a good sign. Philip was in a bed in a small section of the cardiac wing. He was in a private room but the walls were all glass. It made it feel as if all the patients were sharing one big suite, like in a college dorm. The rooms were very small and the bed, patient, and connected tubes and IVs and catheters and measuring devices took up most of the space in each, making the patient look sort of like a fly, stuck in the middle of a small and mostly white spider web. When we entered Philip's room he shifted his gaze to us and no one spoke at first. Mark leaned in and kissed his cheek and sat in the chair beside him and took his hand and held it. I remained standing by the doorway. Philip's eyes were alert and bright, but his coloring was bad. He looked slightly gray and ashen, somewhat yellowish, and it made him appear older. He was bloated and puffy and didn't look all that different from some of the patients I've seen in late stage renal failure.

"Who are we suing?" I asked.

"I'm starting with God," Philip said in the rumbling baritone voice of someone who had just awoken.

"Good luck serving him," I added.

"Hadn't thought of that."

"My mom is coming to New York, Jack," Mark said. "She's coming down to see you," he said to Philip.

"Is she?" I said casually, and nodded my head. Carrie. She'd be a good advocate for him, actually. She might even get him on the list, not that it would matter. He'd just languish there for months and no committee would ever decide to give him a healthy heart, no matter who his father was. From what Philip and Mark related from the doctors it sounded like they could probably extend his life several more months by installing an L-VAD but it's a temporary fix. No one lives on an L-VAD for more than a year, usually less.

✦

If it was only a few years earlier I could have gotten him on a plane to China. We could have gone there with a suitcase of American currency and paid off every fuck with his hand out without some-how attracting enough attention to be thrown in prison. We could have saved this kid, this sharp and cool kid who did nothing wrong other than get sick. They wouldn't put him on the list in New York because he has AIDS despite the fact that every single one of those doctors knew that with a healthy heart he could live for ten or twenty years.

Carrie.

Could she possibly still exist somewhere? Do people still exist when they leave your life and you don't see them or speak to them or touch them and twenty years go by? Is she brilliant and funny and beautiful only now with softer edges and some wrinkles in the corners of her eyes? Does it still say "justice" on her lower back, in Chinese? Did she have an entire life, all completely outside of those two years we spent together in New York so long ago? The thought of it was overwhelming. I excused myself to go and make a call. I didn't want to have that particular conversation while wandering through public hallways, so I left the building. I made my way down Sixty-eighth, and turned right and then north onto York Avenue. He picked up on the first ring.

✦

"Wallace, it's Jack."

"Been waiting to hear from you. Are we going to do this?"

"The guy who needs that part, the big replacement part, he's from New York?" I had to be certain.

"How do you know that?" he asked, casually.

"You said early thirties, rich family . . ."

"That's right, Jack," he said, quietly and suspiciously.

"What's the guy do for a living?"

"Jack—"

"Just tell me what he does."

"You're starting to make me uncomfortable again, Jack. Why are you asking me questions like that?"

"Wallace, for ten years we've done very well together. I've never even asked you to have a social drink. I'm not asking for a meeting or your fucking home address, so don't get jumpy. Just tell me because I am asking, because I'm Jack and you know me and I need you to tell me this. What does this guy do for a living?"

"He's a lawyer."

CHAPTER TWENTY-THREE:
MICHELLE

July twenty-third was my second visit with Mark to go see Philip at the hospital. We wound our way through the hallways and into the cardiac unit and found a beautiful, thin woman with long, dark hair trailing behind her bent over Philip's bed. It only took a fraction of a second before something in my brain rushed a signal down to my heart saying, "Keep the pace! Don't send in the adrenaline." I knew it before she turned around. She wore a smart, white, button-down blouse and I knew that somewhere beneath it the Chinese symbol for Justice was emblazoned across her lower back. I stood still in the doorway, with Mark a half a step in front of me.

She hugged Mark and looked over his shoulder at me. "Jack," Carrie said softly and crossed the small room and took my face in her hands and kissed me on the cheekbone and then embraced me. A mantra kicked in somewhere in my mind saying, "Stay calm" over and over and over and I couldn't really hear what Mark or she might have been saying. My eyes were closed too. It went on for what felt like a long time. Then she stepped back, creating a small space between us that allowed us to face each other and she whispered, "I'm glad you know him," and no one else could hear her but me. No one else in the world.

✦

"He's a really good kid, Jack," Carrie said to me, still speaking very quietly so Mark and Philip couldn't hear us.

"I know."

"Philip too. He doesn't deserve this," she said, and it sounded just a little bit as if Carrie understood what I did for a living and was asking me to take a job.

I nodded but didn't say anything.

"I'm in town for another day or two but I'm going back to Boston for a while after that. Do you want to get together for dinner? Maybe we could talk?"

My gaze was locked on her eyes and in them I was peering into a different time. *Does she have any idea? Could she even imagine the degree to which I was still safe in her apartment near NYU with her, some time twenty years ago?* I didn't respond at first. *Mark knew about Billy Kimball. She knows me. Carrie knows everything, perhaps. Her question hurt me. Of course I want to have dinner with you, Carrie Franco, but what could I do about it?*

"Jack?" she asked again gently.

"All right," I said. I wanted to decline, but it was ridiculous to pretend that I might.

✦

When I left the hospital, it was looking like it might rain. The clouds were blending, throwing what looked like a dull gray dust-blanket over New York, and I just started walking down York Avenue. I didn't really have a particular destination other than downtown, simply because that's where one goes. I walked down Second, with the flow of traffic, past the Fifty-Ninth Street Bridge. The only way to save Philip was to have Mel Wolff do it at Royston. Wallace would make three million dollars. I would earn two million. Somewhere in a shanty-town near Jozi a family would learn that their brother or their son had died on the operating table while selling a kidney. It was his own fault anyway. Pierre would laugh about it over drinks at the Michelangelo. Wolff would sleep fine. In the forties I turned south on Third Avenue. Could I do this? I want to help him but I can't do this. I can't. I needed Scotch to think more clearly.

The news was flooded with nonsense about the debt-ceiling crisis. The US Congress couldn't agree on a plan to raise the amount of borrowing our government is allowed. The US was about to default on its debts for the first time. Our triple-A credit rating was in jeopardy and we all knew that the reign of this empire, at least to some degree, was beginning to come to a close. Maybe it didn't matter at all anyway—that priest in California had miscalculated the End of Days. On May twenty-second, with the sun still shining and the birds still chirping, he must have taken out his abacus and a few lizard toes and figured out that he'd done the math wrong. The world was going to end on October twenty-first, not May twenty-first. It would have made things much simpler if he had just been right the first time.

I passed construction site scaffoldings and waded across crowded avenues, sidestepping double-length buses. I kept heading south, occasionally turning west and inward toward the middle of Manhattan, and then south again . . . and I eventually got to 38th and Lexington when I finally decided to stop walking and get a drink.

◆

It was late afternoon but the bar was almost empty. There was no music on when I first arrived and only a handful of people were scattered at a few tables and at the bar. I got a bar stool and ordered a Macallan's neat with an ice-water back. *Eighteen years*, I thought. After two or three scotches I asked the bartender for a piece of paper and a pen. It was my intention to begin making notes about my plan, start outlining some of the details. The paper remained unmarked. By the time it passed six o'clock and the bar started to fill up with some local happy-hour patrons I had a good five or six drinks in me. I'd killed off what was left of one bottle of Macallan's and the bartender had to retrieve another from the basement.

I got up to go to the bathroom and took the Scotch with me. I placed it on the glass shelf underneath the mirror in the bathroom while I peed. I swigged from it before I placed it down again to wash my hands. I leaned on the sink and stared into my own eyes in the mirror—the eyes that are so much like Mark's—and I knew then that I would do it. All those years, I could have done much better. I felt like crying. My eyes got blurry and moist. I spit into the sink. I could have built a law practice. I could have tried. I turned on the cold water and splashed it on my face and ran my fingers through my hair and did it a few more times, cupping the water in my hands. Then I grabbed a paper towel and wiped off my face but my neck and shirt were still wet, and by the time I reached the door, it was dripping down again from my hair.

I opened the door to leave the small, candle-lit bathroom, and took two steps into the tight hallway. It was early, but dark inside the bar, and there was electronica playing softly. People were swirling by and the absence of smoke was somehow oddly off-putting. I was glad when they outlawed smoking in bars in New York, but it also diminished the allure of quietly getting drunk in public. I miss it now. They should make smoking legal in bars again—if not mandatory. Bars and smoking and driving without seatbelts . . .

I was stopped there in the hallway between a thin glass table and the bathroom doors behind me. There was water in my eyes and I didn't know if it was water from the sink or tears—probably some of both. Then my vision sharpened and she was there, a few steps away, standing out somehow from the bar and the room and the crowd.

◆

Shit, I remember thinking. *It's so primal.* How could I notice a woman, even then, in the midst of all that was happening? But I did. Then I realized that my mouth was slightly open and slowly closed my lips. My eyes met hers and I felt self-conscious. I stood there, stuck in the middle of the hallway, getting nudged back and forth by people squeezing by me to go pee. I still clutched a drink in my left hand, and with the heel of my right hand I dabbed at my eyes trying to look like I was only rubbing them. I had barely blinked but she was standing right there. She was beautiful. I tried not to react.

"Are you . . . ? Do you need help or something?" she asked. She was smiling and sipped a cranberry-colored cocktail, pursing her lips around one of those thin black cocktail straws. I once read that whoever speaks first will always dominate a relationship. She seemed sincere, gently sarcastic, and flirtatious—all at the same time. I still hadn't spoken when she added, "Wait"—her forehead furrowed a bit—"*do* you?" This time she was serious.

"Do I?" I repeated.

"Do you need help?"

"No, of course not," I said, chuckling and forcing a smile onto my face.

"Then you know that you're soaking wet?"

"I am aware of that," I replied softly, nodding a little. I was smiling, slightly but confidently. "Someone had better fix that sink or they'll be hearing from my lawyer," I said, sort of half-heartedly joking, barely making the effort.

"Sure." Another big sip.

"What's your name?" I asked. There were people pushing by us and the music was soft but still out of place.

"You look like *you're* a lawyer," she said, not really grinning enough to seem playful.

"Lawyers can have lawyers."

"So you are. Hmm. That was easy."

"Yeah," I replied, "it was." I already felt helpless. And somehow the conversation didn't feel like it usually did—like a negotiation or the preamble to an acquisition. Instead of comforting me, it made me sad. Maybe something was opening in me, and maybe Mark had caused that, but maybe it was just a wound.

"You're completely drenched. I mean, there's water running down your neck. It's all over the top of your shirt. Did you spill something?"

I laughed a little again. "Clearly," I said, still smiling. "Jack Trayner," I added, extending my free hand. "Your name?"

She took my hand and shook it casually while saying, "Michelle. You know, you're a mess. You're wrecked, Jack." She smiled and sipped again, gently making fun of me.

"I am. I'm wrecked."

◆

I guess I just felt like Jack Trayner when I walked out of that bathroom and saw Michelle and then we talked. Inside each of us is a little polygraph that lights up something in our hearts when we are in alignment with "truth." I told her the truth then and I want to do that now about everything. In the first moments of an important meeting, the less one tries the better one does. It's just like golf—the harder you try to kill the ball, the more likely you are to shank it. I couldn't have tried any less and I think it was appealing to her. I didn't even try to appear as if I wasn't trying.

"I'm soaking wet, I'm drunk, and I'll tell you what else, Michelle. I don't even know what bar we're in. And that's the truth. Quite a thing." And I nodded my head and swigged some of my drink. I hit it straight and long right up the middle of the fairway.

"Yeah. Very impressive," she said. "Come with me, Jack. I think my friends may get a kick out of you."

That's how things start sometimes.

CHAPTER TWENTY-FOUR:
CARRIE TOMORROW

*C*arrie and I will arrange to meet at an upscale, old Italian Ris- torante on the Upper East Side near the hospital. I'll suggest an early dinner at six so she can come directly from visiting Philip, but also because it will feel safer to meet her earlier in the evening, when it's still light outside, when the ghosts might still be sleeping. We'll meet at the restaurant and she'll be dressed casually in a blue and black printed sundress that will cling to her thin frame, and wear sandals on her feet. She will still be beautiful and I'll resent that she won't appear to have put on a single pound in twenty years.

"Do you want to split a salad?" she'll ask.

"Sure," I'll reply automatically, uncomfortable with the suggestion.

"The arugula?"

"Okay."

I won't believe we're there, that she's there, discussing salad choices. I'll be reeling a little and order a double Scotch to help me get a hold of myself and keep it all in check. Carrie will order a Char- donnay. She'll decide to try the artichoke lasagna; I'll get the steak, *although I won't think I can eat. We will of course. And we'll talk about law school, and people we knew, and the law and Boston and what Mark did in junior high. We'll talk about when Mark came out, and his first boyfriend and when he broke his leg in eighth grade by falling off a fence. We'll talk about Philip too. We won't talk much about ourselves, and we won't talk about the "us" that ended twenty years before until the dinner is nearly over.*

After I pay the check Carrie will say, "Jack, what are you doing now?" Her question will hang in the air with the impact of a job offer or perhaps a marriage proposal. At least it will feel that way to me. I won't respond and she'll add, "Come back to my hotel, come have a drink. Let's hang out and drink and talk about things."

"Like we used to?" I'll ask her.

"Fuckin' A," she'll say with a wry smile.

I'll pause, and we'll look at each other, unsmiling, and I'll quietly say, "All right," and we'll push our chairs back from the table at the same time. This is what I imagine.

◆

In the cab on the way to the midtown W Hotel we'll kiss passionately, my right arm draped behind the nape of her neck, my left hand clutching at her breasts beneath her sheer sundress. I won't think about her husband, or her, or me, or Philip, or Mark, or things like love or death and will only think about what I will not want to feel. I'll want the absence of pain, the absence of loss and longing—and let her be the balm on my wound. She owes me that. Let her give me more than she has. Give back. It'll be like coke, like unwrapping a gram, like going forward on a rollercoaster. That rush. The rush of "feeling better." Finally.

We'll go to the bar and order vodka martinis and gulp at the cold, straight vodka but then forego the drinks and agree to go upstairs. I'll pay the tab and take her hand and we'll go to her room on the eighth floor of the W and open the door with the card key causing a metallic click of the bolt. Without speaking we'll undress each other quickly, not frenzied, but with purpose. I'll take her breast into my mouth and think, "Ahh . . ." *and then allow my mantra to return and repeat,* "Don't think, don't think, don't think, don't think," *and push my hand up under her dress and pry my fingers into the wetness between my Carrie's legs and oh God to be there again. She'll rub my crotch and then unbutton my pants and take me in her hand and then place it in her mouth and then soon I will be pushing myself inside of her, on top of my love Carrie, my mouth on top of hers, tongues twisted together and me inside of her and we'll make love again. And time will fall away. Evaporate, and surrender to me. This is what I pray.*

Then, there will be a moment when I will stop, and my vision will focus and our eyes will meet, despite us, and she'll say, "Do it more."

"I still. . . ."

"What?"

"Nothing," *I'll whisper, perched on my forearms, lording over Carrie Franco, inside of her, where I shouldn't be.*

"Finish, Jack," *she'll whisper.*

"I still—"

"You still love me?"

"I still . . . don't feel better."

Carrie will stroke the back of my head with her fingertips. She'll lean her face up to kiss my lips with her lips. We'll renew the motion of sex and I'll come right inside of her and the mélange of feelings will all be there, like the myriad of colors on a palate, all waiting to be chosen and used to have pictures painted with them.

PART V:
THE REPLACEMENT
HEART

CHAPTER TWENTY-FIVE: MY DINNER WITH CARRIE

M eeting Michelle on that particular day, July 23rd, seems to be significant. I'm not suggesting that the world has some kind of a plan—I abandoned Jesus a lifetime ago and all gods are vindictive and good with a grudge—but it was not accidental, and that is a strange realization to walk around with. I had just left Philip and Mark at the hospital; I had dinner plans with Carrie the next evening.

"Sit here," Michelle said to me that day, offering me the only empty chair, and leaving me feeling just a bit emasculated.

"No, please," I said, motioning toward the chair, and she took it without hesitation. She was smiling—took the chair *and* emasculated me. She did it in just two words and then I stood beside her feeling as if I was somehow her attendant.

"This is Jack, everyone. Jack . . . what did you say again?" she asked, referring to my last name.

"Smith. Jack Smith," I said, extending my hand to some of her friends at the table.

"No, really?" she asked.

"Jack Trayner."

I suppose it was my private joke with myself. *Look at me*, I thought, "*so completely fed up and out of control that I am giving out my real last name. Tomorrow I'll go out in the cold without a sweater . . .*" But I was definitely leaving the business.

"Michelle Hammond," she said, taking my hand. I nodded. I finally felt invited when she uttered her last name.

"Jack's drunk," she said to the table, "he's kind of wet, as you can plainly see, and he claims to not even know what bar he is in or why."

"Well, 'e'll fit right in, this one," some guy with an Australian accent said. "Martin," he said, and shook my hand. He had a suit on but no tie. He wasn't well-shaved and his hair was roughed up as if he were about to go onstage with an indie rock band. His elbow was braced on the table for support, face angled down at his drink. He was cocked.

"You all work together?" I asked, and I shook a hand or two and made a little small talk and she trusted me enough, right away, to turn and talk to someone else when I had only joined her group a moment before. "Anderson-Compton," someone said, "interactive advertising." Someone else said, "Agency work, constant stress." "Working for Michelle . . . ," someone quipped with a smile and roll of the eyes.

"Me?" I uttered, when asked about my line of work.

"Radical jihadist," Michelle said on my behalf. "Just look at him."

Michelle was so damn noticeable, and I was struck, yet I was in several places all at once in my mind—long ago, and now, and soon-to-come.

✦

Carrie and I arranged to meet at an upscale, old Italian Ristorante on the Upper East Side near the hospital. I suggested an early dinner at six so she could come directly from visiting Philip, but also because it felt safer to meet her earlier in the evening, when it was still light outside, when the ghosts might still be sleeping. We met at the restaurant and she was dressed casually in a blue and black printed sundress that clung to her thin frame, and wore sandals on her feet. She was still beautiful and I resented that she didn't appear to have put on a single pound in twenty years.

"Do you want to split a salad?" she asked.

"Sure," I replied automatically, uncomfortable with the suggestion.

"The arugula?"

"Okay."

I couldn't believe we were there, that she was there, discussing salad choices. I was reeling a little and ordered a double Scotch to help me get hold of myself and keep it all in check. Carrie ordered a Chardonnay. She decided to try the artichoke lasagna; I got the steak, although I didn't think I could eat. We did of course. And we talked about law school, and people we knew, and the law and Boston and what Mark did in junior high. We talked about when Mark came out, and his first boyfriend and when he broke his leg in eighth grade by falling off a fence. We talked about Philip too. We did not talk much about ourselves, and we didn't talk about the "us" that ended twenty years before until the dinner was nearly over.

After I paid the check Carrie said, "Jack, what are you doing now?" Her question hung in the air with the impact of a job offer or perhaps a marriage proposal. At least it felt that way to me. I didn't respond and she said, "Come back to my hotel, come have a drink. Let's hang out and drink and talk about things."

"Like we used to?" I asked her.

"Fuckin' A," she said with a wry smile.

"I can't get that kid a heart, Carrie." And we stopped dancing around it entirely. The restaurant was real, and Carrie was real, but I was New York Jack, and too many years had slipped between me and the plans I should have made. Happy endings are uncommon.

"What?"

"I wish I could."

"Do you think I want to sleep with you so you'll help Philip?" she said calmly and directly. Carrie.

"I'm just saying that I can't."

"Is that what you think I was doing?"

"I have no idea."

"Really?" she said. "Because I would, Jack. I would sleep with you a hundred times if it would help him. I'd sleep with *anyone* a hundred times if it would help him. Please."

I had fantasized about having a dinner like that with Carrie on and off for twenty years. I had never called her. I had never tried to contact her or to go see her and try to fix things, but I had never let it go either. I never realized quite how strange that was until I was again sitting across a table from her.

"Carrie," I said, "I would help him if I could. You wouldn't have to ask. Even now, all the shit we went through at the end and all the shit I've turned my life into ever since then, I still don't think there's anything I wouldn't do for you. Or to help Mark. That kid is the only beautiful thing I have ever been a part of. He's great, Carrie. He's like you," I said and found myself smiling. It was a parental smile. "If Philip needed a kidney," I continued, "I'd have it fixed by the end of the week."

"That really is what you do?" she asked in a whisper.

"That's what I do."

"I don't need to know details, but that's what you *do*? That's your career?"

I nodded and said nothing.

"Then can't you help him somehow?"

"A heart is different. And he's got AIDS and despite who I know or who his father is . . . some problems just can't be fixed."

"Don't say that, Jack."

"Carrie, I'll try, but Harold Lauer is talking to a guy now who is probably the right guy anyway. It's a small world in my business. I hear things. He's already talking to the best guy to help them."

"That's good. I've spoken to Harold Lauer. He's determined to help him, and he's a very capable man. But I was talking about you, Jack . . . Twenty years ago I was a kid too. You always thought I had it so together, but I was just a kid too, and then I was a pregnant kid. I had ideas about what my career should look like. Now I'm a mother . . ."

I smiled. "What are you talking about, Carrie?" I asked with a laugh.

"I just want you to be okay," she said, her eyes welling up with tears.

I would never insult Carrie by appeasing her with the answer she wanted to hear, as opposed to the truth. "Some problems just can't be fixed," I said.

✦

We stared at each other across the table and she reached out and took my hand. I gasped a little and hoped she hadn't heard me. Suddenly, we were back in her room at NYU. We weren't fighting about coke or the future. It was before then. We had found each other. We were in sync and we laughed all the time and we were better together than alone. We stayed up until five just to talk about random philosophies and laugh about people we knew and delight in feeling together. Carrie was the Xanax in my pocket, the bullet in my gun that I would never use. She wasn't in my life now, but she was alive and functioning out there somewhere in the world and I felt better to be reassured about that.

"You still have snow globes?" I asked her.

"Snow globes?"

"Like you had in college. You had a few. Did you collect them or something?"

"I don't know. I don't really remember."

"Oh." I said.

"I don't think we should see each other for a while, Jack," she said.

I watched her attentively but said nothing.

"Jack?"

"It was great seeing you again, Carrie," I said.

"Yeah, I should go."

She'll get a taxi, I thought. *She'll call Ken to check in when she gets back to the hotel. She's probably having brunch with Mark tomorrow. That's good.* My palms were flat on the table. I kept them there as if I were trying to do a magic trick and levitate the whole thing. I was not. I was trying not to fall over.

CHAPTER TWENTY-SIX:
JACK AND MICHELLE

At the end of July I was holding off Wallace by telling him that I was working on it and wanted to make it happen. Philip was at Cornell. He was stable but in the ICU and my guess was that he would not be leaving unless it was to go to South Africa, or a cemetery. Despite those circumstances I emailed Michelle and flirted like a schoolboy. She agreed to have dinner with me. Bistro Margeaux in Soho. It was great. Drinks at Café Gitane in Nolita the next week. That documentary about the tightrope walker who tiptoed between the Twin Towers that Michelle had been wanting to see. Popcorn and bottles of water and holding hands in the dark like kids.

A few weeks later, on a Friday evening, I was on my way back from JFK. I had just returned from Tucson. I had put off getting the $200K for the liver into the safe deposit boxes because I didn't want to leave her, but after a week or so I felt compelled to go. I hated keeping too much cash in my closet under the luggage. I told her I had to go to London for some sort of corporate closing.

When I called Michelle from the car she said that if I picked her up at her apartment, she'd let me buy her dinner.

"I might still go to the Hamptons tomorrow," she said. "You wouldn't want to come . . . ?"

"I don't know," I replied, driving down Third toward her place in Soho.

"I just want to get out of the city but I don't have the energy to deal with going now," she said when she came downstairs and got in the car. It was already about nine. She had peep-toe pumps on. Her legs were glistening as if they were covered with a thin sheet of condensation.

"We could go somewhere," I said.

"You mean go to the beach? Now?" she asked, looking ahead and sounding tired.

"Or somewhere else."

I turned my car east, onto the FDR, up toward the Thruway, and headed north. "To the woods," I said to her. She pursed her lips, furrowed her eyebrows a bit.

"Woods? Jack, I don't even have a change of clothes."

"We'll buy some."

More nodding. One eyebrow lifted perhaps. I didn't know why she was going along. I didn't know why she let me call her late and then show up at her apartment and sleep with her. I didn't even know why she took my calls. I'm not that funny anymore. I'm not charming. I don't know why she let me lie to her when surely she doubted most of it, or at least some. I don't know why she didn't ask me about my life, like the others always did. Instead, in my car that night under the star-filled country sky above the Thruway, I asked her, "Why don't you ever talk about where you're from?"

"Funny, coming from you."

"I'm from Queens. I've told you that."

"Whatever."

"Flushing. You know that."

"Yes."

"So why don't you talk about it?" I asked her.

"Because it doesn't matter. It's not like I try *not* to talk about it."

"I'm interested."

"Then Harrisburg."

"Pennsylvania?"

"Uh, huh. But I don't go there or anything and I moved to New York right after college. It just doesn't matter much."

"Do you have family there?"

"No."

"I don't know," I said, tentatively, "you're just very unusual, you know that?"

She turned toward me in my Jag's bucket seat and said, "I am? I'm unusual?"

"Well, most women I've met, they like to talk about those kinds of things. Where people are from, their families. It's just a little unusual."

"Unusual," she mimicked quietly.

"Yes. It is."

"Well, let's talk about something else, then. Something more usual. Why don't you tell me about London, Jack? Did you see Big Ben? Was it rainy?"

"Where does your mother live now?" I asked.

"She's dead, like my father. But you probably know that, Jack."

"What does that mean?"

"It means that you measure and gauge and evaluate every nuance of everything anyone says. Or do you not know that? Perhaps you aren't quite so aware when it comes to yourself. Do you not know that you spin and misdirect every detail about yourself? You're pretty unusual yourself, pal. And my parents died when I was a kid, but I don't need you to feel bad. It was a long time ago and I'm fine."

It was silent for an uncomfortable moment and then I just said, "Okay."

"And we've been in the car over an hour now and I want to have sex soon, so start looking for a place to take me before I change my mind. Is that unusual?"

It was silent for another long moment. Then I said, "No, M'am," sarcastically and quietly. She merely nodded a bit, smiling slightly. Point made.

✦

About an hour or so after we had sex in a roadside motel, and before we fell asleep, Michelle said, "My mother killed herself when I was ten. I was an only child. So when my dad got cancer that made me his caretaker. I was still in high school."

"Oh hell," I whispered.

"I was shitty at it," she said softly. "He died when I was nineteen."

"I'm sorry."

"That's when I left Princeton for a year and just went to Europe."

"To get away?"

"No," she replied, seeming confused. Nothing more was said.

My own mother is still alive. I have an older sister who lives in California now. They are Mark's grandmother and aunt. We don't speak anymore. I lied about some of those things too. I couldn't forgive either one of them for not even trying to stop him. I wasn't the first kid to get abused by an alcoholic father, and I didn't have to blame them too. Unusual. I made my own aloneness.

✦

The next day Michelle and I parked at Minnewaska and walked along a trail that led around a mountain lake. There was a gray moistness permeating the woods but the scent was fresh and alive, with the smell of ozone in the air. Gravel and wood chips and branches crunched under the sneakers we had bought at a sporting goods store in New Paltz.

Michelle said, "I could buy some land here. Maybe near a lake like this." Everything was quiet. There were very few people on the trail. When we passed them we just nodded and half-smiled and respected each other's private moments with nature. "Build a house," she said. "That would be really nice." I didn't say anything. "Maybe not. I couldn't do it alone."

"Why would you have to do it alone?" I asked her.

"You're a piece of work, Jack," she said, feigning a little laughter.

Philip was dying at Cornell and I was casually hiking around a lake with my new semi-girlfriend, who already found me to be inaccessible. Yes, I am. I am Jack Piece-Of-Work.

✦

In the short time Michelle and I have been together I've had several cell phone numbers and some of those numbers have already changed. She's asked me about it once or twice, teasing, but she's never pressed me. I think that Michelle just hoped for the best. But I have sometimes wondered why she does *not* wonder why I have three different cell phones and why the numbers keep changing. This has been the ongoing and unspoken discourse between us now for months. We didn't talk much about my work. "International law..." "Oh," she'd say. "Um hmm." Multi-national deals. Contracts. There must be currency issues sometimes . . . She knew there was something unseemly about me but it was not a problem because for some reason she seemed to like it. And what about Mark?

✦

A day or two after we got back to the city I heard from Wallace again.

"Jack, this guy, this guy has late-stage cardiomyopathy. AIDS complications. What's going on?"

"I want to do it," I said.

"Of course," Wallace said. "But if he has to travel we need to get going. If this guy starts to tank and it's too late we're going to lose a lot of money, New York."

"Something like this isn't done the usual way. Frankly, I have no idea how it's done and don't want to know anyway. But I'm going to have to go there and talk to them again. I am going to have to go there and set it up personally. It's too big."

"Then may I suggest," he said, "that you book a flight?"

"I'll handle it. Just sit tight. He's stable for now."

"Did I say that?"

"What?"

"That he's stable?" There was tense silence.

Then, I said, "You'd be screaming bloody murder if he wasn't, Wallace. Relax. I am on it and Jack is getting this guy the part."

"You mentioned L-VADs before. Do you know much about them?"

"Why?"

"Because I don't want us to lose five million fucking dollars. I'm thinking that if he starts to tank that maybe we could keep him afloat with an L-VAD long enough to get him on a plane and get him there. Maybe if we could get enough money up front we could walk away with the deposit when he finally dies overseas. They might advance half of it. That's still a lot of money, Jack. Someone has to be thinking about contingencies."

"That's not good business."

"It's circumstantial. Sometimes things don't work out."

"It's not a good plan, Wallace."

"Well, a lot is at stake here. We need a Plan B."

"Plan A is fine. I am going to get this guy the part and you don't need to worry about contingencies."

"Well, it's getting into the late innings. This is too big a bet not to hedge," Wallace said quietly.

It was all shit. I was talking to a guy who would have gladly sold Philip to a black-market cadaver dealer as long as he got his fee—that's how much he cared. I knew that Wolff could do this at Royston. Pierre could set up the seller. They clipped that poor bastard's liver. True, it will grow back—but only if he survived the post-op trauma after losing a kidney and a third of his liver and getting minimal medication and no proper aftercare . . . Okay, one can't re-grow a heart. Sometimes you can't even mend a broken one. Pierre Kleinhans would greedily accept the assignment, and Mel Wolff would rationalize the whole situation so poetically that by the time he was done, and four or five double Scotches were in my gut, I might even believe that he was right and we were noble.

"There's something else." Wallace suddenly said. "I talked to The Siren."

"Please tell me you're joking," I nearly whispered in response.

"It's getting done, Jack. I am tired of this shit, and need a break, and I am not passing up this fee."

"Wallace, there is no Siren. Those stories about kidney thieves from Vegas are impossible. You know that."

"Tell that to the man I spoke with."

"If you spoke to someone who called himself The Siren . . . just think for a minute about who that man might really be, what he might really want from someone like you. Please stop it. I am on it. Just let me handle it."

"I know that guy's a risk, but I am not passing. So tell me now, Jack. Swear it. Tell me you're New York Jack and we're good and it gets done and I'll forget him. But think, if you were me, and you needed someone who had the guts to cut out part of a man against his will, would it be so crazy to call someone with experience?"

"Maybe not if he was real. But whoever this guy is, Wallace, I am telling you this for me but I am also telling you this for you, whoever this guy is, you ever meet that guy and you're going to prison, or you're dead."

"Then tell me what I want to hear and make it good."

I sighed. I was the protagonist at the end of "1984" when he finally admits that two plus two is five. I would have said anything. "I'm New York Jack, Wallace. We're good and it is getting fucking done."

◆

Murder is a black and heavy word. We've become desensitized to it, but still it sits like a brick on the brain. Can one even say "murder" in a sentence that isn't a reference to a news report or television crime show? To my surprise, I could, and that carried weighty implications. In China it would still have been murder, but it would have been crudely rationalized by a crooked legal system because it would have been a death-row prisoner who was due to die soon anyway.

Who's to say that the parts contained within your body remain somehow your property, or the property of your descendents, after your death? If we had "presumed consent" in this country, even with the option to opt out, a large part of the organ shortage would be solved with one swipe of a pen and parasites like me would be out of business. But here in Jesus-land-America some people seem to think He demands that you never give anyone a kidney. I haven't read the Bible in thirty years, and I didn't listen much in Church as a kid, but isn't that completely ass-backwards?

✦

The plan was this: I tell Kleinhans that we need a heart and he goes into his vast database of potential sellers who had been tissue-typed in advance. He finds an O positive male between 160 and 190 pounds, between fifteen and fifty years old, with various other matching criteria that matter for a heart (and which would also dictate how much cyclosporine Philip would need to take—when his system could handle very little). Pierre would sign up that guy to sell a kidney, advance him a few thousand rand, bring him to Royston where Philip would already be prepped, and then Mel Wolff would cut his heart out. Pierre's people would tell the guy's family that there were complications and he died on the operating table while selling a kidney. "He's lucky he didn't end up in jail," they'd tell his family. "Do *you* want to end up in jail?" they'd say to the one family member who asked questions. That's what they would say to the indignant one. And that would be it. There are certainly no investigations or autopsies done in South Africa on blacks who die in well-regarded hospitals.

Wolff had asked for two hundred and fifty grand. Wallace suggested that "on this first one" we voluntarily pay double what he asked. "It's a good investment, Jack," he had said. It was notable that Wallace was suddenly looking out for Wolff and our relationship with him. It was also notable that he had a long-term view.

I thought about it constantly. Could I do this? The money was no longer my focus. I could do it for Philip, but mostly for Mark, and for the right reasons. Philip was a good man. He had integrity, even if he was a little obnoxious about it. It was about Mark. I have never wanted something the way I wanted to save Philip for Mark. It was a deep and powerful feeling, tugging at my gut. I desperately wanted to do one good and important thing that I could chalk up on the right side of my karma ledger.

Mark. Carrie's son. And mine. I never knew him, because she was right to keep him from me. I have hurt so many people. I've turned down so many beautiful things that this life has to offer. Every single day, on every street corner in New York there were invitations that I side-stepped. One God-forsaken organ was all I needed. Frankly, Philip needing a heart was a great gift to me.

I needed to organize the transaction and also plan for contingencies. I didn't know if he'd ever be able to travel, or from where I could source the part. But one thing is certain, I remember thinking, I need to get this guy over to Columbia Presbyterian right now. Just in case. That's the first thing. We've got to move him to Columbia.

CHAPTER TWENTY-SEVEN:
LOST TIME

Over Labor Day, Michelle and I rented a suite in Montauk and drove out Thursday night in the rain. My telescope was in the trunk and I was disappointed because I had wanted to show her some stars. I felt the pressure of time growing short. The tip of Long Island is different from the Hamptons, only a half hour away. It's become more "hip" (and therefore more crowded) in recent years, but there's still an element that remains dark and calm and natural. There's a lot less light pollution. I wanted us to look together into the light from the past in the skies above the beach, but it rained. I'd like to show Mark that as well. Instead Michelle and I ate lobsters at Gossman's among families and strange couples and some elderly and weathered folks who looked better suited for Boca. We drank Scotch at a local bar with fish mounted on the walls and a pool table in the back and a few old men sitting alone on bar stools listening to loud rock songs from the eighties. That was good too.

I was always proud to be seen with Michelle. She's one of the few people I know who is capable of making fun of you in a way that makes you feel cared for, leaves you feeling better about your-self. She genuinely meant no harm. Behind her sharp-witted barbs she was simply kind. From the beginning, I thought, *She should run for office.* It seemed like everyone around her wanted her atten-tion, yet more and more it was reserved for me.

That night we left the tacky curtains open, their paisley pattern bunched up at the sides of the large window. We let the blackness of the beach sky into our room and the raindrops blew into the glass with the sound of a soft and far-away drum roll. The water glistened with the light of the one lamp shining above the beach, beyond our hotel, but mostly it was dark and the sky looked like syrup.

Michelle whispered, "It's like we're alone out here."

I was drunk. We did not have sex. "Maybe we should just stay here," I said.

"Stay here?"

"Yeah."

"Forever?" she whispered and I could see her smiling in the dim light, teasing me.

"We should. We should move to the beach. Just live here," I said.

"Could you do that? Could you stay with me?" she asked, and the delicate balance of that moment was splintered.

I shrugged my shoulders and shook my head as if to say, "I don't know."

Then she said, "You could, Jack."

"Yeah?" I think I was hopeful. *Please convince me, Michelle.*

"Maybe people like us. . . ." It was silent for a while, except for the rain.

"What?"

"Maybe we could, is all . . ."

That's when I would usually make a joke, or sometimes leave. With most women, that would prompt me to put my pants back on and drive back to the hotel bars in downtown Manhattan looking for new friends before last call.

I did neither of those things that night with her in Montauk. I pulled her in close to me and I could taste the salt that had settled on her lips. The sweat that had dried on her neck behind her small ears. I didn't say anything. To have that time together, and now, to have these memories—it's important.

I lay in bed that night and thought about Tucson. It's rarely crowded at the pool during the week. *Maybe it wasn't impossible*, I thought. *Maybe it wasn't too late.* What if I just stopped—did this one last thing and saved Philip and then stopped and settled in at my place in Tucson? What if I got a job at a local golf course as a pro teaching retirees how to let go of all of the habits that were screwing up their swings? I could convince Michelle to come and maybe we could even move to LA and she could keep working. I'd have enough money. I could go to confession. I could say, "I used to practice law in New York . . . back in the nineties . . . International mostly . . . Oh, currency issues, yeah, all that . . ." What the hell have I done for all of these years? What have I done?

Before I met Mark I don't think I could have seen Michelle the way that I do now. Sometimes when she's sleeping I try to stay awake just to have the pleasure of being in bed next to her. It's harder to do after sex but easier if I go to her place and she's already sleeping. The digital alarm clock on the dresser in her apartment makes a fake manual clicking sound when it changes hours. The vibrations of the 6 train become barely perceptible in the tunnels far below her bed between two and five in the morning on weeknights when all the world is sleeping. She grinds her teeth sometimes, but not every night. She is so perfectly real that sometimes I find her impossible to believe in. I did it then. I watched her for a long time that night in Montauk. Time is limited. Does Mark ever do that with Philip, I wonder? He's only twenty-two. I was twenty-two when I was with his mother. Does he love Philip the way I loved Carrie? When you're twenty-two you think that love changes everything. You think it matters so much and that feeling can stay with you for a long time.

There are consequences no matter how sorry one might be or how much time has passed by, like dirt thrown over the graves of our mistakes. Yet, every moment of every passing day we have choices, opportunities, one right after the other, to do what's right—or not. Now . . . now . . . and there it goes again . . . Now. Now, again.

"What is it about us?" I asked her in a whisper.

"What do you mean?"

"Why are you with me?'

"Ah, that," she said, grinning a bit. "Well, I like you because you're so deeply flawed."

"Hmm? You mean, *despite* the fact that I'm flawed?"

"No. Because." We stared into each other's eyes in that motel room. She smiled at me.

"It makes you happy to be with me?" I whispered.

"It means more to me to be understood than distracted."

"How'd you do it Michelle?" I asked quietly. "When your mom died, and then your dad, and things were hard, how'd you travel around Europe and go to school and build such a great career and, and make people like you?"

"You gotta make lemonade, Jack. It's the only thing to do."

"How'd you do that without feeling bitter?"

"I'm talking about you, Jack. *You* need to do that. It's still not too late."

I didn't say a word. I felt less alone than I had in as long as I could remember, but that made me sick with guilt.

◆

And that night in Montauk, I also had the dream again. I was at a dinner table with fine china and white linen and lace napkins. The plates were pearl white, with thin, swirling spirals of dark red along the outer edge. I was at the head of the table, dining alone. On my plate was a large piece of meat garnished with a sprig of parsley, and roasted potatoes adorned with rosemary. There were etched crystal glasses in front of me, one filled with water and one with red wine. Beyond the glasses was a floral centerpiece, thick with red and white flowers. The table was very long and I could feel the presence of unseen others in the room, outside of my field of vision.

In my left hand was an ornate fork; in my right, an elegant, all-metal steak knife. I clutched the utensils, pointed up at the ceiling, in fists that rested on the linen tablecloth. The pose was aggressive. The meat looked delicious—tender and rare but slightly blackened. It appeared to be a steak, but I didn't recognize the cut. It wasn't familiar to me. Slowly, my gaze drifted down the long, white table, past the red and white flowers. I felt a heightened sense of apprehension as the far end of the table finally came into view, twelve or fifteen feet away. There were men standing just beyond the table, and women too, all of them dressed in black. There were seven or eight of them there, and more lined up in tight rows behind them, one after another, fading back into the black shadows.

The men were all dressed in black suit pants. The women wore black or gray dresses. They were all silent. I pressed my hands down more firmly on the table. I felt sweat start to rise on my forehead, and my breathing quickened. They were all silent. As my eyes scaled very slowly up their legs it was then revealed to me that they were all shirtless. The men had no shirts at all; the women's dresses had been peeled down to the waist to display their naked bodies. The old ones, their bodies wrinkled and marked with age spots, were mostly white. The younger ones were mostly black or Latino. "Why the hell are they undressed?" I thought in a panic, my pulse quickening.

I felt compelled to begin eating. I was breathing heavily, audibly, but began to cut into the meat with the knife and fork clutched in my sweaty hands. Juice oozed from where I cut. It was a beautiful meal. It looked delicious, I thought, but there was a tension in my temples and tears began to well up in my eyes. "What?" I finally shouted at the crowd standing there. They watched me, shirtless, still and silent, and I saw that the young ones were all missing organs. Every one of them had gaping surgical wounds in their torsos, revealing emptiness where their parts had been. There was no bleeding, just raw, red tissue, each wound ragged and unique and menacing. It was monstrous. The old ones had ragged scars, red and raised lines where they had been sewed up after nephrectomies. Their expressions were not pained, but rather, blank and resigned. I shook my head as I pushed the first bite of meat past my teeth and locked my lips around it helplessly.

As I began to chew, I felt terrified. I made eye contact then with one of the women and saw that it was Marlene Brown. My heart raced as I looked at the other faces and made out Tom Walsh, his fat gut protruding over the edge of his pants, a gruesome scar on his lower left side. I saw Kimball, and he smiled very slightly. Standing right beside him, several inches shorter, was Michael the janitor. "It's good, no?" he asked me, "What?" I said quietly around a mouthful of delicious, buttery steak. I saw the faces of Lesedi, and Max from Miami, and some whose faces were familiar but whose names I could no longer remember. No. "You deserve it," Michael said to me, his Jersey accent distinct in the otherwise silent room. "That one's mine!" he added, pointing at the meat on my plate. No. I felt myself vomiting, unsure if it was coming from the dream or the waking world. I was dizzy and woke up.

✦

Michelle went to Europe after her father died because she was running *to* something. That's what she's told me. She thought that if she allowed herself to feel cheated, or victimized, that those feelings would crawl up her legs like quicksand. She was running to things of beauty, and to the old and lasting feelings of Rome or Geneva. To be surrounded by the trappings of stability and romance, and the patient pace of places that would continue to be there for everyone, forever. She met men but didn't sleep with anyone for months. She drank wine everywhere she went. She sketched, and she has the sketch books, but no one else has ever seen them. She cried sometimes, on trains, at night, and sometimes in taxi cabs, crazed with the feeling of being lost, but also in front of polished statues, and at the Louvre and on the Ponte Vecchio and at sunset in Oia, Santorini, at times when she felt terribly happy. She has explained this all to me. Now I want to see those statues, and the Louvre, and walk across the Ponte Vecchio and sit on the cliff in front of the small church that stands at the edge of Oia, facing west at sunset over the sleeping volcanoes in the bay, which Michelle has described to me.

✦

It was the middle of September before I broached the subject of moving Philip. Wallace was losing patience and while he remained controlled in our conversations, he was clearly displeased about

the pace of our progress and the risk of losing the biggest transaction of our lives. "I don't understand your methods here, New
York," he would say. Or, "Please tell me that I am reaching you on
an international roaming carrier in South Africa."

He had even begun pitching me by adding, "The kid's father
is tweaking, Jack. He is looking for other ways. What if he finds
someone else, maybe that lunatic from Dallas? What then? That
asshole will have the guy on a plane to the Philippines within
twenty-four hours for just a couple of hundred grand. Granted,
the guy would die waiting, but still, so would our fee. . . ."

✦

"Mark, it's Jack," I said as I finally began the first of several conversations I had been putting off.

"Hey. Where've you been?"

"Traveling," I lied casually. "Listen, I want to talk to you about
Philip. Are you alone?"

"Yeah. I'm at home."

"How is he?" I asked.

"The same." The same is good.

"Mark, I may be able to help him. There are some things I can
actually do to help, but I need you to coordinate this for it to work.
I can't explain all of the details, but like your mother said, I did that
thing for Billy Kimball when I was younger and . . ."

"Yeah?"

"Some of what I do, it's complicated, and there are clients that
require great confidentiality . . . Anyway, you just need to understand that I can help if you'll let me do that."

"Of course. But I'm not sure that I know exactly what you're
talking about, Jack," Mark said calmly and quietly.

"I know. Listen . . ." I was thinking about what he'd told me, about coming out to Carrie when he was only fifteen. Such a gutsy kid. "Mark, I need you to get Philip moved to Cornell's sister hospital, Columbia Presbyterian," I said. "To do that, you're going to have to talk to his father. That's the way this will go. Once he agrees that Philip needs to move, Harold Lauer can get it done in a day."

"But why?"

✦

The day that I visited Philip in the hospital the second time and first saw Carrie after all of those years, that was really the first time it occurred to me. That was the first time I started to consider yet another option. And it was gray and humid that day but it didn't rain. I just kept walking, turning south and west and south. I came out of the bathroom and Michelle was standing right there in front of me, noticing me, looking beautiful and grounded, but somehow serious. It pushed me off course.

✦

"Mark," I began carefully, "Cornell has a good cardiac practice but Columbia is where they do heart transplants."

"Jack, he can't get a transplant. You know that."

"This is the tricky part, Mark. You'll have to trust me. There's no downside to trusting me so just do it and do what I am asking. Philip has to be moved to Columbia and I can—"

"I trust you," he interjected.

"Really . . ." I said, sort of involuntarily. A moment passed without either of us speaking.

"Because my mom does. She trusts you."

"Oh. Well, he has to move, so you have to talk to his father."

"Jack, they tried to get him on the list and they won't take his name. That's why he's at Cornell. It didn't matter so they just admitted him on the east side, because it's closer to his parents' house. I mean, his father is Harold Lauer. He offered to give Mt. Sinai a new wing and they didn't take it. Even with the money his father was offering them. Because of the AIDS. But Philip's father's been saying there's a chance that he might be able to get Philip help. Apparently, he's been talking to some people who can maybe find him a donor overseas."

I thought, *that's us Lauer's talking about, me and Wallace.* Lauer should shut up, even to Mark and his family. Then I said, "That's fine, I hope he finds a donor. But Philip needs to move anyway, and you need to trust me, and you need to deal with it tomorrow, Mark. And Mark. . . ."

"What?"

"Do *not* tell Harold Lauer, or anyone, that I discussed this with you. Tell him that Columbia is just better for cardiac care and trauma. Get upset. Tell him Cornell is great but Columbia is the best, and Philip needs the very best. Lauer will relate to that. Or come up with something else, but I am not fucking around when I tell you that he has got to be moved to Columbia."

"That sounds crazy."

"I know. But do it anyway."

CHAPTER TWENTY-EIGHT: THE BEACH

A few days later Mark called to tell me that Harold Lauer was pissed about the lack of proper attention his son was getting from the orderlies and nurses at Cornell and Philip would be moved in the morning. The next day Wallace called to relate the same information.

"They just moved the guy to Columbia, Jack." He sounded restrained but angry.

"Really?" This was late September, about six weeks ago.

"Yes. Really. I need to know where we're at, Jack. When the hell are you going over there to work things out? I've been trying to get a hold of you for two days."

"I am going, Wallace. Soon. I'm going to take care of it."

"I don't understand the delay, Jack. What the hell are you waiting for? Do you know how much fucking money we could leave on the table here? The client, the guy's father, he is freaking out already about our lack of progress and now he just had the kid moved to Columbia because of you."

"These things aren't simple," I said slowly and forcefully.

"All the more reason to expedite, Jack. The guy is in precarious shape. You said they can do it. You said they have it typed out in advance."

"They do."

"So do it!" he practically yelled.

"It's still not that simple, Wallace. There are a lot of moving parts to this and there are consequences. This has to be done right. Right is more important than fast," I said, still speaking calmly.

"Jack, maybe we should have a meeting."

"We don't need a meeting."

"Do you know why they moved him? Can you think why they moved him?"

"It doesn't matter. He's going to travel."

"It's one of the leading heart transplant centers in the free fucking world, Jack. Surely you know that. Why would this guy's zillionaire father have him moved to a transplant center, right across town? Because now he apparently thinks he can get a transplant! I have no idea who else this guy is talking to but this is exactly what would go down if the people from Seattle connected with him. Even that asshole from Dallas might send him to Columbia and try to hook something up there."

"No he wouldn't, Wallace! Herman Coburn is a fucking travel agent who also happens to consult for the FBI. He's not going to pull stunts to acquire hearts in Manhattan and end up in jail for conspiracy to commit murder."

"How the hell do you know?"

"Wallace, calm down. I'm handling it. I'm talking to Wolff."

"So am I," he said much more quietly.

"What? So are you, what?"

"Talking to Wolff. At least that guy answers his phone."

I paused, and caught myself before I reacted. "You don't want to do that," I said, with my own quiet-but-threatening tone.

"Actually, I don't. But one way or another, this deal is getting done."

"Well be careful about getting too cozy with Mel Wolff, pal. Sometimes transplant clinics that are on the take get busted and everyone close to them does too."

"Are you threatening to take down Rosyton, Jack?" he said, sounding genuinely amused.

"No one's going around me."

"You're pretty close to Rosyton too, Jack."

"Who is?" I barked in reply. "A guy whose last name is Jack, and whose first name is 'New York'? Just remember, only one of us has a global network of suppliers. So cut the shit and let me do my thing, Mr. Kendrickson." There was a long pause and my cell phone felt heavy in my hand. Wallace was surely weighing his options and I simply waited.

"So it's like that now?" he said. "Now you call me Kendrickson? What other secret tidbits do you know about me, New York?"

"It doesn't have to be like anything. Just let me do my thing and handle it, handle it properly, and everyone is good and gets paid." More silence.

"That's all I want," he finally said, some of the antagonism drained from his voice. "But the clock has been ticking for too long."

"I'm handling it."

◆

When Wallace told me he'd been talking to Wolff, we both understood it for what it was, but also for what it was not. He was pressuring me, but he wasn't overtly threatening me—at least not yet. If Wallace really wanted to cut me out of the loop, Philip would have already been in recovery at Royston. Wallace was a pragmatist. He wouldn't throw a productive ten-year working relationship down the toilet if he could avoid it. Wallace probably knew the names of one or two of my doctors in the Philippines, but he didn't know them well enough to work safely without me. And Manila is not a good place to get caught breaking the law. He knew none of my contacts in Recife; he had certainly never spent any time in Moldova. What if China came back on line? It took me five years to build a network there without getting thrown into prison. Wallace knew that. He didn't need me any longer for this specific transaction, but he did need me for the future beyond it—since he was unaware that there would be none.

That was my leverage—and my disclosure about knowing his real name—but it wasn't enough that I could just ignore him or continue putting him off. Eventually Wallace's sense of caution would yield to his appetite. The minute he decided that keeping me involved was no longer worth the delay, some random resident of Alexandra with type O blood was going to turn up in the morgue at Royston, cause of death listed as post-nephrectomy complications, but the real cause would be New York Jack. They would rip out the guy's heart, sew him back up, and then claim it was sepsis. And if it went smoothly, there would suddenly be more strange deaths around the Dark City. I never signed up for complicity in systematic murder.

All those years, whether I fully believed it or not, I was helping people, saving them, and I wanted to remain on the right side of that. I was determined to get that kid a heart but I was not going to steal one from some naïve victim of a vulture like Pierre Kleinhans. If we got the heart at Royston it would have opened the floodgates to a slew of murders—and the balance in my karma account was already low enough. The door to China had been shut tight. There was no other place I felt safe enough to even raise the question— except for one. So I booked a flight to Recife to go see my friend Juan Guillermo.

Juan Guillermo is not his real name, and he's one of the few worth protecting. It's common knowledge that the hospitals in Recife are corrupt. Everything in Recife is corrupt. No one cares very much, but it's better if he remains anonymous. I hooked up with Guillermo and that schmuck Dr. de Mendoza when transplant tourism was first taking off. When I found better and more sophisticated transplant centers in places like Jozi I still continued to feed Guillermo a fairly steady diet of routine kidney patients in order to keep my suppliers diversified, and also out of regard for our association. Even after 2004, when a ring of Israeli brokers got busted for picking up sellers in Recife and shipping them off to Durbin, South Africa for the procedures, I continued to patronize his facility out of affection for its stout and humorous administrator.

In a country of enormous natural resources with a very large population and scattered pockets of deep wealth, Brazil was still completely backwards in regard to golf, but Guillermo was a prince among paupers. On his best days, if he got me drunk on the back nine, he could even close within a few strokes. I emailed Guillermo from a new account and arranged to meet to play at nine a.m. on Wednesday. I had considered having the conversation by phone, but it was not the time to get careless so I made the fifteen-hour journey.

I was staying at the Vila Rica Recife in Boa Viagem, a wealthy neighborhood on the beach, ten minutes from Guararapes International Airport. Recife is the most dangerous city in a rather dangerous country, and not the kind of place to go out sightseeing. Nearly 70 percent of the population lives in shanty-towns or *favelas*. As in Jozi, they are often right next to wealthy enclaves. However, unlike Jozi, where the shanty-town townships seem to crop up in indentations between neighborhoods, almost like puddles forming where the land is a bit low, in Recife it is the other way around. Affluent pockets of modern life spring up from a landscape of poverty; affluence is the exception, while poverty is the rule.

Recife is a tourist destination for Brazilians but not for foreigners. It is a poor city with a very high crime rate, but scattered pockets of wealth make for a satisfactory infrastructure. It's an ideal place to pick up Eighties with almost no risk of interference from law enforcement or oversight from any medical agency.

I had arranged for a driver, and on Wednesday morning we set out for the club at Caxanga at seven thirty to beat traffic and ensure a timely arrival to meet Guillermo. I didn't like to drive in Brazil. We left the beach and headed through the middle of Recife. That early, the streets were nearly deserted and we cruised swiftly through the center of the city.

We continued on a local highway, little more than a one-lane mountain road, heading northwest toward the hospital and the golf course a few minutes beyond it. Then, the driver said something to me in Portuguese which I did not understand and accelerated abruptly, throwing me back against the seat. The Mercedes we were riding in, like most cars in Recife, had blacked out windows to prevent outsiders from seeing in, but I could see out. There was a motorcycle with two men on it, back and to the left of us, in what was probably the driver's blind spot. They accelerated and pulled even with the rear window on our left side, and my driver slammed harder on the gas, jerking the car forward and past them.

"What's the problem?" I asked.

He replied in Portuguese.

"English," I said. "What do they want?"

"No good," he said.

I glanced at the speedometer; he was doing over a hundred and sixty kph, which equates to around a hundred miles per hour. He tore down the one-lane highway with the motorcycle close behind until it suddenly took a sharp left and peeled off the highway toward what I supposed was some other object of their attention.

Once they were gone for a few minutes the driver turned back over his shoulder and said, "Obrigado, Senhor. I am sorry."

"Don't be," I said, and then I caught his eye in the rearview mirror. "It's good," I said, shaken a bit. I smiled and gave him a thumbs-up. A minute later I asked, "What did they want from us?"

"To rob. Steal the money."

"Is that all? Only to rob?"

We made eye contact in the rearview mirror and he made a face that amounted to the equivalent of a shoulder shrug. *People get killed here*, I thought as we sped away. *People get killed here routinely.*

✦

We arrived at the Caxanga Golf & Country Club at about eight thirty. I changed and went out to the practice greens, where a few members were putting and chatting in quiet, private conversations. Caxanga has operated for nearly eighty years. A few years ago it got a bit of an upscale facelift but there was still a swimming pool where families sat around waiting for dad to finish playing, and it had the atmosphere more of a pedestrian middle-class country club on the Connecticut side of the Long Island Sound than of a prestigious golf course where real players sharpened their skills.

A little after nine my associate strode out onto the practice greens with a wide smile beneath his wide-brimmed hat. Juan Guillermo was a short and rotund man whose ability as a golfer far surpassed what his appearance would lead one to expect. We embraced and he said, "New York Jack," quietly, with the elegance of a gentleman, vastly different from the vulgar manner of a finder like Pierre Kleinhans or the polite pretense of Dr. Wolff.

"It's good to see you, Juan," I said affectionately.

"Maybe not. I have played a lot the last few months."

I smiled but said nothing. I'd be glad to lose a legitimate round to Juan Guillermo. What a sight that would be.

"Did you bring your good clubs, Jack?" he said with a warm smile and a lighthearted tone.

"I did."

"And you are well rested? Slept well at your four-star accommodations? I don't want any excuses when I finally beat you."

"There will be no excuses," I replied, "but neither will there be a surprise upset today."

"Ha!" he exclaimed. "New York Jack! Here in Recife. Come!" He clapped me on the back, pushing me toward the first tee.

Over the years I have probably sent Guillermo a hundred kidney buyers. I may have made him one of the richest men in Recife. There is one thing I have always found notable about playing golf with Guillermo: while he swings with the stilted motion of a plump man, the *sound* of that swing is, for some inexplicable reason, musical. I often closed my eyes to listen to the swing of other golfers. The wind generated by the motion, the grunts or utterances they might release, the concussion of club face on ball. When Juan Guillermo teed off it had the momentary sound of a symphony string section. Perhaps that's why I always trusted the guy.

When we hit the turn it was only a little past eleven and without asking, Juan ordered me a Scotch, but only sparkling water for himself. We both laughed—he was trying to get me drunk. Throughout the back nine, he kept my drink refreshed and entertained me with a string of stories and dirty jokes in an intentionally transparent attempt to distract me, but by the last few holes he was throwing his clubs at seagulls on the edge of the rough. On three occasions he asked me, "So, are you going to tell me what you came all this way to discuss?" Each time I prevailed upon him to play first and talk later.

✦

When we were settled in at the clubhouse in the early afternoon, a Scotch in front of each of us, Juan Guillermo turned and looked at me with the warm, familiar gaze of an old friend. "It must be something bad," he said.

"Why do you say that?"

"You flew a whole day, wouldn't discuss it on the course, and then barely let me keep the score close. You usually at least let me stay *close*," he said with a laugh.

"Juan," I said and lowered my voice, "I've got a guy in New York, a very wealthy guy, from a wealthy family. He needs a heart."

"Ooohh," Juan Guillermo replied with a small grimace. "Jack, we don't do many heart transplants. Why come to me with this? You would need to go to Rio or really, better yet, to South Africa."

"There's more to it. He's also got AIDS."

Juan did not reply. He took on a more sober expression and patiently waited for me to continue, listening intently when I did.

"He's got full-blown AIDS, cardiomyopathy, and Stage Four congestive heart failure. He's going south and has very little time."

"So he'll never make the list in the states," Juan said thoughtfully. "You can't pay someone?" he asked, now matching my own low level of volume.

"AIDS," I said. "None of my domestic guys would ever take that kind of chance. You go to jail for that. That's how you get caught."

"But not in Brazil?" he asked with a touch of sadness.

"Well, no. Maybe not. I'm sorry."

"But that's incorrect, Jack. Even Brazilian hospitals have records. And even Brazil has a government. Plus, there's no way to do it," he said.

"The fee is very large."

"But there's no way to do it," he repeated, this time a little more forcefully.

✦

I had traveled for fifteen hours and played eighteen holes to get to this moment. "Juan, let's say we brought him down here and set him up under your watch. Maybe we even install an L-VAD to keep him going for a while longer while we wait—"

"An L-VAD? Jack, we do *very* few of these."

"Hold on. Maybe I even bring a surgeon down."

"How rich is this family?" Juan Guillermo asked. The look in his eyes was not greed. It looked like the same discomfort I feel when someone says they'll pay me 500K for a liver.

"Juan, they are that rich. So if we did that, and waited, and you kept him at the top of the list . . . What then?"

"Jack, my friend, anything is possible, but to have one come in brain-dead, with matching blood type and MHC, the right age and size . . . You could wait a long time. If he were stable, maybe. He could live somewhere near the hospital. But if he is weak and getting worse. . . ."

"What are the odds, Juan? What are the odds that you could pull it off?"

He frowned in frustration and shrugged his large round shoulders. "One in three, maybe? Thirty percent?"

"That's not good enough," I replied, more to myself than to him.

Something about my reaction prompted Juan to say, "I'm sorry, Jack. Is it a lot of money?"

"Yeah, but, I know the guy. I know him."

"He's a *friend* of yours?" Juan asked, surprised.

"I fucking know the guy. It's personal, Juan. It's my. . . . I really have to help this guy and you were kind of my last option." I felt trapped. "Shit," I whispered. I never felt rage at the system the way I did at that moment in Brazil with Juan. Why should Philip die? Why should some unlucky native from Alexandra die just so bastards like me can drive golf-carts around country clubs? Juan

Guillermo put his fat, stubby fingers on my forearm. I looked up at him. *He's a good man*, I thought.

"There's always one other way, Jack . . . in Recife you could get something like that for a price. You could find a heart, *intentionally*, for the right price." We looked at each other for a moment. "But you'd never do that, Jack. You wouldn't be part of that."

"That's true," I replied, shaking my head slightly. And it was. That much was decided. That was the very reason I was in Brazil.

"Right," he said, looking away. He sipped his drink and seemed far away in his thoughts. "Jack, are you okay?" he asked then. I turned and looked at him but did not answer. Then, Juan Guillermo said, "Hey, do you think I'm a good doctor?"

I laughed a little. "Better than you are a golfer."

"Really," he said, soberly.

"Do you mean . . . do I think you're a good man?" I asked him. "Have you done good? I don't judge people that way. That's your business, Juan."

"Jack, my family, we have a gated home in Leblon, near the water in Rio. I have no brothers or sisters. It's mine since my parents died. I take my family there occasionally, but not too often the last few years. It would be a good place for someone to stay if they needed a place to get away for a while. Rio. It would be a good place for an American who wanted to avoid attention for a while—"

"Oh," I interrupted him, quietly, "I'm fine, Juan. Thank you."

"It's yours if you ever need it, Jack," he said, and he put those stubby fingers to my wrist again for a moment. "Just so you know. . . ."

"Thanks. It's nice to have a friend," I said. Guillermo raised his eyebrows a little. "A good friend . . ."

He nodded silently without smiling. Somehow it was Guillermo's reaction that alerted me, perhaps for the first time, to the fact that I really was in trouble.

CHAPTER TWENTY-NINE:
THE LESSER OF TWO EVILS

The next day I didn't go back to New York. Instead, in the morning I went to Juan Giullermo's office at the hospital and showed up unannounced. His assistant led me into Juan's interior office. It was carpeted and rather elegant. Juan sat behind a huge oak desk. The room was cluttered but it was also large and did not feel cramped. Rather, it just felt lived-in. Guillermo eyed me and motioned with his hand for me to sit.

"I need to talk to you," I said.

"Clearly," he said, a smile breaking out across his robust cheeks. I didn't say anything. "Give me a few minutes," he said. "The café two blocks up, to the west of here . . ." he said. "Meet me there in a half hour."

✦

Guillermo arrived a little sooner than he had said he would and I was sitting at a counter in front of an untouched espresso. He sidled up onto the stool beside me, sat facing forward and sighed. "So? Why are you still here, my friend?"

"Juan," I began quickly in a low and raspy voice, "I've been thinking a lot about what you said yesterday, what you said I would never be a part of, what I wouldn't do . . ."

"I see," he said, seeming to be holding off on any sort of reaction beyond simply acknowledging my words.

"Well, we were talking about how someone *innocent* would have to get hurt in order to get what my client needs. But I've been thinking, what if it wasn't someone innocent? What if it was the very guy putting others at risk? Juan, I mean, what if you knew someone was going to hurt someone innocent, is it wrong then to stop them? Are there different degrees?"

"Degrees of killing a man?" he asked sternly and under his breath. He looked right at me but neither of us said anything for another long moment. "Jack, I'm a Christian."

"Well, I've been doing this so long," I said. "Juan, I'm not sure I even know anymore what's right and what's not. Really."

"I can't answer that kind of question," he said. "But you know, the business we've done on the kidneys, over all these years, those fees paid for a big portion of the new wing. Kids who have cancer. It's children who would die here without ever getting to Rio or San Paulo. Now they get help . . . The sellers from Recife, would things have been very different for most of them? Probably not. But now there's a new wing."

"So what we've done, you think it's justified now?"

"I didn't say that. I have my own peace to make. But there *is* a wing. That's all."

I sat silently looking down at the yellow countertop. I sat quietly for a long while and Juan Guillermo sat beside me and said nothing. I felt like I might cry. I felt like going to sleep. Finally I turned to Juan and began to conduct business by saying, "Well, the guy who is the root cause of this situation I have, he's no good. If no one does anything, then there will be a lot of innocent people affected. I don't know his blood type, this guy. But what if he came here, if I brought him, and something happened to that guy, something that allowed for a healthy heart to survive," I said in a whisper. Guillermo looked at me with a furrowed brow and a look of despair in his eyes. It was the look of a family member receiving the bad news. "If that put a heart into the system, and if my client was here too, at the same time, could you pull together a domino transplant and justify the AIDS factor?"

"Domino?" he said out loud, but apparently talking to himself.

"That guy's heart goes to a patient he matches and then my AIDS guy gets a match out of your list, justified by the domino chain. They could still never do that in the states because of the HIV. Could you do that here?"

"I know 'Domino transplant,' Jack, but not here," he said, and I felt sicker. I felt like the temperature in the room—already uncomfortably warm—had just risen another ten degrees. Then Guillermo added, "In Rio. We'd have to go to Rio. I have a relationship. I think I could do that in Rio with my counterpart there. We just don't do those surgeries, but they do. It would be very expensive, but I think he could do that. I think a domino could get your guy the part. I think they'd be willing to cover the paperwork at the facility in Rio. For a lot of money, Jack. American money. But I do think they could." He shook his head a little and added, "I wouldn't take anything. Just pass it along."

"You wouldn't have to do that," I replied.

"Yes I would."

"Juan, tell me . . . what should I do? What would you do?"

"Jack, you haven't told me who this is, I mean, you never do, but this is different. . . . . Is this guy family?"

"Yes. What would you do?"

"I said I'm a Christian."

"Yeah. I'm not."

"Then you're going to hell anyway," he said softly with a wry smile.

I snickered. "Juan, could this be done?"

"To kill a guy in Rio? You mean, that part?" he asked and laughed a little. "It's probably easier than throwing a good dinner party."

◆

On the flights coming back from Brazil I had a lot of time to think things through and weigh my options, and the potential consequences. I knew who Wallace Kendrickson was but he didn't even know my real name. . . . I surely had the advantage. If the choice was between Wallace being eliminated by his own immense hubris, and a procession of innocent bystanders turning up dead in Alexandra, which was the lesser of two evils? I could coordinate it with Harold Lauer through Mark. We could get on that plane and tell Wallace we were heading for South Africa but simply fly to Brazil. What could he do? Once he got on the plane there would be nothing he could do. We'd exit in Rio and be followed from the airport by some of Juan's friends. At some point they would pull us over and ask me and Wallace to step out of the car—and they would put a bullet in his head. Then we would rush his lifeless vessel to the transplant hospital run by Juan's friend where his heart would be transplanted into the matching recipient waiting at the top of the list, freeing up the next O positive heart with matching MHCs for Philip. He would have a good chance. He'd make it. I believed that. Guillermo would see to that. I wouldn't be able to return to the states for a while but there are worse places to spend a year or two in exile than Rio. Michelle. I didn't know about Michelle. It's

too much, probably. And there would be just one other thing—
Royston. Even without Wallace, and without my help, Wolff and
Kleinhans would not go back to sitting on their hands. I had shown
them the blueprints and given them the keys to the city. They would
have to be handled as well. And so, when I got to JFK, I reluctantly
made the call I had hoped I would never have to make.

CHAPTER THIRTY:
WHO TALKS TO WHOM

The phone rang twice. There was a click and then a man's voice said, "Vinny Pearl."

"Vinny, your name is?" I asked.

"Yeah. Who's calling?"

"My name's New York Jack. Do you know who I am?" There was silence. "Hello?"

"Yes. I do."

"Really," I said, more to myself than him, disappointed.

"Really," he replied.

That's how things start sometimes.

"And organ trafficking is your thing?" I asked.

"It's one of my things. I didn't think I'd ever get to speak to you in person, Jack."

"Me neither," I said flatly.

"So now what, Jack? You want to maybe come here and we can talk a little?"

"Oh, Vinny. That's not what this is about."

"You don't want to get together? Then why'd you call me, Jack?"

"Just getting the lay of the land."

"Jack," he said, a little more sternly, "We should talk, and it's better if you come here. If I have to find you one day, that could be unfriendly. Don't think that you're smart because I haven't found you. Before now no one was really looking."

"Vinny, one quick question: how old are you?"

"Forty-nine. Jack, one quick question: you really from New York?"

"You know I am," I said, and I turned off the phone. I took out the SIM card and slipped it into my pocket—so I could dispose of it safely later—and placed the phone on the floor. Then I casually smashed it with the heel of my shoe.

✦

I still needed to show Wallace and Wolff that things were progressing so after I returned from Brazil I also scheduled the trip to Jozi. I intended to meet with Wolff and Pierre Kleinhans and lay out the details of the plan—the plan they and Wallace wanted to hear—allaying any concern that we weren't moving ahead. That would buy me a little time. I was trying to figure out a way to save Philip without participating in murdering some innocent kidney seller, but I also wanted to spend more time with Mark, and with Michelle.

✦

Only a week later, in the second week of October, I strode through the opulent lobby of the Michelangelo Hotel in Sandton again. I thought about what the black Africans living in shanties in the townships might think if they ever saw where men like me and Wolff and Pierre Kleinhans sipped our Scotch. When Mandela took power he was resolute about moving the country forward without retaliation for apartheid. He did the people a favor. The poor in South Africa have made more progress peacefully than they would have otherwise. Yet, taking in the ostentatious fixtures of that palace of a hotel, I thought that if they could just see it in person, each of them, just one time, they might still storm the castle.

When I entered the main bar I found Wolff and Pierre already seated, a Scotch and a glass of water in front of each of them. Wolff's drink was nearly empty and Pierre's was full. It was not their first. They had probably met early to discuss strategy before I even joined them. As I approached, Wolff stood and smiled. Kleinhans remained seated. I said, "Hello, gentlemen," and nodded slightly.

"Jack, old friend, good to see you again so soon," Dr. Wolff replied.

I kept my attention directed at him and immediately asked, "Why are you talking to Wallace?"

"Wallace? Your friend?" he asked, still smiling. "He's your associate, isn't he?"

"Mel," I said, flatly but politely, "we know each other a long time. If we are going to work together I need your communications to go only through me. I can't have anyone going around me. I am the only point of contact."

"Jack, what do you mean—*if* we are going to work together? That's not necessary between old friends."

"Please don't ever go around me," I said, calmly, and took a seat on the bar stool beside Wolff.

"Jack, you misunderstand. This Wallace, he was concerned about our progress. So were we. He said he had trouble reaching you. No one meant any disrespect."

I demurred. "You can avoid such misunderstandings by talk-ing only to me. I'll discuss the same with him when I'm back in the States."

"That's fine, Jack," Wolff said.

"Let's please be polite, Jack," Pierre said. "Let's have us a drink, please."

"Of course, Pierre." I said, turning toward him. "You look snappy today."

"What?" Pierre asked.

Wolff laughed slightly, breaking the tension a little. *This might be the last time I would see either of them,* I thought. One way or another that kid was getting a good heart, and one way or another my days as a broker were drawing to an end.

My drink came and we clinked glasses and then I asked Wolff, "Did you receive the charts I faxed?"

"Weeks ago," he replied.

"Okay. Good."

"That's why we were concerned, Jack."

"Okay. Is everything arranged?"

"Easily done, Jack," Pierre chimed in.

"You have the part?" I asked Kleinhans.

"We have the seller," Pierre responded. "He's ready."

"So we can move forward when the client comes to Royston?"

"With two days notice," Wolff said.

"It's much easier now than you think, Jack," Pierre said, smiling. "Oh?"

"We've got over five hundred sellers screened and tissue-typed in advance from whom we can now pull anything we might need. Five hundred in advance, ready to go—"

"Five hundred?"

"They're just waiting their turns. They're from this area but also neighboring townships. When they get their turn they think they won the lottery. We are all about to make a lot of money, Jack."

"Pierre," Wolff said, "Moenie roem oor hierdie." Then to me, he said, "Jack, let's focus on one thing at a time. This transaction is a great opportunity for everyone."

"Not for the seller," I said. Wolff looked like he had finally taken offense. There was a moment when no one spoke. I sipped my drink, wiped my brow. It felt hot, despite the air conditioning.

Pierre finally leaned in and said, "The world won't miss one more fucking kaffir."

Kaffir was the Jozi equivalent of nigger, perhaps a bit worse. It was even worse than "floppy."

Wolff said, "Pierre, please," then turned toward me and said, "Jack, let's focus on this thing first. Not get distracted. There is a lot of money to be made for all of us and in the end we are saving this young man from New York and that is what is most important."

Wolff stopped doing surgery personally a few years ago. I wondered who would do the procedure. I wondered about their paperwork, and how he was handling the fact that they were anesthetizing a healthy patient and then removing his still-beating heart. I imagined Pierre in his white suit, with his short-brimmed hat, his cheesy smile hidden behind a surgical mask and clutching a small machete in his hand in place of a scalpel.

◆

"I'll need a week or two to organize everything with the hospital he's in now, square it with the family in New York. Wallace needs to coordinate payment of the advance. It'll be a couple of weeks, but don't worry. We'll be coming back to Royston very soon," I said, looking down, speaking into my glass.

"Good, Jack," Wolff said. "That's excellent. Bring that young man to Royston. As soon as you can, Jack. Let's help him."

◆

I knew that the best thing I could have done would have been to turn and leave that bar, leave South Africa and go home, home to Tucson—not New York—and live out a quiet life, but I turned toward Kleinhans and said, "Pierre, can you get me Thaba on the phone?"

"What's that, Jack?" Wolff asked, smiling sweetly and turning back in my direction.

Pierre looked at me and seemed to be assessing whether the time had finally come to put a bullet in my face. "He speaks to me," he said.

"Who is Thaba?" Wolff asked.

Pierre said something to Wolff in Afrikaans and I interrupted. "No Afrikaans. Let's be *polite*, shall we? I need to talk to your associate so please get him on the phone for me."

"You want to talk to the native herder," Pierre said, angrily. "Fine. I don't give a shit." He took his cell out of his jacket pocket and dialed and handed it to me. "Talk, Jack. I don't care."

Wolff said, "Jack, Jack. . . ." and reached out toward Pierre's cell phone.

"Wait," I said.

"All right," Wolff said calmly, gathering himself up to leave. "Call me at Royston when you're done here." He stood to leave.

Thaba did not answer his phone. I handed the cell back to Pierre.

"Is everything all right, Jack?" Wolff asked paternally.

"It is, Mel. I want to talk to Pierre's man, but everything with the transaction is fine. Get your donor ready. I'll be coming back to Royston with suitcases full of American dollars."

Wolff again seemed offended. He nodded and excused himself.

I turned to Pierre. "I need to talk to Thaba. Can you text him and give him this number to call?" I asked, and read off the number on my new South African cell. Pierre typed it into his phone without comment. He sent the text, took a last swig of his drink, and said, "See you, Jack," as he got up and exited the bar.

"Yes. *Au revoir*, Pierre," I said. It always seemed to annoy him when I addressed him in French. I ordered another Scotch and before the barman returned with my drink the cell rang. I answered it and said "Hello," but there was no response.

"Thaba? This is Jack. New York Jack."

"I know who you are. Why don't you call Pierre Kleinhans?"

"I needed to talk to you."

"What do you want?"

"Thaba, I need to go back to Alexandra."

"No, Jack. That is not good."

"I need to go back and I would appreciate it if you would come with me. I know I can't keep going there and not come out missing an arm soon."

"You can't go there anymore. You saw Alex. Now go back to New York. It's not for you."

"I need to talk to that boy, Lesedi."

"Lesedi?" he asked.

"Yes."

Thaba was silent for a moment, then he said, "Lesedi is dead."

I exhaled involuntarily. "From infection?" I asked.

"Jack, call Pierre. I cannot help you with this."

"How did he die, Thaba? Was it from infection?"

"You don't know the townships. This is not New York City—"

"How did that kid fucking die, Thaba?" I yelled, right there in the middle of the bar at the Michelangelo, drawing a stare from several of the guests scattered at the tables.

"He killed his self," Thaba said loudly. "He cut his own troat." I shook my head a little in disbelief. "In the square where you see him play football. And stand there. With the people. You know the truth. You are New York Jack. You took his kidney. I take. Pierre take. Royston Clinic. But now you want to be his friend?"

"No."

"Now he is dead. Don't you call my number again."

I said nothing, and he said nothing, and after another minute I realized he had already hung up. I pictured Lesedi with that ear-to-ear grin of his playing soccer with a ball made out of tape on a pitch made out of dirt. I imagined him walking into the square one day, the sun beating down on the dust, Lesedi pulling a large knife from underneath his shirt. He had been ostracized, exiled without leaving. His own sisters would not speak to him because he had sold a kidney in the hope of buying them running water and a better life. For them, for God's sake. And this is what they do in some communities. Did he leave a note to explain himself? Did he make a speech, standing there in the dirt of his last day, his only pulpit a makeshift soccer field between one-story concrete dwellings? Probably not. Only an American would think anyone would care to listen. I'm an American, and I'm writing a note to explain myself that has now become hundreds of fucking pages long—but Lesedi was a kid who would have seen no value in committing his final thoughts to a piece of paper that no one would ever care to read.

I noticed the bartender then, cleaning glasses and looking away from me, determined not make eye contact. Wolff was on his way home to his mansion where he lived near Sandton on an estate with an iron gate surrounding lush grounds with an armed guard on duty at all times. Pierre was on his cell telling the seller how much money he would get for a kidney. How he would get women. I realized then that I was crying. I slumped back onto the barstool and sobbed. I think that is the moment when my reluctance finally broke, snapped like smelling salts. Like a glow stick cracking into luminescence, I broke. I never had anyone to cry for before meeting Mark, and before Michelle. Only someone with love and something to lose can feel that kind of pain.

CHAPTER THIRTY-ONE:
TIME IS LIMITED

The second time I called Vinny Pearl, it was through an interchange in Europe I hadn't used in a long time, and wouldn't be able to use again.

"Vinny Pearl."

"Vinny, this is New York Jack."

"Where are you, Jack?" Pearl asked casually.

"Funny."

"Thailand, Jack? Nice beaches there."

"You're wasting time. It's going to cost me another cell phone if you don't stop."

"Okay. I'm listening. I thought I might not hear from you again."

"I have information for you now," I said. He listened patiently and I added, "Do you know what I do, Vinny?"

"New York Jack is a black market organ broker."

"I'm a seller's agent," I said.

"Call it whatever you want, Jack, but it ain't legal, and we know who you are now."

"And you're triangulating the call, so we don't really have time to argue semantics. If it's so illegal then what about the Man from Dallas?"

"Coburn?" Pearl asked, a bit incredulously. "That guy's just a travel agent. Plus, he's a helpful guy sometimes. You wanna be helpful? Doing that could help a guy like you avoid a lot of stress."

"Yes, I want to be helpful."

◆

Vinny Pearl is a Special Agent with the FBI. He has more in common with an accountant than a secret agent, but it is the patient and persistent ones who uncover the hidden gems. Gems like me. In the never-ending clusterfuck known as the war on drugs, our soldiers are so camouflaged that they sometimes struggle to even recognize themselves after a while. In the "war on terror" there's no reason to put on costumes or fake mustaches—it doesn't matter when so few can even speak Farsi. And investigations into violations of the National Organ Transplantation Act of 1986 fall under the more workaday division of the FBI that oversees Interstate Commerce. Very modest resources are directed at this area of law enforcement, and very few investigations ever yield any promotion-worthy results. The agents rarely go under cover; they carry regular 9mm handguns and they wear suits to work. The Manhattan Field Office for Interstate Commerce Violations is on Seventeenth Street over by the West Side Highway, a half a block down from a huge Manhattan Mini Storage that dominates the cobblestoned street. Unlike several clandestine facilities set up in nondescript office buildings all over the city by the FBI, Homeland Security, and the DEA, shrouded by shingles with the names of fake marketing agencies or data storage companies, the building on Seventeenth Street has a black metal plate right next to the door that says, "Federal Bureau of Investigations, New York City Field Office." I got the number for Vinny Pearl a few years ago. I got it from The Man from Dallas during the one conversation we ever had subsequent to that meeting back in 2000. I had let it fester in my contacts waiting to see if it might one day get called upon—and hoping it would not. Until now.

Despite the fact that *I* had called *him*, I didn't think Pearl expected me to make such an offer—"to be helpful"—and I caught him off guard.

"Great," Pearl said in a measured tone, "but you need to come in here and we need to sit down with the DA and write it up. If you are the guy I think you are, and you're willing to really help, I think we can offer you a lot in return."

"It's not like that, Vinny. This isn't about me. I'm just calling to put something important on your plate."

"Okay . . ."

"But you have to wait. You can't do anything yet. You have to build a file and start collecting evidence, and Vinny, you have to get this right the first time, so please don't rush it. If you're patient, and do it right, this is very big for your team. If you rush, you'll end up with nothing."

"Sure. What is it you're giving me, New York?"

He said "New York" facetiously, but the tone of camaraderie, whether fake or not, somehow reminded me of Wallace, and somehow that caused a pang of sadness like a gong being rung in my gut.

"Royston," I said and then clenched my jaw.

"Who the hell is Royston?"

"Vinny, they have Google on FBI computers . . ."

"Okay, Royston. R, O, Y? . . ."

"S, T, O, N. Bye, Vinny."

"Jack," Pearl said, softer and more slowly, "why are you doing this anyway?" The tone was collegial, almost one of concern.

"So I can't back out."

"Back out of what, Jack? Tell me what we need to know, and let us handle it. Let me help you, Jack. Maybe you really do want to do something right here. So that's good. That's the right thing. Let me help."

"You can't."

"Hey, you're in Prague?" he asked then.

"Oh, please."

"Wait—" he said.

I hung up.

✦

That night I had the dream again. I was at a dinner table with fine china and white linen and lace napkins. The plates were pearl white, with thin, swirling spirals of dark red along the outer edge . . . I felt the presence of the others in the room and then I saw them. The men were all dressed in black suit pants. The women wore black or gray dresses. The old ones, their bodies wrinkled and marked with age spots, were mostly white. The younger ones were mostly black or Latino. "Why the hell are they undressed?" I thought in a panic, my pulse quickening.

Then, I was dizzy and there was vomit on my plate, and on the table in front of me. They all stared at me, expressionless, their entrails now exposed in their torsos. "Not to your liking, sir?" asked a man in the second or third row.

"I don't know you," I whispered.

"We never spoke," he said. "Your partner set it all up. But thank you."

"I'm sorry," I said. I was barely audible. I was speaking to myself. I was dreaming and I knew it. Then I woke up.

◆

That was about a month ago. I would stop them all, I thought when I awoke. I had waited long enough. Too long. You see, everything shines just a tiny bit brighter when one feels like time is limited. Well, time is always limited, for everyone, always, and much more so than we ever care to admit when we're running through the city on auto-pilot trying to make a meeting. Of course it's limited. It's *limiting.*

I am very sorry that Mark had to learn the truth about his father and all the pain I've caused, but I'm very grateful to have gotten to know him. I'm sorry for Michelle too, that she ran into me in that bar that night, but I am grateful for having met her as well. Mark had no choice when it came to me. The universe made that choice. DNA did, not us. Carrie made that choice. But he did come looking for me.

◆

Now a guy named Vinny Pearl will become my accidental partner, the way Wallace had been for so long. Pearl's colleagues will Google Royston and all of its executive officers, starting with my friend Mel Wolff. They will search confidential government databases. Pearl will talk with friends at Interpol, and to the South African secret police— but only the one or two guys he knows he can trust to wait and keep it contained.

That may be all it takes. To shine a light on it. Like cockroaches: once you see one, surely there are thousands more just out of sight. Pearl knows that. He's been around. Little facts will start to surface pointing to things being out of sort. The amount of cyclosporine they use. The amount of donors who end up dead. The sellers coming from Alexandra. Wolff's assets and Swiss accounts. . . . Every chain like that has weak links; you just need to start pulling on it. And now I've told the FBI where to pull. New York Jack, FBI informant.

Pearl and his people will need some time to get organized now, to get ready. That's good. This is not a thing I'm in a rush to complete.

I could have built that law practice. Eighteen years ago when Kimball walked into my office I could have just said no and stuck to the plan. I could have overcome things, but I made other choices. That's the reality of who I am. That's how things start sometimes—by accident. I have learned that they only end with purpose.

PART VI: MARK AND MICHELLE

CHAPTER THIRTY-TWO:
TIME

It was on the plane back from Jozi last month that I began to write this down. At first I just started writing a note, hoping to explain some of the things that I thought you had a right to know, Mark. I started with the simple admission of who I am and what I have done. Then I explained the events that led to where I am now, writing for an hour or two when Michelle was at work, or in the shower or at a dinner meeting. I thought it might take a few pages but I seem to have underestimated how much I needed to tell. I wanted to tell you the truth, and Michelle too, and let you decide for yourselves. Like your mother did, Mark. It's more important to me to tell you the truth than to spin the story to make you see it my way. I regret so much now, but listing the reasons for my regret and trying to somehow apologize might add another hundred pages, and this note is already so long, and time is limited.

By the time October rolled around, Michelle and I had fallen into patterns. We had a bit of an Indian Summer this year. During that ten-day stretch, the temperatures were often in the seventies instead of the fifties. I remember thinking that when it cooled back down, that would be the time. But when the weather turned back to fall, I still didn't act. It started to get so that almost every day I would pick another time, but when that time came I would come up with a reason to put it off a little longer, each time buying another day or two. All that time, this note grew longer and started to turn into what it has become: not just an explanation, but also a lengthy and detailed confession.

On one of those unseasonably warm days a few weeks ago, Michelle and I went running down along the West Side Highway. We ran past Chelsea Piers and through the Village and into Tribeca before we slowed to a walk. We turned on Chambers Street and followed it in until the end and walked along the renovated waterfront in Battery Park. There is endless manicured landscaping along that path now. There are trees and babies in strollers and dogs and picnics. There are sailboats on the Hudson River. Some people even swim in it now. Some days, the vibe is more akin to Sydney or London than downtown Manhattan. We stopped and leaned up against a railing looking out over the river and across to Jersey City and Hoboken. Michelle said, "I could get used to this."

"Great day," I agreed. "So warm."

"I mean to us, Jack."

The water was lapping against the dock that supports the path there. There were two helicopters flying up the corridor between Jersey and New York, high in the air and looking black against the bright blue of the sky.

"Yeah."

Michelle turned to me and said, "I don't want to miss out on things because I've been uncompromising."

"That makes sense."

"Don't do that, Jack."

"What?"

"Agree with me."

"You know," I said to her, "I never feel like you want anything from me. I think that's why I like you more than the others."

"What others?" she said with a mock accusation.

"Before you."

"You didn't exist before you met me." She paused, then, more seriously, added, "And I want things from you, Jack. I just don't *need* anything. That's the difference. And I want that for you too. To want things from me, and from life, and to be able to want things without somehow feeling like that's a problem."

She was right, and I knew it right then, standing on the concrete at the edge of the Hudson River, Michelle backlit by the sinking sun. I had avoided disappointment by turning myself off. And by avoiding people. We were both silent for a long moment and I moved closer to her and said, "There's something else I want to tell you."

She looked up at me with what I thought was apprehension.

"I've got a son." She didn't respond and after a few seconds I continued. "His name is Mark. He's twenty-two and lives here in New York. I was with his mother in law school and I didn't even know about him until last year." She moved her hand on top of mine. We were okay. "I'm sorry I didn't tell you about this before. I wanted you to know and I'd like you to meet him one day."

✦

That was one of many times when I decided that it was time to get started. Tomorrow, I thought. Then, I'd do nothing. When one has friends and family, they literally become a sort of fabric you're woven into and that's life I guess.

"Jack," she said quietly, peering into my eyes, "that's great." The water was lapping gently at the concrete, the air was crisp but warm, and she was holding onto my hand with both of hers. It was perfect, and I was present enough to know it.

✦

Michelle and I went to my club at Doring-On-The-Hudson in Westchester that Friday. I had completely stopped working and I was spending a lot of time writing this letter. *Michelle, things will change soon*, I thought, as she pushed a tee into the ground with the ball cupped in her fingers. I cleared my mind of those thoughts and became acutely aware of the conditions and the flag past the fairway on the short par three that is the first hole there. She hit her first shot cleanly and placed it on the fairway, if a bit short, hooked just a hair to the left. I was impressed. I thought she might scoff at golf, mocking the pretentious social aspects rather than appreciating the true meditative nature of the game. I took out my three wood and stepped up to the tee and felt certainty flowing through me.

"Jack!" from Michelle. I turned my attention to her. "So this guy walks into a bar and he says, 'Ow. Shit . . .'" I nodded. "Cause he walked *into* the bar. You know?" she said, almost giggling, "the bar itself."

"I heard you." I recommenced my approach. I let it go. The club, my arms, the tee . . . Thwack.

"What the hell was that?" she asked, incredulous, but smiling broadly.

"I told you I was good."

"Jack, it almost went *in*."

"It's probably about a four-foot putt.'

"What?? Oh, shit. That was amazing." She laughed a little. The sun was in our eyes. The air was rich. "Well give me one good tip. One."

"Your backswing. You bring the club back too quickly. It's a pretty common problem. Come back slower."

"That's it?" she said, laughing a bit. "Even I've heard that before."

"Well, maybe you'll actually listen to me."

"Okay," she said and grasped my forearm. I took a step toward our cart but she held my arm and said, "You're a nice man. The last few months have been different for me. I feel less worried about things now that you're in my life." That was hard for me to hear since I was considering actions that might remove me from her life. "You have a good heart, Jack," she added.

The sound of those words kept creeping into my head over and over for the rest of the day. I shot nine over that day and missed two easy putts. "Good heart," she'd said. Would she be okay if her boyfriend disappeared and didn't call her for months? Could she feel safe again after learning that she had spent months living and dining and making love and sleeping with New York Jack, one of the world's biggest kidney brokers?

CHAPTER THIRTY-THREE: CONFESSIONS

A day or two later the weather turned cold, and shortly after that Philip finally started heading south. It often happens the same way with kidney patients. The descent of their decline suddenly accelerates and you can tell they're on their way out. I told Wallace to have the client charter a plane for me, Philip, and a nurse to go to Johannesburg. I made arrangements with Wolff. Wallace seemed relieved, and Mel Wolff seemed excited.

I was at Michelle's place, late on Tuesday night, November first, when one of my phones rang. It was you, Mark.

"Jack? Jack?"

"Yes."

"It's Mark."

"I know," I said, getting out of bed and walking out into the living room. I stood in front of Michelle's large windows, looking south down along West Broadway.

"I think he's dying."

"What did they say?" I asked, "they" being the *doctors* of course—the gatekeepers between this world and the next.

"T-cells, white blood cells . . . It's all a mess. Blood pressure fucked up. There's a arrhythmia. I think this is it." You were practically whispering. I assumed you must have been in the room with Philip. Were you? You had been in the room with him while I ran along the waterfront and made love and went out to dinners. My last meal went on for weeks while Philip was slowly dying. The thought of that is sickening to me now.

"I'm sorry, Mark," I said, and decided once again that this was the time to act. His heart hadn't stopped. He might still have days. *Tomorrow*, I thought. Everything was in place. There was a plane chartered, but maybe I wouldn't even need a plane. I had gotten Philip moved to Columbia from Cornell. I had typed up the letter. I was nearly done with this explanation. It wasn't too late yet, but it had to be now.

"All this time," you were saying, "I've known it was happening, but he was better for a while and. . . ." You were straining to keep it down to a whisper. "This shouldn't happen to someone so young," you said, sobbing a little.

"He's too young, Mark. I know. And he's a good guy."

"He is, but I meant me. *I'm* too young. I'm too young to lose the person I love like this. I'm too young to take it that someone with AIDS doesn't deserve a heart. What kind of a thing is that?" I said nothing. "Jack, I need to talk to you about something else."

◆

You asked to meet in person and we arranged to meet at the hospital the next day at 11 a.m. I went back into the bedroom and Michelle was awake, sitting up in bed. The light was dim but she was visible, like a movie image or a faint holographic projection. She is so beautiful. When people have sex they are literally connected. Maybe all our lives we're desperately trying to achieve some state of connectedness, even if only for brief and fleeting moments. I sat down on the bed beside her and neither of us spoke. Tomorrow.

◆

The next day I went up to Columbia to meet you as you had asked. As I entered the emergency room lobby, I carefully studied the layout. A revolving glass door separated the building from the sidewalk. There was a large wooden piece of furniture just inside the doorway which held all sorts of literature about different health issues and pharmaceutical products. There were modern-looking leather and chrome chairs gathered around cheaper-looking glass coffee tables. I made mental notes. The security guard, information desk, and entrance into the hospital beyond the waiting room were all slightly to the left.

When I got up to Philip's room, he was sleeping and you were sitting on a black plastic chair looking up at the television on the wall. You stood when you saw me and stepped forward to give me a quick embrace.

"How is he?"

"The same."

"How are you?"

You exhaled a little. "Same." Then I followed you out into the hallway. About twenty feet down the hall past Philip's room were a half a dozen plastic chairs lined up against the wall. We sat, and you turned to me.

"Okay," you said, then took a deep breath and went on. "Here's the thing. This is hard, so please. . . . I lied to you, Jack. I lied to you and I feel really bad about it and I want to tell you." I waited. "Jack, when we met that day at that diner, I knew more about you than I told you."

"Okay."

"Carrie—my mom—wasn't unsure about what you do. She knew you got that guy Kimball a kidney, and she knew that you had done it again. She wasn't uncertain about any of it. And she didn't tell me about you when I turned twenty-one, and she never wrote me some letter a long time ago. I made those parts up."

We stared at each other for a few moments. "So, did you come to find me that day for a reason, Mark? For a specific reason?" I knew the truth, but I figured everyone has a right to say they're sorry.

"Yes, but I want to be clear because what I did was wrong. It's bad and I can't do this without telling you the truth. And because I didn't know I'd like you, Jack. I didn't expect that. I thought I could lie to you and not care. I resented you. I didn't really know anything about you but I had you pre-judged as a coke-dealer asshole who treated my mother shitty and then disappeared."

"Go on."

"Jack, look, I was in New York for years and never gave a shit about trying to find you until Philip got sick. My mom didn't care. I came to find you because—"

"Mark, I knew that. You're not a good liar. It was clear to me as soon as you told me that Carrie knew about Kimball."

"What was?" you asked.

"That you found me in order to help Philip. I knew it wasn't about me. Of course I knew that. I don't blame you."

"Jack, you don't understand. I'm not twenty-two," you said. "I'll turn twenty-one in a few months, Jack. Do you understand what I'm saying?" You were holding back tears.

The truth hit me just as quickly as the lie did that day at the diner. "You're saying the math doesn't add up," I whispered. "It means you were born two years after Carrie and I split up."

"I'm sorry."

"How could she do this?" I asked, still speaking in a whisper. "How could Carrie do that to me?"

"Because the rest is true," you said. "Philip and I've been together since I was sixteen. I met him at a college summer program. And we love each other. I love him, Jack. Can't you understand that? I love him so much. My parents went crazy when we first met. I was a teenager and had just come out and he was almost thirty, but they love him now too. We're a family and my mother is sick over doing this, we both are, but I would do anything to help him, Jack. I would do anything. That's love and please I'm sorry, it was wrong, but please help us anyway. You said you could and I am begging you. I had to tell you the truth. My mother told me not to, but I had to, but please help my boyfriend. This is my fault, not his. Please help him." You were crying by then, coughing and rocking back and forth on the bench a little.

"So, Ken Carson, he's your real father?" You nodded. "And Carrie told you to tell me that story? To find me in a diner and pretend that you were my son? *That was her . . . idea?*" It was impossible to believe. You said nothing. "I get it, Mark," I said. And then, you probably remember, we sat in silence on those plastic chairs for nearly fifteen minutes. Carrie did what anyone would do; she did what was best for her. What was more remarkable to me was what you did when you decided to tell me the truth, despite the massive motivation you must have felt to do otherwise.

You were not my son after all, but again, nothing felt different. I felt no sense of resentment. I liked you more even. We sat there, not speaking, for a long time. You calmed down, but continued to wipe at your eyes and sniffle. My primary thought was this: *I've done more harm with the pain I've held on to than the pain I've caused.* It occurred to me that everyone makes mistakes, every single one of them, and everyone is flawed, and everyone is awful sometimes, and we either let it go someday, or we die alone. And no one else cares what we decide.

You eventually stopped crying and sat beside me for several more minutes. "How did you get involved in this?" you asked me then.

"Mark, you should paint, not be a lawyer. Or become a veterinarian or something. But not a lawyer."

"But I'm not really going to be a lawyer. I'm going to be a lawyer like Philip," you said, speaking with a confidence that seemed new.

"I can help him," I eventually said. "I think I can get Philip what he needs. But I need some things from you." You shook your head, grimaced again against the oncoming tears a little, and still did not speak. "Tell Philip it's okay. Tell him it will work out. Try and get his father to be a little more patient, even if Philip is getting worse. That's going to get very hard soon, but I need you to make sure that nothing happens to change anything. The current plan can save him, Mark. But he can't be moved until I tell you otherwise."

After a moment you nodded. Then you quietly asked, "You'll still help us?" I said nothing. You added: "His father will pay you a lot, you know."

"Yeah. Five million."

"I'm so sorry, Jack."

And you were. You're a good kid, Mark. The world's tough.

"I wasn't doing it for you anyway," I said.

"You're doing it for my mom? . . . For Philip?"

"No. "

I felt like I'd been hit by a truck, but I straightened up and went home.

CHAPTER THIRTY-FOUR: LOVE AND LAST CHANCES

On Friday Wallace called again. I was taking a break from writing this letter, contentedly watching the people and the traffic below on the streets of Soho.

"Wolff says you aren't leaving New York until Sunday. Not doing the procedure until next Tuesday," Wallace said, obviously agitated.

"Why are you talking to Mel Wolff again? That doesn't help things, Wallace."

"Do you really not get this, Jack? I've been talking to Wolff since the day after you started socializing with the fucking family of that Marlene Brown last Christmas."

There was silence. It was one of those moments where you either take your toys, go home, and never see each other again, or you let it go and you grow up a bit.

"Wallace," I said calmly, "I understand that there is a breakdown of trust between us. That we are going to have to reevaluate and sort that out once this is done. But please stay focused right now."

"I am the one who's focused."

"If you want to get this done you can't be talking to my contacts in Jozi. I told Wolff the same thing. I handle it, or it doesn't happen. I have reasons for doing things the way they are done and it has to be done correctly. We are leaving in two days so settle down."

"He is fucking tanking. This guy's vitals are deteriorating. He may not even make it until Sunday and now he has to fucking fly. They're thinking about putting in the L-VAD now and that would mean more delays."

"No L-VAD!" I said. "You're right. It would hold him up. You can't do a transplant directly after surgery like that. Have the client tell the doctors to stabilize him with meds until we leave for his procedure. It will work."

"You should have left a month ago. I can't believe this guy is getting on a fucking plane now and we only got a deposit of one and a half. If he tanks, I promise you that your share won't buy you a pizza."

"He's flying in a bed with an attending nurse and a half a million in medical equipment. This isn't a regular client. It's going to work."

"But it didn't have to be this way, Jack." Then something happened to Wallace's demeanor and he said it again. "It didn't have to be this way, Jack." He said it with a hint of regret, and it was the most threatening thing anyone has ever said to me. It occurred to me that he and Wolff and Kleinhans might have already decided that my continued participation was unnecessary. They were ready to write off a resident of Alexandra in order to procure one needed part. Would they eliminate an unsound partner, if they thought he might get in the way of earning a fortune in coming years?

"We leave Sunday," I said. "I just need to confirm something with you tomorrow. In person, Wallace."

There was a pause. There we were again, my friend and I, acting coy and playing cat and mouse again. Ten years of this.

"We don't need a meeting," Wallace said. "You said it's all arranged. You said you have a plan and a schedule. The client has a plane ready. I know that myself. This Pierre guy, Wolff says he has the part."

"But I need to discuss something with you before I can leave."

"It's a sixty-forty split, Jack. The fact that you're trying to shake me down at the last minute actually makes me feel a little better, like maybe you've come to your senses about priorities, but there's still nothing to discuss."

"It's not the money, Wallace. It's something else. Not for phones. We need to have a brief meeting before I go. Like we sometimes do."

"All right," Wallace said suspiciously.

"Great. Meet me at noon tomorrow at the patient's hospital."

"The hospital?" Wallace asked. "I try to stay away from hospitals."

"Yes, you're much more comfortable at country clubs and hedge funds. I know," I said, trying to lighten the mood.

"That's correct."

"Well, I know my way around hospitals like this pretty well. You'll be in good hands."

✦

I waited a few minutes before making my next call.

"How goes it?" I asked Special Agent Vinny Pearl.

"Oh, not bad. My wife's trying to get me to go to Bermuda over the holidays.

Thinking about it. I don't actually like the beach as much as she does, but you know . . . You? How goes the kidney thieving?"

"This is it, Vinny. It's time." I was keeping it even. After all, I'm New York Jack. But there were tears in the corners of my eyes and I had to think about you, Mark, in order to keep talking at all. My banter with Pearl had taken on an ironic tone, laced with barbed-but-friendly witticisms, reminiscent of how Wallace and I used to talk. I missed him—Wallace—before he was my problem. I missed the old days, when we felt like international spies and still thought we were Robin Hoods, and not Al Capones.

"So does that mean you want to meet, Jack?"

"How good is the file on Royston and Wolff?"

"It's thick. Will you testify?"

"No."

"What if you have to?"

"Vinny, assume that somehow I don't testify. As great a secret agent as you are, imagine for one moment that you can't get me to testify. What then? How good a case can you make against Royston without me?"

"We've got a lot, but it's a fucked up country and different rules, so you never know. Jack, you have to testify. You are obviously doing this for a reason."

"But you have records?"

"I've even had my own people inside the hospital. It was risky. But we have a lot, Jack. We've been working with the South African Hawks—"

"That's their FBI?"

"Yeah. They don't have resources like we do, but they still don't like their toes stepped on, so they were looped in. Also, I've got a colleague at Interpol who has a file of his own. You know, you aren't their only friend at Royston. They distribute to a few of your competitors as well."

"Of course they do. . . ." Actually, I had not considered that or its possible scope. There was some silence again. I had been on the phone too long already.

And then a different question occurred to me. "Vinny, is The Siren real?"

There was silence.

"Vinny?"

"I'm The Siren," he said without further hesitation.

I didn't respond at first. Finally, I asked, "What does that mean?"

"Well, I'm not saying I'm the only guy who goes by that name, but sometimes it's me. And of course I'm not luring drunk salesmen into hotel rooms to drug them and cut out their kidneys. I lure in guys like you Jack. Guys who do what you do but sometimes get greedy or sloppy. Now that I've told you that, you're not going to go and screw that up for me, right? You're trying to do something good you said, so you won't go and tell your buddies about my sometimes-alias will you? . . ."

"Wait. Then you've spoken to Wallace?"

"Wallace from Florida? Yes. Is he a friend of yours, Jack? He's got some scary ideas that guy. I haven't heard from him in a while but I expect I'll catch up with him eventually."

I shook my head and closed my eyes.

"Jack? Jack? So where do we meet?" Pearl asked.

"I'll tell you tomorrow," I said.

"You going to maybe disappear on me now, New York?"

"No," I said.

"So what then?"

"I'll tell you tomorrow, Vinny," I said. "Then it ends. I'm trying to do something right, like you said, I want to do something right and now you can help me. I was just making a living, Vinny. Not like Wolff and the setup at Royston. I never meant to hurt anyone. I'm going to try to fix some of it."

"Wait a minute," Vinny Pearl said, more animated. "What do you mean? What are you going to do, Jack?" he asked, speaking more quickly.

"I'll call you tomorrow, Vinny. Stay reachable."

"No, no, no!" Pearl practically yelled into the phone. "Now, wait a minute, Jack. What are you gonna do?"

"Help you. Just help."

"No. That's Uni-bomber martyr talk! Murder talk! What the hell's going on, Jack? You don't need to do anything. You just tell me what you know and we handle it. The Man from Dallas, Jack. Remember, the Man from Dallas? He's barely ever done time! In France for a few months once, but never here in the states. I can help you."

"Vinny, you're kind, but we've been on the phone way too long. The whole thing has gone on too long," I said. I turned off the phone and unceremoniously tossed it into a garbage can, SIM card and all.

✦

A week or so ago Michelle told me she loves me. It was in bed, in the morning. We had just woken up. It was early and we had time. I stared back at her like a mute dog. Most people seem to think that love lives in your heart or your head, as a thought or a feeling. It's not true, and this much I do know: your pain, your relief, your justifications and your machinations, your joy . . . they don't matter. In the end, we are measured by our actions. And while poets may think it's complicated, I think it may actually be simple: when you put someone else's interests ahead of your own, in your *actions*, that is love. That's what The Man from Dallas meant. That's also what Michelle meant when she said it to me, and it's why I could not respond.

CHAPTER THIRTY-FIVE: CHOICES AND APOLOGIES

When I awoke this morning, Michelle was dressing for work. I stayed in her bed, hands behind my neck, staring at the blank, white ceiling. She had showered while I was still sleeping. She had already put on her makeup. She was nearly ready to leave.

"Jack. . . ."

"Yeah?"

"I'm going."

"Okay. I should go too," I said. I was focused.

"Really? Where will you go? Your office? Is that the story for today?"

"Michelle, what are you talking about?" I said, as I got up from bed and gathered my clothes.

"You off to your secret operation? That office? Or maybe you'll just hang out in the park today."

I was surprised to learn she was aware I didn't go to work anymore. "Things are pretty slow lately," I said, "that's true." I started getting dressed, sitting on the edge of her bed. I wanted to spend the day with her. I wanted to get back into bed with her. But I couldn't tell her the truth. That wasn't the way I wanted to tell her, or Carrie, or you, Mark. I wanted to write it down and present it all fairly. So there was nothing to do but let her go to work.

No one spoke for a long moment. "You'll have to tell me eventually, you know," she said.

"Tell you what?" I asked.

"Everything, Jack. Whatever it is that you still don't tell me."

"Yes, I know that," I said.

✦

I never planned to go to law school. I never planned to get into the business. I never planned to have a son, or not have a son, or become a drug dealer and I knew that I couldn't just let Philip die because of my ambivalence. Does protecting the life of one doomed resident of Alexandra really warrant what I intended to do?

I'm the one who's sorry, Mark. How did I go on not telling you? I began by saying that I wouldn't apologize, that I would just tell you the truth about what has happened—let you all judge everything for yourself, objectively. But that was a lie too. You apologized for your lies, and I'm sorry too.

Remember this, Mark: Doing the right thing when it's convenient says nothing about a man's character. When you told me the truth about you not being my son, you sacrificed your own interests for mine, in order to do what's right. I might have told you to go to hell and not helped Philip, but you stood up anyway. I need to do that. For once. I am so sorry now, I really am, for everything really, and I can't even believe what I've done, and what I haven't done yet, but will, and how sorry I am and how I know that I cannot avoid the massive regret that I am getting paid back with, but it's fair, and I am terribly, terribly sorry and I deserve it.

I am sorry to everyone. To every poor wretch in some third world country who sold a kidney for chump change because I so slickly facilitated it all. To every buyer misled into thinking this was a clean and guiltless transaction. I'm sorry. I really am terribly sorry. I'm sorry. I'm sorry. I am.

✦

Before I left Michelle's apartment I called you on your cell.

"I wanted to tell you, Mark, I wanted to let you know that it's going to be okay."

"For Philip?"

"He's going to get the thing he needs. I promise you."

"You're certain?"

"He's really sick, Mark. I can't say how he'll do. But I can tell you that he'll have a chance. And yeah, of that I'm certain."

"Did you do that?" you asked.

"I've gotta go."

"Wait, Jack. My mother thinks you're a good person," he said in a rush. "You're a good person who just did the wrong things. 'People are complicated,' she says. And even twenty years later, they remain the same deep down. That's what she thinks. And she said she's very sorry that we lied to you. She said to tell you that she's sorry."

"Okay."

"And you never answered me about how you got to doing this? Did you start selling coke because your father was shitty to you and wouldn't pay your tuition, like my mom says? Do you really do this now? As a job? And do you care about these people?"

"And that's how you'll decide if I'm worth knowing?"

"Can we stay friends somehow afterward, Jack? Maybe my parents, maybe they can help or something. . . . They're both lawyers."

"Yes, Mark," I lied. "We'll be friends. And I'll tell you the truth about it all soon," I said, "but not like this. I can't do it over the phone. Let me deal with this thing with Philip and then I'll tell you everything. All of it."

"I'm sorry I had to drag you into this. That I lied to you."

"Mark, it's good. It's given me purpose that I never had that before."

"Helping Philip did?"

"Meeting you."

I hung up without saying goodbye.

◆

It was on July twenty-third that I had left you and Philip at Cornell and started walking south through Manhattan. That was the day I decided that I couldn't let Wallace and Wolff and Pierre Kleinhans go on a murder spree that I had unwittingly helped to make possible. And I couldn't just let Philip die on you, not when I could change it. That was the first time that the idea of how to fix it first surfaced in my mind. But just an hour later I met Michelle. I've heard many kidney recipients say that they didn't know how sick they were until after they got a transplant. Then, after their procedures, they felt so much better that they realized, for the first time, how bad off they had been. I guess the same thing is true of loneliness.

CHAPTER THIRTY-SIX: THE WAITING ROOM, TODAY, NOVEMBER 5, 2011

Michelle went to work a few hours ago. There were several moments this morning when the urge to tell her how I feel almost overcame my drive to get this done. I never really told her that I love her, and now it's too late in a way. I suppose she knows the truth. Surely now she knows. And I want you to know, Mark, that I'm not mad at you, or at Carrie. Frankly, I'm more inspired by the fact that you finally told me the truth than I am disappointed by the fact that you lied to me for almost a year before then. The fact that you're not really my son doesn't actually change anything for me. The current that I'm swept up in now started pulling me toward this end long before you and I even met at that diner. You know, very few things are unstoppable, but I can tell you with certainty that one of them is time. It's time for me to go and surprisingly, I feel grateful more than I feel regret. Really, I do.

✦

I will pause outside the entrance to the lobby of the emergency room at Columbia Presbyterian, one of the best transplant centers in the world. I'll be anxious, but not afraid, and I'll try to appear casual. I will have already brought three copies of this long note to Fed Ex and overnighted one copy to your apartment, one copy to Michelle's office, and the last copy to Vinny Pearl. As I survey the room through the window I'll probably feel solid, like a dam quietly holding back a massive wall of water. In my hand will be fifty copies of the letter I wrote. It is addressed "To Whom It May Concern." In the interior left pocket of my jacket will be the 45. I bought it from a guy selling guns out of the trunk of a car near the Grand Concourse up in the Bronx. It was easy and inexpensive to get such a capable murder weapon. I decided not to take a chance with Wallace. I am going to stop them, and for the chance to do something good I'll feel grateful to everyone in the world.

Before I enter the lobby I will make one last call to Pearl.

"Vinny, it's Jack," I will say.

"Hi. You okay?"

"It's time, Vinny. Come to the emergency room at Columbia Presbyterian. But no cops. No lights, no sirens. Just you. Come up here and you'll know who I am when you arrive."

"Now?"

"Yes. Right now, Vinny. Thanks a lot," I'll say softly.

"Okay. So wait for me, Jack. I'll head uptown right now, so just wait for me and don't do anything until I get there, okay? Then we'll talk and work this all out, Jack. Okay?"

"Okay, Vinny."

"I'll be there soon, Jack," he'll say anxiously.

"I know. Thanks." I will hit "end call," leave the phone on, and toss it aside into the bushes that decorate the entrance to the hospital, before I step through the revolving doors.

In the foyer of the hospital emergency room there will be a security guard sitting behind a small podium, like the Transportation Safety guys who check your ID at the airports. It will be a bad day for him. It's one more terrible thing I need to do in order to accomplish my noble goal. Noble? Well . . . I'll kill time by pretending to read email on my mobile. Then, I'll study the room, checking the position of patients, doctors, visitors, children. . . . There might be a mother with a kid in a stroller entering through security. I'll have to wait for Wallace to arrive. I'll think about you, Mark, in those slow-moving moments and I'll download my thoughts into my heart, as many as I can. It will be important that they get there. I will not be doing this despite you. I will not be doing this despite the fact that Michelle and I have each other now and I am not alone. I will actually be doing it because of her, and because I am no longer alone. I know that is going to be hard for her to take or understand. It was hard for me too and I struggled with it for a long time. Now I am clear.

Then it will be on. The revolving doors will spin more quickly and through it will emerge my associate, padding along silently on the tiled floor like a leopard. Wallace was wrong and we are different. There is a line that no price can make me cross and he'll know it very soon. He won't even look up. He'll address me only with his presence, approach me using his peripheral vision. Our business was always dangerous, but the danger was never between us, and the threat of violence was remote. He will not expect me to have a weapon. He would never dream of a man like me taking a risk in a hospital with cameras and an armed guard. . . . He must be disappointed in my frailty right now but he won't be disappointed for much longer. There is another Afrikaans expression that I learned from Pierre Kleinhans: "Wie nie waag nie, wen nie." Pierre said it to me many times over the last few years, always with a smug grin. "He who doesn't take risks, doesn't win." I want to win.

Wallace will approach me without humor, and he won't be in the mood for our usual banter. There will be no "New York!" greeting, or

"Strange place for a meeting. I hear the food's not so great." His hair will be gray at the temples. He'll look common, a little thicker in the middle these days, no different than any other guy walking down West A-Hundred-and-Sixty-Eighth today thinking about his prostate medicine or whether he'll make his year-end bonus.

I imagine our conversation will go something like this:

"So what's the problem, Jack?"

"Don't you know?"

"I think I do, but I was hoping I'd be wrong."

"This isn't what we signed up for," I'll say. There will be animosity in our eyes, but also affection and regret.

"I didn't sign up for anything, New York. I'm just running a business."

"The one you started at the Cleveland Clinic?" I'll ask.

Wallace's eyebrows will go up at the mention of his old employer. He'll glance to the left and right and survey the room, taking in the position of the security cameras. He will probably look at every middle-aged man in the crowded room and try to discern if they might be FBI agents, or perhaps some kind of mercenary working directly for me.

"So I guess we have a big problem," he'll finally say.

"We do," I'll reply.

"Why would you want to ruin things now, Jack? Now, when there is so much money to be made. We help people, Jack."

"Not really. We help some, but only at the expense of others. And this is different. I told you from the beginning this is a different thing. A heart."

"It's getting done, Jack. No matter what you say now it's still getting done."

"What if I asked you not to? Wallace, what if I asked you to leave here, and go get a drink, and tell Harold Lauer that in the end you just couldn't get the part? Could you do that? Could you consider that maybe we've taken enough and just go get that drink with me instead?"

He'll look at me, concerned and also sorry, but mostly he'll be unflappable. I know that's what will happen. So I'll have my answer and it will not be a surprise.

"That sounds almost like an ultimatum, Jack. I've got one for you. Walk out of here, and go home, to wherever the hell you go, and get on that plane tomorrow and get this deal done and you can have two million dollars and then a whole lot more. If you don't, we'll do it without you. Either way, it's getting done."

"Not if I stop you."

"You can't. You'd only be implicating yourself."

"There are other ways."

"None that end well for Jack."

"That's a matter of perspective now."

Then I will turn to my left, away from him and the entrance, and toward the guard. I'll step forward and one foot will pass the other, planted firmly on the polished stone floor of the hospital lobby and then be passed by the other. In slow motion I'll step toward the small security station. "I'm sorry," I'll say politely, "I need you to read this." I've rehearsed this all in my head so many times. He'll squint at me while he reaches out to take the flyer from my extended hand. He'll begin to read the letter and I will turn back toward the entrance to see Wallace making his way toward the revolving glass doors. In one sweeping motion I will fling the stack of forty-nine other letters into the air above us, scattering them all over the lobby and the emergency room. My other hand will then plunge inside my jacket and remove the 45. There will be motion all around me, noises everywhere, but I will remain completely focused. The gun will be an extension of my arm, like a golf club. Everything else will recede, leaving only me and the gun. Wallace will be visible through the glass of the revolving doors. I will quickly place the muzzle into my mouth. I might faintly make out the security guard shouting, "No!" as he jumps from his chair, far too late, but I will pull the trigger, unleashing a slug into *my own upper pallet and brain. It will be a perfect shot, straight up the fairway.*

◆

That was my plan . . . for a while—but no. I'm not good, and I couldn't trust myself. Of that, I was more certain than anything else. Jack could not be trusted. Too much was on the line for it all to depend upon Jack. I drafted the letter:

◆

November 5, 2011
To Whom It May Concern:
This is extremely important, so please read this very carefully. The first few sentences of this letter are here simply to delay you for a moment while I take the necessary action. In a moment you will get to the real point and you will understand that I am very sorry to involve you in this situation today, but it is unavoidable. I ask that you please act quickly, try as hard as you can not to judge, resent, or evaluate what I am doing, but rather, work immediately to save an innocent life.

My name is Jack Trayner. For eighteen years I have been a black-market organ broker. I have done terrible things and I am trying to do something good today. In room 1705 in the cardiac unit of this hospital is a patient named Philip Lauer. He knows nothing about what I am doing. Philip is O positive and has been tissue-typed for a heart transplant that he desperately needs. However, he has AIDS and will never get a heart through conventional means off a UNOS list. I am also O positive and have also been tissue-typed and we are a good MHC match. I hereby consent to have the transplant surgeons at this facility give my heart to Philip Lauer—and ONLY Philip

Lauer. TIME IS OF THE ESSENCE. *They have only four hours to complete this procedure, so please do not delay. Do not think, and do not question, at least not until my heart is again pumping inside of Philip Lauer. Once that is done, the hospital may harvest every organ in my body and give them to whomever they deem to be appropriate recipients.*

An FBI agent named Vinny Pearl will be here soon as well. Please tell him to expect a long letter from me tomorrow. Tell Agent Pearl that Wallace from Connecticut, Wallace Kendrickson, another organ broker, will be visible with me on your surveillance video right before this shooting. He has houses in Coral Gables, Florida and South Norwalk, CT. He was once a nurse at the Cleveland Clinic Transplant Center. More recently, he was my partner. He won't stop now unless someone stops him.

Please tell them that I had money, but neither Mark nor Michelle really needs it, and my pal Vinny would have seized it anyway, so I made other arrangements. I sent a hundred grand to a guy who does research on cryogenics with a note that merely said: "You helped me once although you didn't even know it. Good luck with your research. I hope you live forever, but in the meantime, get some freaking air conditioners. And stay away from The Siren. –New York Jack." The rest I gave to a friend in Brazil. I trust him to use it to pay for a bunch of kids' cancer treatments.

Now please, do not delay. Please help give Philip Lauer a chance to live. I am glad and feel lucky for what I have done today. Thank you. –Jack Trayner

✦

That was my plan; if only Jack could have been trusted. I didn't print the letter. Even as I was writing it I could feel the uncertainty creeping into my gut. Pangs of self-preservation were collecting in my throat with each sentence. I needed a certain plan—one that didn't depend on an act of nobility. You see, everyone is flawed, Mark. Anyone who's been alive for a while has nicks and dents in the front of their shinbones from running into life's many tables. Some are just more flawed than others. What's incredible, just as much for the fact that it's true as it is for the fact that I never knew it, is that we're constantly afforded opportunities for a little redemption. I wanted to do something good, but no one leaps from a cesspool like the life that I have built into being any kind of hero. Evolution takes place in steps, and maybe it can for people too. I know this much: I'd rather be a rat than a killer. I may not have sacrificed myself in that emergency room lobby, but I did get Philip on a plane to Brazil.

CHAPTER THIRTY-SEVEN: BURNING DOWN ROYSTON AND ANOTHER JACK

When I told you to convince Harold Lauer to move Philip to Columbia Presbyterian that was for your benefit, Mark, not Lauer's. I had already reached him the day before and explained how it was going to go. It wasn't the first time that I negotiated with the rich father of a son who needed a life-saving organ. The conversation was dry and pragmatic and lasted no more than a few minutes. I introduced myself to Lauer and once he understood that I was the partner who sourced the parts, he also believed that I had all the cards and Wallace had none, because time was running down more than usual. I explained that Lauer could have what he wanted for Philip, and that the transaction would cost two million dollars—not five—but only if he did it exactly as I game-planned that it needed to be done. I told him that you would call. I told him that you would beseech him to move Philip to Columbia. I told him to pretend to resist but then concede, and move him. I didn't want you to know that I was talking to Philip's father until we were already over the ocean. And of course Harold Lauer did what I asked. At that moment he would have done anything I said, absolutely anything. This time, however, I did not squeeze a few extra drops of cash from him to ferment in the bottom of my apartment closet. I took nothing.

Part of the fee was to cover the cost of three private jets. The first one left with Philip, his father, an attending physician and nurse, and a few hundred grand in medical monitors and emergency equipment—bound for Rio. That flight was safely in the air long before I went uptown to meet my old partner.

◆

The conversation began much the way I had imagined that it might for weeks. He's just making a living, Wallace said. He's not a part of anything. He's just running a business.

"The one you started at the Cleveland Clinic?" I asked. Wallace's eyebrows did go up at the mention of his old employer, just as I thought they might. He glanced to the left and right surveying the room and taking in the position of the security cameras, checking out every middle-aged man in the crowded room trying to discern if they might be FBI agents or perhaps some kind of mercenary working directly for me.

"So I guess we have a big problem," he finally said.

"We do," I replied.

"Why are we here, Jack?" Wallace asked calmly, so calmly that it sounded like a preamble for violence. I pointed to one of the security cameras. He exhaled deeply and closed his eyes against the magnitude of us both unravelling right there in that lobby. After all of those years. All of those kidneys.

"Why would you want to ruin things now, Jack? Now, when there is so much money to be made. We help people, Jack."

"Not really. We help some, but only at the expense of others. And this is different. I told you from the beginning this is a different thing. A heart."

"It's getting done, Jack. No matter what you say now it's still getting done."

"What if I asked you not to? Wallace, what if I asked you to leave here, and go get a drink, and tell Harold Lauer that in the end you just couldn't get the part? Could you do that? Could you consider that maybe we've taken enough and just go get that drink with me instead?"

"That sounds almost like an ultimatum, Jack. I've got one for you. Walk out of here, and go home, to wherever the hell you go, and get on that plane tomorrow and get this deal done and you can have two million dollars and then a whole lot more. If you don't, we'll do it without you. Either way, it's getting done."

"Not by killing someone innocent."

"So what's the plan Jack?" Wallace nearly whispered. "What are we doing here?"

"Burning bridges," I said, matching his tone and feeling a tightness in the back of my sinuses, tears starting to well up in my eyes.

"Mine?" he asked, sounding defeated.

"Everyone's." He waited. Then I added, "The Lauer kid is already on his way to the airport. His father has a charter waiting there for us to go to Jozi. We all go. Including you and me."

"Me?" Wallace asked, sounding weak. "I'm not going to Johannesburg."

"The FBI gets here in five or ten minutes. We've been filmed. I am doing this last deal and then I'm out. You and me and Wolff are going to sit down and work through things—"

"I am not getting on a fucking plane to South Africa, Jack."

And this is where my acting skills kicked in. "But the bridges are already burned . . ." I said. I knew he needed a minute to process. He would have been physically unable to walk had he not been granted a few moments. But Pearl was truly on his way to Columbia and we had to go. "Call Mel," I said. Wallace looked up from the floor. I drew a phone from my pocket and held it out to him.

"I have it," he said softly. He put his own cellphone to his ear. He spun on his heel, away from me, pushing choice words into the mouthpiece, nodding intermittently. Then, we looked at each other. He nodded again, yielding, and we exited to the car I had waiting for us on the street. Whatever their own plans might have been, and despite what other schemes Kleinhans and Wolff might have been formulating at that moment, they did believe that the patient was on his way, and that we were both coming with him.

◆

The clouds above us were a bit blurry through my watery eyes and I surreptitiously dabbed at them with the heel of my hand, self-consciously, trying not to let Wallace see me. There were thick, over-lapping waves in the sky that looked like foam gently spreading out above a massive cappuccino. We sat in the back seat of the town car, each orienting his body toward our respective windows and away from each other. The entire way to Kennedy neither of us uttered a word. I casually led the way up the ladder-like stairway and into the private plane. I crouched to sneak under the low ceiling and turned to see Wallace enter behind me. I felt dizzy, like I had a flu coming on, scared to stop walking for fear that I would somehow sink into the quicksand that must really lie on the floor where it appeared to be carpeted. Wallace's momentum carried him a few steps into the plane before he seemed to realize that there were three tall, young men in the cabin who closed ranks behind him, cutting off access to the doorway. They had dark and smooth South American skin. They were Juan Guillermo's guys. They wore suits and their ties were loose at the neck and it appeared that they had flown all night from Brazil only to wait for hours on the runway, to wait for us, and to gather in Wallace like a car service and then to return to Brazil with him.

Our eyes met for the final time and his appeared fearful and wild, not somber.

"Where's Lauer?" he asked.

"He's already on the way. On another flight."

"Why?" Wallace asked, knowing that anything I said would be a lie, perhaps just stalling while he tried to figure out the best pitch.

"I'm not going with you," I said. He did not reply. This was it. This was how our moment would be. The universe didn't care. No one cared. I loved him somehow. And I missed him already. Wallace started to shake his head slightly from side to side and only said, "Jack," quietly, as if to mean, "Wait, let's just talk this through now. How much? How much, friend? Okay, we can work this out. . . ."

"Don't worry," I said, clenching my teeth. "I'm just taking another flight. I'll meet you there."

"What?"

"I'm just taking the other flight. But I'll meet you there. With Wolff and with everyone. We'll work things out then. We'll talk in Jozi. Don't worry. I'll see you. We're going to end up in the same place."

I turned quickly and Wallace suddenly yelled, "Jack!" and it stunned me and I stopped. One of Juan's men put his hands up in front of his chest and pushed his palms toward Wallace. It seemed to exert an energy which literally pushed him down into his chair. Another turned to me and said, "Go. Go now," and I did. My eyes were blurry again, my breath came shallow and I felt sick. I pushed my fingers back through my hair. Wallace's flight was not going to Jozi. It was headed for Rio. In the car from the airport to the hotel it would be pulled over by two men on a motorcycle. Those men had already received a half a million dollars in a wire transfer from

Harold Lauer. Lauer didn't know why. I made all of these choices alone. That's important.

◆

I did not go to Rio. I did not return to my Jozi of Joburg and the golden days of my ascension as a golfer, and a broker. I went somewhere else. I didn't get away with anything, nor have I truly been punished. I simply "am" now, but no Jack, no matter how new, has ever been without a plan. So these words are for my new associate, Vinny Pearl:

You won't find me. I have gotten quite adept at laying low. But I also need you not to try. We have some mutual goals now and trying to find me would actually be counter-productive. Everything I've told you about Mel Wolff and Royston, that's all true. Now go and burn that place down. Have your SA counterparts put Kleinhans and Wolff away, and if the case isn't good enough, use a fucking drone strike. But don't let that place stand.

Everything I have written here about my friend Guillermo, in Brazil, is of course inaccurate, including his name, and even the cities he might frequent. Perhaps even the countries. His biggest interest is saving kids in poor South American countries who have cancer. That's not something you need to upset. Tracking down the email address I used to send you this, the IP address. . . . That won't give you anything. Neither will the cellphone I may call you from in a few months. You know that.

Philip got his heart in a domino transplant, just like I dreamed that he might a few months ago. If you want to go after his father I don't even give a shit but for what it's worth, the guy had no idea what was happening and didn't really conspire in anything illegal, nor was there intent. Philip has been in recovery for four days now and he's doing well, but his prognosis is still far from rosy, and never will be. Perhaps you can leave that alone as well. He has a shot now, and that's all anyone really ever has, but his comes with much longer than average odds.

You'll hear from me from time to time, Vinny. That won't remain possible if I feel like you are looking for me, but if you leave me alone, I will definitely get in touch. I might be able to help you out a bit. It's like I said earlier—everyone's flawed, but some are just more flawed than others. Anyone who works in my old business who's just getting by, trying to make a living, stretching the truth and doing a little damage along the way, that's okay. I'm not concerned with them. They all have their twisted rationalizations and victim perspectives and I have my own. Let them think they saved a few fat Americans. Let them think they're working in secret, safe from the fluorescent office lights the rest of the world lives beneath. As for the rest of them, the ones who would do harm even when it isn't necessary, they are all in my Rolodex. I know the vampires and the leaches and the Kleinhans counterparts in every third-world shithole of a city where they prey upon the poverty of organ sellers. Let me work some of it out. I'll let you know how it's going. I'll ping you every now and then to let you know how your guys can help.

As for the money. . . . Yes, Vinny, my money, more than a grunt like you could ever imagine getting his hands on . . . neither Mark nor Michelle really needs it, and you would have seized it anyway, so I made other arrangements. Some of it I need. I sent a hundred grand to a guy who does research on cryogenics with a note that merely said: "You helped me once although you didn't even know it. Good luck with your research. I hope you live forever, but in the meantime, get some freaking air conditioners. And stay away from The Siren. –New York Jack." The rest I gave to a friend in Brazil. I feel no satisfaction from any of that. I'm not sure why.

I have one last thing to say to Mark: Don't ever be confused. You saved me. -Jack

AFTERWORD

While the preceding story is fiction, the organ shortage in America is not. It is dire for over 120,000 people currently on the waiting list and of deep concern for over three hundred thousand others who are on dialysis but not on a waiting list for a transplant. So what can we do to help save the lives of some of the people on those waiting lists, some of whom might even be people we know, or know through only one or two degrees of separation? First of all, register to be an organ donor. A now-famous Gallup Poll conducted in 2005 found that 95% of Americans approve of organ donation and yet, today, nearly half of those eligible remain unregistered. If you are one of them, you can rectify that right now, in a few short minutes, by visiting www.donatelife.net and registering. Doing so will ensure that when you pass away, if it is possible for a hospital to make use of your organs to help others, you might potentially save as many as eight other people's lives.

We also need sensible, modern and effective public policies to address the problem that is quickly growing into a quiet epidemic. There aren't enough donors and in addition, the current system doesn't efficiently convert those who have signed up to actually become donors. The shortage of critically-needed, life-saving organs has created a black market that harms countless other people in poor nations around the world who are victimized by the illegal transplant tourism system as described in *The Organ Broker*.

In my article published in Salon.com on March 23, 2014, I proposed a realistic three-pronged solution:

1. Presumed Consent. Like many European countries, the United States would benefit from a policy of Presumed Consent (wherein those who do not want to be organ donors must register to opt out, as opposed to the current system where one must register to opt in). There is debate over the ultimate impact of such a policy, but this much we know: in European countries that switched to an opt out system on average only three percent of citizens bother to opt out. On its own, a policy of Presumed Consent would not solve the problem, but it could dramatically raise the number of organ donors and can be part of an overarching solution.

2. Binding Consent. In America, when you die, if you have left a will, no one at a funeral home, hospital, or government agency asks your beneficiaries whether they want to honor your will or just split up your money some other way. If we get to determine the disposition of our money after death surely we should also get to decide the fate of our own bodies and organs—and not be overruled by anyone, even our own families. Yet, that is not the case. Each year, thousands of potentially life-saving kidneys get thrown out because distraught families, approached at the very worst time, refuse to donate the organs of their loved ones, even if they had registered as donors. It's not right for us to ask families

to make such choices, and it's wrong for us to allow them to contradict the stated wishes of their family members (which are often legally-binding, but ignored anyway) who wanted their organs to be used to save others.

3. Education. With Presumed Consent and Binding Consent in place, we still need modern and comprehensive educational programs to help individuals understand their rights, to help families navigate these difficult circumstances and to better empower hospital and transplant center staff to manage the difficult process.

Whether you agree, or disagree, with all or some portion of my proposal, we can all agree on this: something needs to be done. While you read my book, people died who might have otherwise been saved by new legislation. Twenty people will die today while waiting for kidneys. Twenty more will die tomorrow. The most ironic part of all is that creating greater access to organs for transplantation might also cut down on the enormous expense of dialysis, most of which falls on Medicare, and save US taxpayers billions every year. Please register to be a donor, and to learn more, visit www.theorganbroker.com.

Please visit www.tengrade.com/tornado/theorganbroker to rate various topics discussed throughout this novel, and compare your opinions with your friends and people like you.

Thank you,

Stu Strumwasser